"I'VE FALLEN IN LOVE WITH YOU ALL OVER AGAIN!

"And it just isn't right for a man to have to go through that twice in a lifetime!" Blake growled.

A few seconds passed before the full implication of his words hit Shannon. She was stunned. "Are…are you talking about when we lived on this farm?" A vision of the shy boy he'd been crossed her mind. Could he really have been lovesick?

"Yeah, a long, long time ago. My first love. It was more like senseless worship. Unfortunately, unlike most first loves, this one didn't fade quietly into memory. I never forgot you."

A tiny laugh escaped Shannon's lips. "Blake, that's the most…incredible, romantic, and…farfetched thing I've ever heard!"

ABOUT THE AUTHOR

Barbara Kaye's mellow style and gentle humor
make her books great favorites of Superromance
readers. Now that her five children have flown
the nest, she is able to devote herself to writing
full-time and is already hard at work on her
next Superromance.

Books by Barbara Kaye

HARLEQUIN SUPERROMANCE
46—A HEART DIVIDED
124—COME SPRING
161—HOME AT LAST

HARLEQUIN AMERICAN ROMANCE
19—CALL OF EDEN

These books may be available at your local bookseller.

Don't miss any of our special offers. Write to us at the
following address for information on our newest releases.

Harlequin Reader Service
901 Fuhrmann Blvd., P.O. Box 1397, Buffalo, NY 14240
Canadian address: P.O. Box 2800, Postal Station A,
5170 Yonge St., Willowdale, Ont. M2N 6J3

Barbara Kaye

SOUTHERN NIGHTS

Harlequin Books

TORONTO • NEW YORK • LONDON
AMSTERDAM • PARIS • SYDNEY • HAMBURG
STOCKHOLM • ATHENS • TOKYO • MILAN

Published April 1986

First printing February 1986

ISBN 0-373-70206-X

Printed in Canada

CHAPTER ONE

SHANNON STABLED OMAR, her magnificent chestnut thoroughbred, brushed him down and replenished his water and feed. The day had been an unusually mild one for a Long Island February, and Shannon's face was flushed with the excitement of the first ride she'd had since before Christmas. In winter her visits to the Post-and-Paddock, the exclusive riding establishment where she had boarded Omar for two years, were infrequent, for the course was frozen most of the time. Today, however, the footing had been a little better. She had managed to give Omar some real exercise, though the ditches and fences would have to wait until spring.

Leaving the stable, she fell into step beside Peg Thorpe, her best friend and the afternoon's riding companion. The two women, whose friendship went back many years, made a striking contrast, for Peg was as blonde and round as Shannon was dark and angular.

"The course was miserable today," Peg muttered. "I thought you were going to break your fool neck."

Shannon grinned. "Never. I know what I'm doing."

"Vic would have a king-sized fit if he could have seen you."

"He won't ever see me, because he wouldn't be caught dead here." She looked out over the open, immaculately-kept hunt course of the Post-and-Paddock, beautiful even in winter. "He refers to this place as a barn. Some barn!"

"Let's stick around for coffee and horse talk in the tack room," Peg suggested.

Shannon glanced at her watch. "Oh, Peg, you know I'd love to, but I'm running late, and I want to talk to Vic before he leaves."

"Ah, I forgot. He's on his way to Vegas, right?"

Shannon nodded. "He'll never forgive me if I'm not home before he leaves."

"Yeah, husbands can be positive turkeys about those things." Peg paused to giggle. "Well, while he's gone we'll have to do some fun things. Lunch and shopping. The most divine new boutique has opened near Jerry's office—I'm talking très chic. We'll have to check it out. Maybe you can spend one night in town with us, and we'll have dinner at Tavern on the Green."

"Sounds great. It's been ages. I'll call you in a couple of days."

"Enjoyed it," Peg said gaily and strode off in the direction of the tack room. Shannon stood and watched her friend's retreating figure for a moment. She wasn't one for wasting time on envy, but occasionally she envied Peg, and not only because of her friend's sunny disposition and perpetual air of good will. Peg's husband, Jerry, not only supported her many causes and activities, but even seemed to encourage them. It was easy for a woman like Shannon to envy someone like Peg.

Giving herself a quick shake, Shannon made for the parking lot and her sleek tan Mercedes sedan. A passing stable hand smiled and waved.

"Bye, Mrs. Parelli. Don't stay away so long."

"Goodbye, Stan. Tell the weather to behave and I won't."

Driving faster than she normally did, Shannon reached home in less than twenty minutes. She passed through the iron gates and continued up the sweeping drive of the fifteen-room Tudor mansion she called home, silently praying that Vic had been so busy with preparations for his trip that he wouldn't have noticed the time. Not bothering to put her car in the garage, she parked in front of the house and rushed inside. "Vic?" she called.

"In here, Shannon," responded a husky masculine voice.

"In here" was the large paneled den that functioned as her husband's favorite retreat. She hurried into it and found him seated at his impressive mahogany desk. Unfortunately, two other men were present also—Boots Williams and Joe Something-or-other, two of Vic's hangers-on. The men were a constant source of irritation to Shannon, though she did her best to conceal it. She had no idea what they did or why Vic wanted them around, other than the fact that Vic seemed to need constant companionship. She nodded to them and forced a smile, then proceeded to ignore them.

Vic glanced up when she entered, but there was no welcoming smile on his handsome face. He took a quick look at her riding clothes and made no attempt to hide his disapproval. Smiling through her discomfort, Shannon crossed the room and planted a kiss on his cheek. He was freshly-shaven and smelled of his expensive aftershave. Impulsively, she bent and kissed him again.

"You smell divine," she told him.

"And you, my sweet, smell like hay. You're late." His tone was openly censorious.

"I'm sorry, darling. Peg and I were enjoying the beautiful day, and the time just got away from me."

"It always does when you're at that...barn. I must say I fail to see the attraction."

I will remain pleasant, Shannon thought. *We won't argue just before he leaves town.* "That's because you aren't a horse fancier," she said evenly.

"I was beginning to wonder if I would see you before I left. Frank wants to take off before four, if possible. That'll get us to Philly before dark."

"Would you like me to drive you to the airfield?"

"No, Boots and Joe will. We have business to discuss on the way."

What "business" he could possibly have to discuss with the likes of those two Shannon couldn't imagine. "I wish you were taking a commercial flight," she said with a frown. "Those little planes look so flimsy to me."

"Well, they aren't, and Frank is a great pilot. He's after me to take lessons from him, and I just might do it."

He would if the notion took hold of him, Shannon knew. Vic was one of those fortunate souls who could afford to do anything he wanted anytime he wanted. He was constantly picking up and discarding expensive hobbies. All the more reason for her to wonder why he begrudged her a few diversions.

Yet, she conceded, she wouldn't have Omar if it weren't for Vic. In one of his expansively generous gestures, he had presented the magnificent animal to her on her birthday two years ago. So typical of Vic, she thought. On one hand he disliked the time she spent at the Post-and-Paddock; on the other he had given her such a wonderful horse that she felt compelled to visit the stables frequently.

While mustering the courage to bring up the subject that was on her mind, her eyes darted around the elegant room. Its walls were lined with hundreds of momentos of Vic Parelli's recording career, a career that had spanned three decades. Looking at her husband now, Shannon found it hard to believe he had been a singing star since she was in the first grade. At fifty-seven he was still so attractive and admirably fit. His dark good looks photographed beautifully, and on television he hardly looked a year older than he had when his weekly show had been number three in the nation. That was fifteen years ago, when she'd married him.

There no longer was a Vic Parelli Show and hadn't been for a number of years. His smooth, mellow, romantic voice didn't appeal to modern young people, the audience television aimed for, but he still was a star and would remain one even if he never sang another note. Now his professional life consisted of doing TV specials, making guest appearances and recordings, and he continued to play Vegas twice a year, always to packed houses and rave reviews.

Normally Shannon would have been accompanying her husband to Las Vegas, but this time Vic had asked her not to. This trip was to be an outing with "the boys." He loved the company of his male cronies and liked doing "manly" things; he had even agreed to play in a Pro-Am golf tournament while there. Shannon had been only too glad to remain behind, for she hated the life they were forced to lead in Vegas—up all night, asleep by day. She liked getting up before seven and being in bed by eleven. A holdover from a youth spent on a farm, she supposed.

She took a deep breath, hating the fact that she found talking to him so difficult. "Vic, before you leave, I'd like to talk to you...alone." She emphasized the last word.

A second passed. Then he looked at the two men and gave a jerk of his head. Like robots they stood and left the room without a word. After watching them go, Vic directed his attention to his wife. "All right, dear, we're alone."

"I want to know if you've given any more thought to Mike and the school."

His dark eyes flashed momentarily; then his face settled into an inscrutable cast. "Actually, I have, and I'm afraid the answer has to be no."

A heavy moment of silence followed. Shannon was mildly disappointed but not at all surprised. She and Mike Erickson, the choreographer on Vic's now-defunct show, had excitedly discussed opening a dancing school for years. The cost of such an enterprise would be prohibitive for Mike, but for Vic it would amount to little more than pocket change. However, she had warned Mike from the beginning that Vic would probably oppose the idea. There wouldn't be a solid reason for the opposition. It was just that he opposed everything she wanted to do outside the house.

She was trying to think of a forceful argument in favor of the school, when Vic spoke again. "Shannon, you haven't danced professionally in fourteen years."

"I know that, but dancing and teaching the basics of dance to young kids are two different things. Mike says I can do it."

"Oh, he does, does he?" Vic smiled an unpleasant smile. "Well, as long as we're discussing Mike, I think I should tell you that I would prefer you didn't see so much of him. People might talk."

Shannon's mouth dropped. "About me and Mike? Oh, come on, Vic! Mike's been our friend for years, and everyone we know knows it."

"Nevertheless, it doesn't look good for a married woman and a single man to run around...."

"We don't 'run around'! We only meet occasionally to talk about the school."

"And since there isn't going to be a school, there's no need for you to 'meet' occasionally anymore, is there?"

Her chest rose and fell as her annoyance increased. That remark had been totally uncalled-for. It hurt that he would imply there was anything but friendship between herself and Mike. There couldn't possibly be a more faithful wife than she, and she suspected Vic knew it. She'd never even engaged in the casual, harmless flirting that most of her women friends considered a normal part of conversation with men.

That afternoon she wanted very badly to tell him that, then to ask him why he persisted in trying to make her feel guilty when she'd done absolutely nothing wrong. She wouldn't though, because the conversation would have degenerated into a quarrel, and arguing wasn't the way to get anything from Vic. So she tried a different tactic. In her calmest, sweetest voice she said, "The school's very important to Mike, Vic. Please reconsider."

The corners of his mouth quirked. "Your Southern accent gets as thick as molasses when you beg, dear."

Shannon masked her irritation. "I'll stay out of the school, if you want, but Mike thinks the world and all of you. I'd hoped you would give him a little encouragement and some financial backing."

"I don't think so."

"May I ask why not?"

"The project doesn't interest me, and I don't put money into things that don't interest me." The voice that had charmed millions turned as cold and hard as granite.

That didn't have a thing to do with it, Shannon knew. It was simply that Mike had grown to be more her friend than Vic's, and Vic couldn't stand that. A male friend was unacceptable; he even found fault with her female friends. In fact, he wouldn't tolerate anything that diverted her attention from him. He had become overly possessive in a way that was exhausting. According to him, she spent too much time at the Post-and-Paddock, or on the tennis court, in art classes or with any of the activities she engaged in, although she did so only to fill up her days and expend some of her unused energy.

Once again Shannon found herself standing before her husband, feeling frustrated and impotent, wishing she knew how to storm and yell and demand her rights. Poor Mike wouldn't get his school because he had shown the bad sense to make friends with her.

Vic's eyes again fell on her expensive riding clothes—ivory shirt, tan jodhpurs, brown boots. "I have some phone calls to make before I leave, dear. Why don't you go upstairs and get out of those clothes? Then we'll have a drink together."

"Yes, of course," she said icily, as she turned on her heel and left the den, feeling like a child whose teacher had just dismissed her. Stalking up the stairs, she could feel her face growing hot. She jerked at the buttons of her shirt as she strode into the luxurious master suite on the second floor, only to encounter Ralph Winston, Vic's valet and the household's majordomo. Ralph was finishing Vic's packing. Shannon clutched her shirt together. "Ralph, do you mind?" she asked tiredly. "I have to get dressed."

"Of course not, ma'am," he said and hurried out of the room.

Ralph was another person whose presence she didn't understand. Vic had simply shown up with the man in tow five years ago and announced that Ralph was going to be his valet and butler. Shannon had no idea what Ralph's background was, but she was sure it was neither a valet nor a butler. His chief job, it seemed, was to make sure Vic wanted for nothing from waking to sleeping.

Ah, well, at least the fellow had a viable job, which was more than she could say for Boots and Joe. Shrugging out of the shirt, she tossed it on a nearby chaise. Then she sat on the edge of the bed to take off her boots, her thick knee-high socks, and the jodphurs. Clad only in her bra and panties, she hurried into her ivory-tiled bath for a quick shower before choosing a silk shirtwaist from her walk-in closet. The dress was expensive, just like everything that surrounded her—the furniture and all the room's perfect accessories, chosen without a thought to their cost. *I have everything money can buy,* she thought, *yet sometimes I feel I have nothing.*

The scene downstairs had been so predictable, and her feelings were so familiar—a sense of inadequacy, even failure. Perhaps the impressions weren't merited, but she felt them nevertheless. When did this wonderful marriage start turning sour, she wondered. When did we stop being close? It seemed to have happened in the blink of an eye, but she suspected it had eroded over a long period of time. Fifteen years ago Vic Parelli, then enjoying the zenith of his spectacular career, had fallen in love with a starry-eyed, twenty-one-year-old dancer. Against the advice of everyone he was close to, he married her. "You make me feel young, Shannon," he'd told her. And for a few years he'd thoroughly enjoyed her youth and vitality.

All that had changed. Now he seemed to want a serene companion, someone who made no waves and "knew her place." And he'd become sensitive to the years that separated them. He squelched her vibrancy at every turn. Now what he wanted in a wife more than anything was a pretty, poised, elegantly dressed *hausfrau.*

Well, he would be gone ten days, and during that time Shannon intended taking a long, hard look at her marriage. Somehow she would find that inner reservoir of strength she knew had been submerged through the years. She would confront her husband with honesty and determination. Something had to give. *I am suffocating,* she thought bitterly.

CHAPTER TWO

BLAKE CARMICHAEL STEERED his jeep past the sagging wooden gate and drove up the weed-choked dirt path leading to the house. As he drew nearer the structure he studied it with appraising eyes, and the sight confronting him caused a pang or two in the region of his heart.

It was a big old-fashioned farmhouse, two-storied, with a covered front porch made for sitting and rocking. All of its tall windows were flanked by shutters, some hanging askew; many of the windows were broken. Once it had been painted a pristine white with gray-blue trim, but now the paint was soiled, cracked and peeling away in places. Once there had been a fine fragrant stand of honeysuckle bushes lining the driveway, but most now were dead. An unchecked forest of scrub pine and wild dogwood had advanced on the house, considerably reducing the size of the clearing. The property was in pitiful condition, much worse than had been apparent from the road.

Blake halted the jeep at the foot of the front steps and uncurled his five-eleven frame from the driver's seat. Pulling himself erect, he stood with arms akimbo, the angular planes of his handsome face set. He was dressed in the working clothes of his trade— clean, crisp khakis that fit his muscular physique so splendidly they looked tailor-made. By profession Blake was a builder of fine homes, and he could see the possibilities lurking behind the house's sad exterior. His dark eyes missed nothing as he surveyed the structure. The farmhouse was familiar to him; he knew it had been built in the late 1940s by a devoted owner who had expected it to stand for generations. Once it had been the most beautiful rural homestead for miles around, and he saw no reason why it couldn't be again. It was a damned shame to let it stand idle, doing no one but the tax collector any good.

His passenger in the jeep, a stocky middle-aged realtor named John Foreman, scrambled out of the vehicle and hurried to Blake's side. As Blake ambled around, the realtor stayed hard on his heels, making a comment or two but mostly just watching. John's eyes followed the younger man's as they wandered leisurely and critically over the decaying buildings and untidy pastures. He was more than just a little curious about this man's interest in the old Jameson farm. No one had even looked at the place in over a year. It was in deplorable condition, and although Carmichael had vaguely mentioned wanting something that needed "some fixing up," John doubted he had anything like this in mind. Restoring the Jameson farm would be a Herculean task for anyone, to say nothing of a mighty expensive one.

"How long's this place been for sale?" Blake asked quietly.

"Long time," John said. "On and off for seven or eight years. There've been a few tenants through the years, but renters don't look after a place properly. It's still owned by the Jameson family, though,

what's left of it. Used to be Jamesons all over this
part of South Carolina, but they've about died off.
Both Harry and Beth, who owned this farm, are
gone now. Beth died of complications following
surgery about ten years ago, and Harry was killed in
an automobile accident seven or eight years ago.
That just about did the family in.''

Seven or eight years? Sadness gripped Blake. Had
it really been that long ago?

John continued. ''There's a daughter, but she's
married and lives up north somewhere. Been gone a
number of years, I guess.''

Eighteen of them, Blake instantly recalled. Shannon had left in the spring of '67, just after her eigh-
teenth birthday. Her departure had thrown him into
a long bout of depression. At the time he thought his
life had ended. ''Yes, I know,'' he said to John. ''I
knew the family.''

The realtor looked at him in surprise. ''You from
Fountain Inn, Mr. Carmichael?''

''I used to live here.''

''Carmichael? Don't think I know any Carmi-
chaels. Are your folks still living around here?''

''No, they never did. They lived down south, near
Sumter. I was orphaned at an early age and lived in
a succession of foster homes. This farm was the
last.'' And the best, he thought. My salvation. The
hold it had on his heart was firm and everlasting.
Even he was surprised by the hodgepodge of emotions it aroused in him.

In an instant, as often happens with momentous
decisions, Blake made up his mind. He had to have
this farm; it seemed only right for him to be the one
to own it. The decision brought on problems, of

course. He hadn't expected to buy property so soon, and it would be months before he could devote much time to getting it in shape. But at the moment that didn't seem important.

Returning to the Jameson farm after all these years had been nothing more than a sentimental journey, simply an uncharacteristically nostalgic move on Blake's part. He often came to Greenville on business, but he'd always avoided returning to Fountain Inn. He didn't know why today had been different, but ever since arriving in Greenville he'd been plagued by a desire to see it again. The For Sale sign by the side of the road had brought him up with a start, for it had seemed something of an omen. Normally he was no believer in omens, but to discover the Jameson place was for sale at precisely the time in his life when he was yearning for change, a challenge. . . .

Well, if it was a coincidence it was a damned timely one, and every instinct he possessed told him to act on it. He had immediately driven back to town and looked up the real estate agency that had it listed. Now his probing brown eyes methodically scrutinized every aspect of the unimpressive scene before him.

Most of the decrepit outbuildings were obscured by the thick pine forest. The barn looked as though one strong gust of wind would topple it. Blake remembered the day it was raised, the high-spirited party following its erection, and the late night walk through the woods with a beautiful dark-haired girl. An ache, a longing impossible to stifle stirred inside him.

"Well, I'll be!" John exclaimed. "So you lived with the Jamesons!"

"Yes."

"That means you knew Shannon Jameson. Was she as pretty as everyone says she was?"

"Yes, she was." To this day she was the prettiest lady he'd ever laid eyes on.

"I guess she's the closest thing to a celebrity Fountain Inn ever had. She was a dancer, wasn't she? Folks around here claim she could've been a star in her own right if she hadn't married Vic Parelli. Didn't she dance on his TV show for a while?"

"I really don't know, Mr. Foreman," Blake said. It was a lie. He'd watched that blasted show every Saturday night during the year Shannon had performed on it, choking on his jealousy of Parelli and convinced that Shannon was the greatest dancer since Pavlova. "I don't know how close to stardom she came. I left Fountain Inn shortly after Shannon did. Joined the Air Force, which seemed a pretty good place for a kid who was all alone to be. I . . . I lost track of her."

Blake's eyes clouded. So had everyone else. Once the hoopla surrounding her May-September marriage to singing star Vic Parelli had quietened down, Shannon had disappeared from the limelight. Parelli, whose days as a teenage heartthrob had long since passed, still did occasional television specials and guest appearances, and Blake had heard he could still pack the house in Vegas. But his private life remained private. He never made the gossip column, and there were no photographs of his home or his family. Blake didn't even know if Shannon had any kids.

What difference does it make, Carmichael, he asked himself pointedly. *Would anything change if you knew all about her? Would it make you happy to learn she had a passel of kids, had put on weight and sported some gray in that gorgeous raven hair of hers? Fool!*

Blake's long silence prompted John to thumb quickly through his realtor's directory. "Now, Mr. Carmichael, I'm sure this place is a disappointment to you. Looks a little better from the road, doesn't it? But I've got plenty of others we can look at...."

"Nope," Blake said decisively, "I want this one."

John closed his directory. "For sentimental reasons?"

"Maybe, but I've been looking for some country property for quite some time. I've given some thought to homesteading. Seems to me this place has just been sitting here waiting for me to come along and find it."

The realtor digested this. *Well, to each his own,* he thought. *Takes all kinds to make a world, lucky for me.* A triumphant smile touched his lips. Finally unloading the Jameson farm after all these years was going to make him the fair-haired boy around the agency.

"How much?" Blake asked succinctly.

John mentioned a figure that might have had merit some five or six years earlier, but Blake knew it would go for a whole lot less now. At the moment, however, the price wasn't uppermost in his mind. "Tell me, Mr. Foreman—if I buy, will the owner be required to put in an appearance in order to finalize the deal?"

"That's the usual procedure, but there are exceptions. Shannon Jameson...er, Parelli is the sole owner, and I imagine business decisions are made for her by a manager or accountant. In fact, the only address the agency has for her is an accounting firm in New York. If she prefers to send someone to represent her, well, we won't let that stand in the way of the sale. Ah, would you like to come back to the office with me? We'll draw up a contract, and I'll get it in the mail by five."

"All right." Blake reached into his shirt pocket, withdrew a business card and handed it to John. "You ought to have one of these. You can reach me at that number in Charlotte almost any working day. If I'm not in, leave a message with my secretary, and I'll get right back to you."

John glanced at the card. "You have a construction business? How're things going for you these days?"

"Pretty good right now, but we had some lean years."

"Yeah, same with real estate. Say, don't you want to look inside the house?"

"No, I don't think so. I remember quite a bit about it." And Blake thought he'd indulged in enough reminiscing for one day. It was a depressing indulgence at best.

HOURS LATER, however, as he drove back to his home in Charlotte, he couldn't stem the flood of memories that washed over him. He had been an incorrigible kid with a smart mouth when Harry Jameson had taken hold of him. He could smile now as he recalled himself at seventeen. Not bad exactly, but having been in and out of more foster homes than he could remember, he was totally unfamiliar with love and warmth and was determined to desert people before they could desert him. In those days his normal reaction to friendly overtures from others was a sullen stare and an unkind retort.

But Harry had quickly taken the sass out of him. Blake learned the rules straight away: he was expected to work his butt off on the farm, finish high school and go on to trade school, and there would be no nonsense about it. Somehow from the beginning he'd sensed he'd met his match in Harry. He supposed he owed much of what he was today to that fine man.

And to Shannon. The Jamesons' daughter had been the most beautiful thing he'd ever seen, a dark-haired, dreamy-eyed girl whose driving ambition was to be a professional dancer. Nothing had been as important to her as those twice-weekly lessons in Greenville. He could still see her, dressed in black leotard and tights, ponytail flying, climbing into the old pickup for the drive into town. And she was forever practicing, practicing. To his inexperienced mind she had seemed a goddess.

At first she'd wanted nothing to do with a smart-aleck, surly kid who couldn't relate to softness and kindness from others. Desperately wanting her to notice him, he had shaped up fast and was rewarded by his dream girl's approval. Anyone who believed love couldn't conquer all should have witnessed the transformation in that disagreeable boy. Within a year after arriving at the Jameson farm he and Shannon had become, in her words, "best friends," though Blake's hopes had lingered on something more profound than friendship. He'd wanted her to know how he felt about her, so for months he'd rehearsed how to tell her.

Before he could, however, Shannon gave him a jolt. He could still hear her words as clearly as if she'd spoken them yesterday. He could still see the light of excitement blazing in her dark eyes. "I'm not going to waste my life on this farm, Blake. I'm going to leave South Carolina just as soon as I graduate. Do you remember Marianne Henderson? Well, she's living in New York now. She says I can live with her while I make the rounds of the auditions. Oh, I know it's going to mean a big fight with Daddy and buckets of tears from Mom, but I've got to do it. I just know I'm going to make it big! I'm going to be somebody!"

He had been so shaken he hadn't mustered the courage to tell her he loved her. For years he'd regretted that deeply. Not that it would have made any difference.

As he drove into the familiar outskirts of Charlotte, Blake reflected on life's strange twists and turns, as well as on the whims of human nature. When he had crawled out of bed that morning it certainly hadn't been with the idea of going out and buying a farm. Although he had long harbored the desire to homestead some property, he'd imagined that would be in the future, ten or twelve years down the road. He had gone to Greenville on business only, to look over a tract of land that could be developed into a business park.

But curiosity or nostalgia or something less definable had urged him to return to Fountain Inn and the Jameson farm. Buying the place was probably the most ridiculously impulsive act of his life, but it felt good, for once, to do something not carefully rooted in thought.

Ordinarily Blake was a sensible man, for life had forced him to be. He had been twenty-two when he left the Air Force—strong as an ox and filled with a steely resolve to make something of himself. He'd considered settling down near Fountain Inn, a place where he'd known a measure of happiness, but one visit with the Jamesons had cured him of that. He had politely listened to Harry and Beth as they rhapsodized over Shannon's recent marriage to Vic Parelli, and had looked at the mementos of her scattered throughout the house before making a hasty exit.

Instead of Fountain Inn, he had gone to Charlotte and taken stock of his assets. Trade school had trained him to be a carpenter, a good one, and he'd put aside a nest egg while in the service. So he'd bought a small parcel of land and built a house with his own hands, sub-contracting only the plumbing and wiring. Two weeks after completing it he had sold it for three times what it cost him to build. Convinced he had found his forte, he began Carmichael Construction Company, a shoestring operation that had prospered in glittering fashion.

The years had been good to him financially; at thirty-seven he had already made all the money he could spend, for he was basically a simple man who had no extravagant tastes to indulge. He lived alone in the comfortable but unpretentious town house he had purchased ten years previously. He liked to fish and to work with his hands. And nothing pleased him more than settling down with a good rip-roaring adventure yarn at the end of a busy day. No workaholic, he knew how to relax and entertain himself. He dressed well, dined well and associated with a small circle of successful people he called friends. Most of them envied his life.

He couldn't complain, but some things had been postponed. Living alone didn't bother him, for he had been alone most of his life, but he'd always meant to marry and have children. He thought he would have liked having progeny, a link between the past and the future. Now, as he began to approach forty, he wondered if he ever would.

Only once had he become seriously involved with a woman, and that had been a mistake. He'd met her at a party two months after starting up his business. Her name was Norma Grayson. She had black hair, worked in a bank and took ballet lessons for "figure control." He'd often speculated on the coincidence. She was a realist, she'd told him, a modern woman who had no illusions, and he'd believed her. The affair had lasted six months, and in the end Norma had been good and disillusioned. Guilt feelings persisted after all these years.

But he shook them off. There had been so many women since Norma. A successful man of intelligence, virility and good looks didn't have to look far for feminine companionship. Some of the women had interested him beyond mere male curiosity; some, happily, were still his friends. But he'd never found that one special someone who could fulfill all his needs and desires.

Maybe Norma was one reason he hadn't married; certainly she had colored his subsequent relationships with women. No more mistakes, he'd vowed.

Norma had made him cautious, and cautious men, he reflected, didn't fall in love easily.

Or maybe he had been too busy. The business had taken most of his time and energy for years, although now it pretty much ran itself. Maybe he had been looking for something that didn't exist. More than likely, though, too much of him was tied up in dreams and memories of someone else—the one he could never have.

He had heard it said that no one ever forgets the first love, so that could account for Shannon's failure to slip comfortably into the dim fringes of his memory. God knows he should have forgotten her by now, or at least remembered her only occasionally. She was married, happily so he guessed. She and Parelli had been together fifteen years, which was unusual in this day and age, and in show business circles it must have been a novelty indeed.

Yet, not all the common sense in the world could prevent him from wanting to see her again, if only for a minute. Just to see for himself if being Mrs. Vic Parelli had turned out to be "somebody" enough for her. He'd know, he was sure. He'd know with one look.

Damned fool! He turned onto the street where he lived. Most of the year it was a quiet, postcard-pretty avenue, but in February it looked rather bleak. In a couple of months the dogwoods and azaleas would be in bloom, and for a few short weeks the Carolinas would be transformed into a breathtaking panorama of white, pink and red blossoms. Then even dilapidated farms like the Jameson place would seem to have been touched by a fairy's wand. The dogwoods had been in full flower when Shannon left Fountain Inn for good.

He eased the jeep into his private parking space and gave a little growl of self-disgust. The one disturbing aspect of his successful, well-ordered life was his inability to rid himself of his foolish obsession with a woman he hadn't seen in eighteen years!

BLAKE DIDN'T EXPECT to hear from John Foreman for a week or more, so he couldn't have been more surprised when the realtor called him four days later.

"Isn't it a damned shame?" John asked. "I guess we can forget about hearing from Shannon Parelli anytime soon."

Blake's heart lurched. Had something happened to Shannon? "Why do you say that?" he demanded sharply.

"Haven't you seen a newspaper this morning?"

"No, I haven't. Why?"

"Damned shame," John said again. "Vic Parelli was killed in a light plane crash last night."

Blake gripped the receiver tightly. "His . . . wife?"

"No, she wasn't with him. Parelli, the pilot and Parelli's manager were the only ones in the plane. Happened somewhere out in Colorado. They were on their way to Las Vegas where Parelli was due to start a one-week engagement. It says here that . . ."

John read the newspaper account of the tragedy, but not much of it registered with Blake. One consideration, however, pounded over and over in his brain. He knew it was unconscionable of him to think it, but . . .

Shannon was a widow!

CHAPTER THREE

THE WOMAN NAMED ANNA MARTINO took the envelope, clutched it to her ample bosom and flicked away a tear with a forefinger. "Bless you, ma'am, and bless your dear husband most of all. I don't know what the kids and I would have done without..."

Shannon Parelli silenced her with a small smile and a wave of her slender hand. "Please, Mrs. Martino, don't thank me. Me least of all. You just take care of yourself and the kids. That will be all the thanks Vic would have ever wanted."

The plump woman nodded humbly, opened her mouth to say something else, but quickly shut it and turned away from the desk. With a mixture of sadness and relief, Shannon watched Anna leave the room, vaguely wondering why Mrs. Martino was a recipient of Vic's philanthropy. If she remembered correctly, Anna was the widow of a musician in Vic's band, the one who had died of a drug overdose a year earlier. But she easily could have the woman confused with someone else.

Shannon knew very little about any of the unfortunates and down-and-outs whom her husband had chosen to take care of. She only knew that this monthly task was difficult for her. Vic had handled it with aplomb, even seemed to enjoy it, but she

couldn't. To sit behind the impressive mahogany
desk and dole out checks to once-proud, now pa-
thetically humble people, while she herself was surrounded by baronial luxury didn't sit well with her.

Anna had been the last of the day's callers, thank
the Lord. Shannon sighed and closed her appointment book. She would have given anything if the
philanthropy could have been handled in another
manner, by mail or through Vic's accountants. But
the surprising personal note to his wife in his will had
been specific: the checks were to continue to be given
in person on the first of every month. The note had
been accompanied by a lengthy list of names and
addresses. Although Shannon had known about the
list, just as she'd known about the dozens of callers
who trooped into her husband's study on the first of
every month, the extent of his generosity overwhelmed her.

From her vantage point behind the desk, she stared
across the great expanse of the paneled den. Everything around her spoke of wealth. Mahogany tables, leather furniture and brass lamps stood about
on thick burgundy carpet. Rare paintings and photographs of Vic with various celebrities lined the
walls. Recessed lighting in the ceiling created a subdued, serene effect. The room resembled the interior of an exclusive men's club and reflected
something of the personality of the man whose room
it had been—masculine, elegant, even a bit preten-
tious. The last time Shannon had seen her husband
alive they had been in this room. Vic had been seated
where she was now, and he had been displeased.

A lump formed in her throat. Would she ever be
able to forget that last time they were together? As

had often been the case, Vic had been irritated over something she'd said or done or wanted to do. Why had she even mentioned Mike and the school? She'd known how Vic felt. Had she done it deliberately to antagonize him? She had been in a very rebellious frame of mind.

Part of her lingering melancholy, she knew, stemmed from guilt. At the very moment her husband had been flying to his death, she had been ensconced in the beautiful world he had given her, snug and comfortable and planning a confrontation with him when he returned. Only an hour before that awful phone call from the highway trooper in Colorado, she had been enjoying a solitary dinner in the gracious dining room, rehearsing what she intendedto say, imagining his reaction. She had been prepared for outrage, disbelief, indifference....

Abruptly Shannon gave herself a shake. Why dwell on such things? She told herself to think instead of all the good times. There had been many of those. And to think of the passion and dreams that had been poured into their marriage. Above all, to remember that if Vic had tried to force her into an idealistic mold, it was a mold she had willingly accepted fifteen years ago. Only lately, in the last four or five years, had she found it confining.

Hugging herself, Shannon rubbed her arms briskly. In spite of the weight of her bulky heather-gray sweater and the heat from the fireplace across the room, she couldn't banish the chill in her bones. Sometimes it seemed she'd never be warm again.

She stared through the French doors to the garden in the rear of the house. It was the first week in April, but nothing of the scene outside suggested the impending arrival of spring. A steady rain had been falling since daybreak, and it was now late afternoon. Everything was gray, gray, gray, and the forecast was for more of the same tomorrow. The room was so still and hushed she could hear the ticking of the clock on the mantle. Vic had been gone two months, yet his presence permeated the house, especially this grand room he had loved so. She still had the feeling he would walk through the door at any moment. And every so often she thought she heard him humming in his rich baritone. Even though she had been through similar periods before when she'd lost her parents, she found death the most difficult thing in the world to accept.

In some ways the weeks immediately following her husband's accident had been the easiest for her. There had been so much to do, not the least of which had been answering the hundreds of letters from fans all over the world. Now the days seemed to plod, and a permanent weariness had settled over her, although she was more inactive than she'd ever been. Her mother, who'd had a saying for every conceivable situation, used to warn, "Doing nothing will just wear you out." For the first time, Shannon fully understood what she'd meant.

Sighing, she stood and crossed the room to the fireplace. Lethargically pushing open the firescreen, she jabbed unnecessarily at the logs with a poker, sending up a shower of bright sparks. She stepped back just as the sound of footsteps in the hall reached her ears. A light tap on the door followed; it opened to admit Nicole, one of the household's domestics.

"Ma'am, Mr. Thorpe is here."

Shannon snapped out of her melancholy reverie. "Please show him in, Nicole."

"Yes, ma'am. And about supper tonight, Mrs. Parelli. Ginger's made some nice bean soup."

Shannon smiled fondly at Nicole. The little woman had been clucking over her like a mother hen for weeks. And Shannon ruefully realized she hadn't done justice to Ginger's superb efforts in the kitchen. She accepted the grand meals set before her, and ate them dutifully without thought or taste. That wasn't an appropriate way to treat a kitchen artist like Ginger. "On a day like today, Nicole, bean soup sounds marvelous. Tell Ginger I'm looking forward to it."

Nicole nodded and scurried away, leaving the door open to admit the tall distinguished figure of Jeremiah Thorpe, Vic's trusted business manager and her best friend's husband. He strode into the room, closed the door behind him and advanced on Shannon, who straightened and walked to meet him in the center of the room, hands outstretched. "Jerry, how nice of you to stop by."

Jerry took her hands and clasped them warmly. "I've been meaning to get over for days, but it's been one damned thing after another."

"You work too hard. It's probably not worth it, you know."

"You sound like my wife. I'll tell you what I tell her—work's what I do best."

"Peg stopped by yesterday."

"I know. She told me."

"She's been wonderful, she really has. Let me get you a drink or something."

"No, thanks, dear. I really can't stay long."

She smiled. "You never can stay long. You're busy then?"

"Very."

"Then come, let's sit by the fire. This room seems so dreadfully cold."

"Miserable day, isn't it? I'm ready for winter to end."

"Aren't we always?"

When they were seated opposite one another in front of the fireplace, Jerry regarded her with interest. "How are you, Shannon? You look wonderful."

She smiled wanly. "Thanks, Jerry."

"Your tax return is about finished. I've been working on the thing for weeks. It gets more complicated every year."

"I know. When the lawyers were filing in and out of here, trying to explain everything to me, I wondered if Vic ever realized just how complicated his life really was. He always declared he wanted to keep things simple."

"Well, one doesn't acquire the kind of money Vic did without also acquiring a bunch of people and some complex machinery for taking care of it."

"I suppose you're right." Of course Shannon had known her husband was a wealthy man, but she hadn't been prepared for the scope of his fortune. Large bequests to charitable organizations, to his children and to associates who had been with him for years, to say nothing of those names on the list, had still left her with a staggering sum of money.

"So, Shannon, what's been going on?" Jerry asked. "What did you do today?"

"It was the day for Vic's list, remember?"

"Ah, yes, the list. I still don't understand why he didn't leave that to me. I could mail those checks from the office, and you wouldn't have to bother with them."

Shannon also thought that would have been the best way to handle the gifts, but she didn't say as much to Jerry.

"Damned if I don't hate to say this," Jerry immediately went on, "but Vic was too easy a touch. Some of those people have been on that list for years. Did he intend taking care of them the rest of their lives?"

"I don't suppose we'll ever know, will we, Jerry? That list was Vic's private business. He barely discussed it even with me. He only told me he was helping a few folks over some bad times."

"And you don't think any of those folks are ever going to admit to good times, do you? Not when all they have to do is stick out their hands."

"Don't be cynical, Jerry. It obviously was something Vic wanted to do."

Jerry scoffed, then changed the subject. "Have you seen much of the kids?"

The "kids" he referred to were John and Rosemary, Vic's adopted children by his first marriage. "Recently, no. They've made their duty calls."

Jerry frowned. "Now, that doesn't seem right somehow."

"Oh, I never expected to see much of them. After all, they were almost grown when Vic and I married, and my relationship with them has always been cordial, but not close. That's not so surprising, is it? They're both married and have their own lives to lead. I certainly don't resent their absence." In fact, she thought it refreshing that none of them went through the pretense of being real family.

"Ralph left, I understand."

Shannon nodded. "There really was nothing for him to do here, and he was miserable without Vic. The will provided for him handsomely."

"How about Boots and that other fellow... Joe?"

"I haven't seen them since the day the will was read. You know how generous Vic was to them."

"Fair-weather friends?"

"They never were my friends, Jerry. I don't think they were even Vic's 'friends.' They were users, pure and simple."

"I could never understand why Vic allowed it."

"Nor could I," Shannon said tersely.

"You know," Jerry mused thoughtfully, "I wish you and Vic had had some kids of your own. They would have helped make all this easier for you."

"Do you really think so? I wonder. Seems like that's a lot to expect of kids." This was the kind of offhand remark she used whenever the subject of children came up, but the one abiding regret of her life was being childless. She knew she would of enjoyed being a mother. Vic had wanted kids, too. They'd excitedly discussed it in the early days of their marriage. Shannon had even studied the rhythm method, though for the reverse reason that most women did. When she failed to conceive she'd been concerned enough to see a gynecologist, who'd pronounced her hale and fit for pregnancy. She'd related the news to Vic, but he'd dropped the subject, and never mentioned it again. Since his first marriage hadn't produced a child either, Shannon accepted the fact that her husband was probably sterile.

She doubted he had accepted it, however, and he'd certainly never gone to a doctor to find out. Vic had harbored a vast array of antiquated ideas, among them the notion that masculinity and fertility went hand-in-hand. She imagined he had convinced himself that he'd simply chanced to marry two infertile women.

It was a shame, she thought, and not only because she had been robbed of motherhood. It would have been good for Vic to have had to share her with someone else. He might have been less possessive.

But it simply hadn't happened, and it was easier to pretend to others that her childless state didn't bother her at all. A good many of her friends thought she'd actually planned it that way.

"Have you been out today?" Jerry asked.

"No, I had to make out all the checks and then see all those people."

"Have you been anywhere this week?"

She shook her head. "I meant to, but the weather has been so miserable."

"My God, what do you do with yourself in this big old house all day every day? I'd be climbing the walls."

"Oh, I manage to stay busy," she said feebly.

"This can't continue, Shannon. Vic's been gone two months."

She averted her eyes. "I know. And I intend to get out and get busy soon, although I'm not sure doing what. It's difficult, Jerry. Vic was so much a part of my life for fifteen years. Just about all of it, if you want the truth."

Jerry leaned forward and spoke earnestly. "All of us feel that way, everyone in the group. The boss was our lives, too."

Shannon nodded. Vic had kept himself surrounded with people like Boots and Joe, but "the group," the people he had trusted most of all, consisted of his lawyer, his agent, the road manager who had died in the plane crash with him, and Jerry. To a man they had been as devoted to "the boss" as aging cocker spaniels, and to a man they had been flabbergasted fifteen years ago when Vic had married a woman twenty-one years his junior. But they had always treated Shannon with deference, with almost obsequious courtesy because she was Vic's wife.

All but Jerry. From the beginning he'd treated her as an interesting individual who just happened to be married to Vic Parelli. And his wife, Peg, had become her dearest friend. Peg was all the things Shannon imagined herself not to be—vivacious, charming, ebullient, passionately involved in the business of living. Shannon admired her tremendously and adored Jerry.

"How is everyone?" she asked. "I haven't seen any of them in weeks."

"We're all muddling along, doing what you should be doing—filling the void Vic left in our lives. Vic would be the first to tell you that if he could."

Would he? Shannon doubted that.

Jerry went on. "He married Marie when they both were kids, nineteen or something like that. Then one day she was gone, he was forty and convinced his emotional life had ended. But he met you. He found someone else and so will you."

"No, Jerry, not another man. Never another man. You can't imagine what living with Vic was like." A wealth of meaning lurked behind those words, but she doubted Jerry would guess what it was.

He didn't. "Ah, Shannon, I know you and Vic had a fantastic marriage, perfect maybe, and I don't suppose anyone can expect that twice in a lifetime. But you can have something pretty good."

"I'll find something to do, but it won't involve the heart."

Jerry sighed. "I hope you change your mind. You probably don't think thirty-six is all that young, but it is. Much too young to draw up into a shell. There are so many options open to you."

"For instance?" Shannon asked, hoping to change the subject.

"Well . . . to begin with I think you should sell this mausoleum." His hand made a sweep to include the house as a whole.

Shannon gasped in mock horror. "Jerry! If Vic could hear you refer to his beloved house as a mausoleum . . ."

"This place suited Vic perfectly. It's exactly the sort of house a poor kid from Philadelphia would build when he hit it big, but for you it will be nothing but an encumbrance, a place full of memories. If I were you, I'd sell it."

She had thought of doing just that several times since Vic's death, and the idea had had nothing to do with the memories associated with the house. The grand Tudor mansion simply wasn't to her taste, that was all. She would have adored something smaller, lighter, with great expanses of glass and natural wood. Or even a vine-covered cottage. Anything but the Tudor. Yet she balked at selling. "Vic loved this house so," she murmured obscurely.

"Shannon, it costs thousands of dollars to run this place every month."

"Money doesn't seem to be one of my big problems, Jerry."

Jerry sighed again, this time dramatically. "What in the devil are you going to do with it? Live in it alone? Why?"

She lifted her shoulders and spread out her hands. "It's been my home for fifteen years," she said, as though that explained it all.

"Well, I know change is never easy. It's easier to get set in concrete, and the prestige associated with this house is enormous."

"I don't give a flip about the prestige."

"Well, you need something, some interest. I've often wished you hadn't given up your career."

Shannon looked at him in surprise. "You have? Why on earth?"

"Because of this, because you must have known you would be a relatively young widow someday."

"But not so soon," she said pensively. "He shouldn't have gone at fifty-seven."

"No, he shouldn't have, but he did. And if you had a career to occupy your time and thoughts..."

"Oh, Jerry," she interrupted with a little laugh, "surely you don't think I'd still be dancing at thirty-six? Not as a chorus line hoofer, and that's all I ever was. I'd never have been a star, you know that. I never deluded myself that I was giving up a fabulous career to marry Vic. In South Carolina I might have been a big deal, but in New York I was just one of many."

Jerry opened his mouth to say something, then shut it, apparently changing his mind. A moment of strained silence passed before he reached into his breast pocket and produced an envelope. "Which reminds me . . . besides wanting to see how you're doing, I had a reason for coming. I need to know what you want to do about this."

"What is it?"

"The letter and contract from that realtor in South Carolina. I've had it two months now, and I need to tell him something."

"Oh, yes, the farm. I'd forgotten all about it." The letter had arrived the day Vic left for Vegas. She had told Jerry to put it aside until her husband's return. Not surprisingly, she hadn't thought of it again.

"Do you want to sell?" Jerry asked.

"I don't see why not. I can't imagine ever wanting to do anything with the old place."

Jerry studied the contract. "The offer seems fairly reasonable to me. I suppose it's the best you're going to get. According to this Mr. Foreman, it needs a lot of work, so that has to be taken into consideration. You'll be selling at a loss, but that might be a good thing tax-wise."

Shannon shrugged her indifference. "Whatever you think. That's your department."

"Okay, we'll sell. So why don't you go down there and take care of it?"

"Me? Is that necessary?"

"No, I could take care of it for you, but it would give you something to do, get you out of this house and away from this miserable weather."

"Oh, Jerry, I haven't been back since my dad died. I don't think . . ."

"Don't think about it, just do it. Seems to me you'd welcome the chance to get away."

"Yes," she said thoughtfully, "I would. I've been thinking about the house in Florida."

Jerry growled his disapproval. "Where there are more memories of Vic? Do you really think that would be such a good idea? That house isn't much more than a glorified recording studio. You ought to sell it, too. What do you need with it? Go to South Carolina and take care of the old homestead. It's something that needs to be done, and the break in routine will be good for you."

Shannon got to her feet and crossed the room to the French doors. Jerry watched her, noticing that she still moved with the grace of a dancer. Tailored gray gabardine slacks fit smoothly over the curves of her hips and the length of her shapely legs. Her figure was as trim and supple at thirty-six as it had been the day she married Vic. The group's wives, his own Peg, especially, had collectively decided that Shannon had kept her admirable figure because she'd been spared pregnancy.

She was wearing her dark hair shorter, about chin-length, and Jerry thought it looked great. For years he had been a Shannon-watcher, as had most of Vic's friends, and he had marveled at the transformation from wide-eyed ingenue to elegant young matron. She'd always been a pretty woman, but maturity and the advantages of wealth had turned her into a striking one. Coupled with her good looks were a softness and graciousness that made her seem fragile, but Jerry knew how deceptive that was. He'd occasionally glimpsed a reservoir of strength beneath that delicate-looking exterior.

Unfortunately, Jerry thought, Shannon had lost something along the way—a certain zest for living, the quality that had probably captivated Vic in the first place. And Vic probably was responsible for the erosion of all that enthusiasm. God knows, he couldn't have been an easy man to live with—another reason to admire Shannon tremendously. Although he'd loved Vic like a brother, he'd always realized that a great deal of the famous Parelli charm had been strictly reserved for the public.

Jerry's gaze remained fastened on Shannon. She seemed a million miles away. He would have given anything to know what she was thinking.

Shannon braced one arm on the doorjamb, the other on her hip and stared out at the drenched garden. The rain was coming down harder now, in dismal gray sheets. Long Island winters had the most unpleasant habit of over-staying their welcome, and though she had lived with them for years, the Southerner in her had never made peace with them. Inevitably, along about the first of April, her mind wistfully recalled flowering dogwood, winding paths packed inches deep with pine needles, the smell of honeysuckle and freshly-plowed earth. She could see her father sitting high atop the tractor in a distant field, and she could hear her mother saying, "I do believe the English peas and new potatoes will be ready in time for Easter dinner."

It was good, she now thought, to remember there had been a life before Vic. Remembering that, perhaps she could realize there would be one after him. She had made a career out of being Mrs. Vic Parelli because Vic had needed her in ways difficult to explain. It had been a time-consuming career, exhausting at times, not always fulfilling, yet she had pursued it with determination.

But she didn't want to make a career out of being his widow, and if she wasn't careful that would happen before she knew it. Jerry and the others would continue to do for her as they'd done for Vic. For the rest of her life she'd only need to lift a finger or a phone, and anything she wanted would be hers. It would be so easy...

And the worst possible thing for her! How could she make a new life for herself if she clung tenaciously to the old? Jerry was right; she needed to get out of this house. Vic lingered in every nook and cranny of it. It had been his house long before she'd ever set foot in it, and not fifteen years of her personal touches had done much to make it hers. It had all the warmth of a castle on the moors. She couldn't imagine why she had persisted in remaining locked away in Vic's luxurious world, seeing only Peg and Vic's friends and associates.

Abruptly she turned around. "All right, Jerry, I'll do it. The weather back home should be lovely about now."

"Good, Shannon, good! I honestly think it's what you need—a change of scene." Rising to his feet, he said, "I'll call this fellow in the morning and tell him to expect you... when?"

She gave it some thought. "Thursday, I guess. Yes, Thursday. That should give me time to get ready."

"All right. I'll make airline and hotel reservations for you, and I'll arrange with the realtor to have someone meet you at the airport. Better still, maybe I should get someone to travel with you."

There it was—the easy way. For so many years everything had been done for her. It was appalling to realize she'd never made reservations, never traveled alone, never rented a car.

"Jerry, do me a favor. Stop looking after me, please. I'm not Vic. I don't need an entourage to protect me from a curious public. I need to learn to do for myself." She offered him a small smile. "I'll make my own airline and hotel reservations and rent a car myself. I don't need a traveling companion, and I don't want anyone to meet me at the airport. Just tell the realtor to set up an appointment for...oh, for Friday afternoon sometime. I'll contact him when I get to Greenville to find out the actual time. I think...I think I might like to wander around alone for a day or two. After all—" her eyes swept the big room, and the smile died on her lips "—there's no reason to hurry back here. Not anymore."

THAT EVENING after she had dressed for bed, Shannon took the time to read the letter and the copy of the real estate contract Jerry had left for her. A twinge of regret or guilt or something stirred inside as she thought of selling the farm her parents had devoted their lives to. But that was nostalgic nonsense, and she knew it. Her father, who had epitomized practicality, would have been the first to tell her that. She unfolded the contract and began reading, then paused and frowned when she encountered the prospective buyer's name.

Blake Carmichael! Surely it couldn't be the same one. Not that somber-eyed boy who'd lived with them when she was in high school. She had been accustomed to having parentless kids in need of a temporary home staying with them; her parents had done that sort of thing for years. But Blake had been different. Older for one thing, and such an unpleasant sort at first, a kid with a king-sized chip on his shoulder. Living on the farm, though, had changed him, and she'd grown to like him a lot.

He had been a year older than she and was the first male "best friend" she'd ever had. They used to take long walks through the woods and talk with adolescent seriousness about the future, although she'd done most of the talking, since he'd been such a quiet one. She'd wanted to become a famous dancer, and he'd wanted a big house with a wife and a bunch of kids. Lord, that seemed to long ago! If the would-be buyer wasn't her old friend, it was one heck of a coincidence.

She refolded the contract and placed it on her bedside table. Switching off the lamp, she snuggled under the covers and silently prayed for sleep. It had been weeks since she'd taken the sleeping pills the doctor had prescribed, for she'd realized she shouldn't continue using that crutch, and besides, she disliked the way they made her feel in the morning. Sometimes, though, doing without them made for long, long nights.

She closed her eyes and allowed her mind to carry her back in time. Blake Carmichael, for heaven's sakes! What she remembered most about him were his eyes, dark and intensely earnest. He'd been such a serious, thoughtful boy, entirely unlike the boys at school who had nothing but sex on their minds and lunged on the first date. Blake had been almost painfully shy around her and utterly respectful. She couldn't recall that he'd ever so much as touched her.

Shannon smiled. So he had gone back to Greenville after the Air Force. Occasionally she had wondered whatever happened to him, how life had treated him. Shannon Jameson certainly hadn't ever become a famous dancer. She hoped Blake Carmichael had gotten that big family. Maybe that's why he wanted the farm.

CHAPTER FOUR

A SPONTANEOUS LIGHTNESS LIFTED Shannon's spirits as the plane touched down at Greenville-Spartanburg Airport. Her decision to make the trip was the best thing she could have done. For three days she had been so caught up in preparations that she'd had no time to feel lonely or to think about Vic. She had been determined to make all the arrangements herself, something legions of women did routinely, but for her it had been something of an adventure. No one could have been more surprised than she when she arrived at Kennedy and discovered she did indeed have reservations.

She was just as pleasantly surprised now to find her rented car waiting for her. A sense of accomplishment, of self-reliance swept through her. And wasn't that something! Here she was, thirty-six years old and learning to do for herself again.

She had depended on others for so long it was hard to believe life hadn't always been that way. Once she had possessed a stubborn independent streak that propelled her to seek the pot at the end of the rainbow. The move to New York, for instance. It had meant openly defying her father for the first time in her life and suffering through her mother's dire predictions of what could happen to a girl all alone in a city like that. It had meant leaving behind all that was familiar and comfortable for the unknown and difficult. In those early New York days she had been a "gypsy," an itinerant dancer racing from audition to audition, hoping for the big break while waiting on tables in an Italian restaurant at night. There hadn't been anyone to rely on then. She had mastered the art of making do, doing without, and looking after herself.

But all that was before Vic. Looking back, their marriage still seemed pure fairy-tale stuff. The media had had a field day with it, one of the reasons Vic had guarded their privacy so strictly afterwards. Prince Charming had carried Cinderella off to the castle on Long Island, to live happily ever after in the lap of luxury. And they had been happy, blissfully so in the beginning. She had been so young, so in love, so overwhelmed by Vic's personality and the beautiful life he had given her. The years had simply flown by, and in time it seemed that she had always been Shannon Parelli, that Shannon Jameson hadn't existed at all.

Maybe, she thought as she sped along the Interstate toward Greenville, it was time to find her again.

The motel she had chosen was one she remembered from years ago. It no longer was the newest and swankiest in town, but it had been well kept and was centrally located. After checking in and getting settled in her room, she telephoned Jerry. He and Peg were the only souls on earth who would really care where she was. Then she called John Foreman and arranged to meet him in his office the following afternoon at two o'clock. That done, she changed out of her beige traveling suit into khaki slacks and a rose-colored blouse for the short drive to Fountain

Inn. She wanted to see the farm one more time before it passed from her hands forever.

The countryside was putting on its spring show and was as beautiful as she remembered, with riots of color everywhere. A swirl of emotions assaulted her as she drove the rented sedan past the farm's sagging wooden gate. The car bounced along the dirt path leading to the house. Seeing her childhood home in such sad condition prompted a rush of melancholy, the last thing in the world she needed. Too late she decided she shouldn't have come. The impromptu visit only served to remind her of how alone in the world she truly was—no parents, no husband, no one. And once the farm was sold—no roots.

Shannon braked and stopped the car at the front steps. For a moment she simply sat still, debating whether or not to get out. She did finally, and while she slowly mounted the steps, her eyes wandered over the depressing scene around her. She took a moment to be glad her parents couldn't see their home this way. They had both worked from dawn until sundown, weekends and holidays included, and they had received very little in the way of financial reward. But they had always kept the homestead looking like something out of *Gentleman Farmer*.

It wasn't until she reached for the doorknob that she realized she didn't have a key. Trying the knob, she found the door locked. Her arm fell to her side. Just as well, she thought with a sigh. She wasn't sure she wanted to go inside after all. What possible purpose could it serve? South Carolina, this farm, Fountain Inn were no longer part of her life, and she had traveled too far from them ever to come back.

With a sigh, she turned to leave, but at that moment the door opened. Startled, Shannon turned toward the sound, exclaiming "Oh!" as the figure of a man filled the doorway.

He was five or six inches taller than she, tall enough to force her to tilt her head to look at him. A handsome, well-built man dressed in casual tan slacks and a cream-colored pullover stared back at her. She wondered if he was John Foreman, the realtor. Whoever he was, he shot her a charming, lopsided grin; it was so infectious that she grinned back. Then her eyes locked onto a pair of intense masculine ones, and the first dawning of recognition overtook her.

"Hello, Shannon," he said in a husky, slightly unsteady voice. "It's been a long time."

"Blake!" she breathed. "Oh, Blake—so it is you after all."

Blake's heart thudded so erratically inside his chest he found breathing difficult, and he tightly grasped the doorknob in an effort to steady himself. She was here! Very real, no mirage, no fanciful flight of his imagination. And she had recognized him. For two days, ever since John had called to tell him she was coming, he'd planned what he would say if she didn't. He had pictured himself awkwardly explaining who he was, while she vainly searched her memory. But all that could be forgotten and he would bask in the irrational pleasure her recognition brought him. Unfortunately, he was as rattled as he feared he might be.

He knew he was gawking, but he couldn't help it. He would have known her instantly, no matter where he'd encountered her. Although there were changes, certain things were the same—the color of her hair, the depth of her luminous eyes, her sweet smile, the erect way she held herself. She'd kept her figure, but other things had changed. The ponytail was gone, along with the ingenuous prettiness. They'd been replaced by a mature beauty that took his breath away. And she'd developed style, he thought as his gaze took in her simple but obviously expensive clothes, and that indefinable something called "class." Drawing deep within himself, he called upon all the poise he'd ever been able to muster.

Shannon stepped toward him and offered both her hands. "Oh, Blake, it's so good to see you again!"

He took her hands and clasped them in his, feeling their smoothness. "It's good to see you again, too, Shannon. You look . . . wonderful."

"So do you. You look healthy and prosperous. Are you?"

"Yes, thankfully I'm both." He dipped his head briefly, then looked at her and smiled. "You've lost your southern accent. You sound like a Yankee."

Shannon laughed. "Back home my friends say I sound as southern as corn pone."

She cocked her head slightly and studied him. He had gained some weight, which was all to the good. "Filled out", she supposed, was a better description, and in all the right places, too. His mature muscular physique was admirable. He had been such a wiry, gangling boy, but all traces of that boy were gone now. Time had treated him kindly. His features were strong and rugged, etched with character. Thick brown hair tumbled across his forehead, its tips sun-bleached a lighter shade. His brown eyes were as warm as a summer morning. Yes, he was a distinctly handsome man, and she hadn't remembered him as being especially good-looking. But then, in all honesty, she probably hadn't thought of him more than half a dozen times since she'd left Fountain Inn.

He hadn't released her hands, and she made no attempt to remove them. Something about the way he was looking at her made her feel welcome. "When I saw your name on the contract I wondered if my buyer would turn out to be you."

"Yes, the moment I discovered that the farm was for sale, I knew I had to have it."

"Good, good! I'm glad someone who really wants it will own it." She gave both his hands a shake for emphasis, and a small giggle escaped her lips. "Isn't this something, meeting again after all these years!"

"Yes, it's... it's really something." The odd inflection in his voice irritated Blake. He wondered what Shannon would think if she knew how often he'd thought of her over the years. She had no idea she'd been the first love of his life, so the thoughts dancing on the periphery of his mind would probably send her fleeing in horror. He cleared his throat and said, "Come on inside and let's talk. I was just doing some measuring."

"All right."

Blake dropped her hands and stood back to allow her to enter. Shannon took a hesitant step forward, and the moment she entered the house she felt a sharp stab of grief. The exterior of the house was in deplorable condition, but inside it was just as she remembered. It had a musty, unlived-in smell, but it looked the same. She hadn't recalled that most of the furniture was still in place, but she should have.

She'd taken very few things, only a few of her mother's most cherished mementos, and there hadn't been anyone else to give anything to.

Dear God, it looked so shabby! Had it always looked this way? On her right the living room was furnished in no particular style, just a mishmash of items her parents happened to like. On her left, in the dining room, the big oak table stood waiting for company or Sunday dinner. A railed stairway rose to the bedrooms on the second floor. Shannon's breath was expelled in labored puffs. She had left Long Island to get away from memories, only to find herself overwhelmed by different ones. "There's a lot to do," she murmured distractedly.

Seeing her distress, Blake stepped closer to her. "Not so much, not really. The outside needs a lot of attention, but I was pleasantly surprised by the inside. Paint, wallpaper, new carpet...you'll see." Would she ever see it once he had finished with it? Not likely. Gently he touched her arm. "Let's sit down. I brought a thermos of coffee. Would you like a cup?"

"I...yes, I guess so." She walked into the living room and sat on the worn print sofa while Blake poured their coffee. "How did you get here?" she asked. "There's no car outside."

"My jeep's parked in back. Ever since John called to say you'd accepted my offer, I've been driving over every day, just to look around and take notes." That was so much garbage. Something had told him that Shannon would want to see the farm; it seemed only natural. But she hadn't told John when she would arrive in Greenville, so Blake had been haunting the place, fearing seeing her but afraid of missing her.

"Over?" she asked. "Over from where?"

"I live in Charlotte." He handed her a Styrofoam mug full of coffee. She took it and held it in both her hands. He noticed that she still wore her wedding ring, a stunning diamond-encrusted band of gold, and still on her left hand. Taking a seat beside her on the sofa, he tried to study her without seeming to, casting surreptitous glances at the gentle contours of her profile. The excitement of seeing her again had subsided somewhat, and he was able to look at her more honestly, satisfying his eager curiosity.

She had changed more than he'd thought at first. Or perhaps not changed so much as settled into someone very unlike the Shannon of his memories. That Shannon had fairly blazed with life, but perhaps one only experienced such vigor at seventeen. Gone forever was the soft, innocent girl he had loved with mindless devotion.

Hardly surprising, given the passage of years and her recent bereavement. Recent—that was the key word. In Shannon's lovely dark eyes he fancied he could discern a sadness of long-standing, mingled now with doubts and confusion. She was unhappy long before her husband died, Blake thought, or, if not exactly unhappy, then resigned to something less than happiness.

In some curious way he felt disappointed, all the while acknowledging the absurdity of the disappointment. Time changes, he reminded himself. Certainly he had changed; why had he imagined Shannon wouldn't have?

Nonetheless, he felt a loosening taking place inside him. He hadn't expected this. How wonderful it would be if this meeting with Shannon, instead of renewing his passion, finally and forever put an end to the fascination she had held for him for far too long.

Shannon carefully sipped at the coffee. It was black, strong and bitter, probably made hours ago. Her mother had kept a pot going all day. "Have a cup," was the way Beth Jameson had greeted visitors, and by mid-afternoon that brew had often been powerful. Ginger, on the other hand, refused to serve coffee that was more than thirty minutes old.

What made me think of that, Shannon wondered. Is it this house reminding me of my drastically altered lifestyle?

She forced her thoughts back to the man seated beside her. "Charlotte? What sort of work do you do there?"

"I have a construction business."

"Your own business? Blake, how wonderful! You've come a long way."

He grinned. "A long way from that miserable kid who first moved to this farm, that's for sure."

"Harry's doing." Instantly he sobered. "I didn't learn about either of your folks' deaths until many weeks after the fact. My fault. I should have stayed in touch. I came to visit Harry a few times after your mom died. Not as often as I should have, I'm afraid. His death hit me pretty hard."

Shannon stared into the coffee cup. "I came down for Mom's operation, so I was able to comfort Dad a little when she died. But his accident . . . Vic and I were in Bermuda when it happened. I . . . I remember thinking how glad I was that he didn't have to go on without her any longer. I think he died inside when Mom died."

Blake rubbed a hand across his chin. There was such quiet desperation in her voice, that he wondered if she felt the same way. Did she wish she had gone down in that plane with Parelli? Then, because he felt it needed saying, he murmured, "Shannon, I'm awfully sorry about your husband."

"Thank you." Something in the tone of his voice touched her. For two months people had been telling her how sorry they were that Vic was gone. But Blake, who hadn't known Vic, was sending her a different message: he was sorry for her because she had lost her husband.

A moment of silence followed while Shannon took another sip of coffee. Blake averted his eyes, not wanting to study her further. He thought about leaving. Nothing in her expression or manner told him whether or not she considered his presence an intrusion. Could she use some company or did she want to be left alone? He wished he knew.

Actually, Shannon couldn't have been more grateful for his company. It was good to see an old friend, even if he was virtually a stranger after all these years. Had Blake not been there she feared she would have given in to tears, and a crying jag would have left her feeling miserable for hours. Sensing that her pensive silence was making him uneasy, she forced a smile. "So, Blake, tell me all about yourself. Do you have children?"

"No, I've never been married."

"Never?"

He shook his head. "You sound surprised."

"I am. That's unusual. We have single friends, but they're mostly products of divorce."

Blake took note of her use of the plural "we." "I think I prefer never being married to being the product of divorce."

"True. When I left Fountain Inn I could count on the fingers of one hand the people I'd known who were divorced. Now it's just the other way around. Now someone on television announces he's been married twenty-five years and he gets a standing ovation. Maybe people just don't try hard enough anymore."

"Or maybe they expect too much."

"Yes, maybe so."

Another pall of silence descended. Blake sifted through the dozens of questions he wanted to ask her: chiefly, how she had met Parelli, why she had married a man so much older than she? Not very appropriate. What did you ask someone you hadn't seen in eighteen years?

It was Shannon, however, who asked the next question. "If you live in Charlotte, why on earth do you want this farm?"

That was something Blake could talk about at length. "Oh, it's something I've been thinking about for a long time. Has to do with the lure of the land, I guess. And a longing for some new challenge. It's not easy to explain. My business doesn't demand as much of me as it once did, and farming is a day-in, day-out challenge, no question about that. Your dad was the one who told me there's no satisfaction to beat working your own land."

"You mean you're actually going to farm this place?"

"Actually I was giving some thought to home-steading."

"Working it, you mean?"

"Well, Shannon, homesteading means more than just working a piece of land. It has to do with a return to the simple life, to the kind of self-sufficiency our grandparents took for granted, the kind of life that disappeared with supermarkets and freeways."

Shannon looked at him blankly. Why on earth would anyone want to return to that kind of life? Her grandparents' life had been hard, and her parents hadn't had it much easier. Farming was a lot of back-breaking work, worrying about the weather and counting yourself lucky if you showed a profit every other year or so. Frankly, it sounded terrible.

Blake could tell she didn't understand. Not many people did. Homesteading, according to popular belief, was for society's nonconformists and drop-outs, people who couldn't hack it in a modern tech-nological world: not for successful men like himself. And there was no good way to explain what he wanted to anyone who didn't already understand it.

"Would you like to come outside with me and look around? Maybe I can show you what I have in mind."

Shannon shrugged and set the coffee on an end table. Why not? What else did she have to do?

"Sure," she said and stood when he did.

THEY MADE A SHORT WALKING TOUR of the area im-mediately surrounding the house. Shannon, accus-tomed to the meticulously manicured grounds and formal gardens of the Long Island house, saw nothing but neglect and decay, but Blake's enthusiasm was unrestrained.

"In homesteading this place I'm starting out with a plus," he told her.

"You are?" she asked in surprise. Everything she saw looked like a definite minus.

"Sure—the house. Admittedly it's what a real estate ad might refer to as a 'handyman's delight,' but it's sound. I always figured I'd have to start out by building one, then go on from there. I imagine I'll spend the first year on the house, putting up a new barn, clearing the area and planting a garden. After that I'll plant crops and buy some livestock. I can use the stream for irrigation, for energy, too, if the velocity proves adequate. Someday I'll be raising and preserving every bite I eat, and I'll be using wind, water and sun for power." He folded his arms across his chest and smiled with satisfaction.

All that should have had a stronger impact on her, she supposed, for her roots lay in that kind of life. However, she felt so far removed from living close to the land. Her life now was one of the utmost comfort and convenience. "You know," she mused, "I've noticed that whenever people 'return to the land,' or whatever it's called, they tend to get so caught up in it that you can't talk to them about anything else."

"How's that?"

"Well...we had a friend who left the city and moved to a little farm in Pennsylvania. We visited him once, only once, I might add, because he bored Vic to tears. Here was a man who had been one of New York's most successful advertising executives, the last word in sophistication, and all he could talk about was how something or other repelled cucumber beetles."

Blake chuckled. "Nasturtiums."

"What?"

"Nasturtiums repel cucumber beetles."

"Maybe that was it. Who do you suppose discovered that in the first place?"

"Probably some farmer who happened to plant the flowers next to his cucumber patch and found he wasn't infested with beetles that year. Look, Shannon, I'm not entirely obsessive about these things. I do believe in indoor plumbing and modern appliances, and I'm all in favor of electricity. I'd just like to generate as much of my own as possible."

"It all sounds very ambitious," was all she could think to say.

"It is."

"What happens to your business in the meantime?"

"Oh, I'll keep the business for several more years. This farm will have to be a weekend project for a long time. But in ten years or so I plan to be living here full time, and if things go well, I won't have much need for the outside world."

They had reached a spot near the barn where the woods grew thick and tangled with undergrowth. Shannon studied the dilapidated structure. "Lord, look at that old barn! Do you remember when it was built?"

"Yes, very well."

"The folks threw a party afterwards, and you and I sneaked off for a walk in the woods and one of our long serious talks."

"I remember." In fact, he probably could have quoted that long ago conversation almost verbatim. What would Mrs. Parelli think of that? He'd wanted to kiss her so badly that night he could taste the desire in his mouth. Those days had been such a time of conflict for him. When he was with her he'd been happy and miserable at the same time. First love had been hard to live with and, as he'd discovered, all but impossible to outgrow.

Shannon pivoted and stared at the rear of the house, now some distance from them. She supposed a lot could be done to make it attractive. As a young girl she had thought it pretty—although she had itched to get away from it—and her mother had kept the yard picture-perfect.

"Gray," she mused aloud.

Blake looked puzzled. "I beg your pardon?"

"Gray," she repeated. "I think the house should be painted gray... you know, a soft blue-gray with white trim. And you should plant a lot of things that bloom red, not just azaleas for spring, but zinnias and salvia and geraniums. Climbing roses, too. Definitely. A house like that needs climbing roses." She smiled up at him. "At least, that's what I think."

Blake returned the smile. "Sounds nice. I'll make a note of it. Do you garden?"

"I fiddle around in our greenhouse and occasionally pinch a petunia or two, but the garden is much too large for one person to take care of. We have a team of groundskeepers who work on it all the time. Perpetual care, like a cemetery." She had always loved their garden, but Vic hadn't liked for her to, as he put it, "muck around with the hired help, then come in smelling like manure." Strange she should have remembered that now.

Blake cupped his palm under her elbow, and they strolled back toward the house. "Tell me about your house, Shannon."

"My house?" She had always thought of it as Vic's house, seldom as hers. "It's on Long Island, and it's big. Tudor and big. Fifteen rooms, and we live in maybe five of them. At one time Vic must have envisioned it full of children."

Again the collective "we," Blake noticed. She hadn't accepted the fact that he was gone. She must have loved him a lot. Probably she'd remain primarily Mrs. Vic Parelli for a long time.

"Then you don't have children?"

"No, I don't."

Blake thought he detected a twinge of regret in her voice. "Forgive me if I'm prying. Does it bother you to talk about these things, Shannon?" he asked gently.

"No, not really." And it didn't; at least it didn't bother her to talk about them with Blake. He had a way of making her feel he was really interested, which she knew he couldn't possibly be. Still, it was nice he made the effort. How many people would? "You wanted children, didn't you? I remember that. You wanted a big house and a big family."

Blake was astonished that she'd remembered that, of all things. "Well, at least I got the big house."

"Yes, and I'm glad you did. Whenever I think of it, I'll be glad it's in your hands."

"Will you be going back to Long Island when you leave here?"

She nodded. "For the time being. There are still some things requiring my attention. I really don't know if I'm going to keep the house. It's much too large for my needs, but . . ."

"But it was your husband's, and you hate to let go of it," Blake finished for her.

"Yes," she said without hesitation. "Amazing you would know that."

"Not really. As a builder I've learned how people feel about houses. Most tend to cling to them, particularly when they've lived in one a long time, and you've been in yours . . . how long now?"

"Fifteen years."

"That's a long time. It's hard to move when you don't have to. Staying put is the path of least resistance."

The path of least resistance, Shannon silently repeated. She'd hardly strayed from it these past fifteen years. She thought about the house on Long Island, as well as the one in Florida. Neither of them held much promise for her, she decided dispiritedly. She could live anywhere in the world that struck her fancy, have several homes if she wanted. She could go anywhere, do anything, yet her mind was a blank. No spot on earth held any particular lure for her, save maybe this old farm, and that was nostalgic nonsense. Besides, after tomorrow the farm no longer would belong to her.

They reached the house and walked around the side to the front. Shannon fumbled in her handbag for the car keys. Blake probably had a dozen things he wanted to do, and she was keeping him from them. She would go back to the motel and read, watch TV or something, then take a bath, and order dinner from room service. It didn't sound very appealing—it was downright depressing, in fact. She couldn't for the life of her recall what she hoped this trip would accomplish, other than the sale of the farm, but whatever it was hadn't come about. She would have to remember not to listen to Jerry so readily.

"I do wish you luck with this place, Blake," she said, fighting back a silly sense of loss. "It seems to me you've taken on a gigantic task, but you appear to be ready and willing to tackle it."

"Maybe someday you'll get curious enough to stop by and see how it's coming along." He wasn't sure why he'd said that; it seemed to pop out of its own accord.

"Maybe," she said with a smile. Withdrawing the keys, she clutched them in her left hand and extended her right. "It's been so nice, Blake, and I'll see you at the realtor's office tomorrow afternoon. Two o'clock, I believe."

He took her hand. "Yes, two o'clock."

Forces warred inside Blake, things he didn't understand. At that moment he honestly thought he could let her go and be at peace with himself. Their encounter had been more enlightening than thrilling. The girl of his dreams was gone, and the woman standing before him lived in another world, light years removed from this South Carolina farm. He could say goodbye and, except for a few minutes tomorrow afternoon, never see her again without too much regret. Let her go and be done with it!

Yet, something compelled him to spend more time with her, to get to know this Shannon a little better. Maybe it was his natural curiosity about people. Or a normal male interest in a lovely woman. In spite of everything, he couldn't let her just walk away.

"Ah...Shannon, I was wondering...are you here alone? Is anyone traveling with you?"

"No, why?"

"Well, I'm staying overnight in Greenville, and I'm alone, too. Both of us will have to have dinner tonight. Why don't we have it together? I detest eating alone."

Shannon had never grabbed at an invitation so quickly. She hoped her relief wasn't evident, but she could have kissed him. Instead of a lonely dinner in her motel room, she could dine in the company of this pleasant man, reminisce a little, and pass the time. "Why, Blake, thank you. I'd like that."

"Where are you staying?" She told him, and he asked, "Is eight o'clock all right with you?"

"Eight is perfect."

"What kind of food do you especially like?"

She laughed lightly. "All kinds."

"But are you in the mood for one kind in particular?"

Shannon thought about it. "You know, it's been ages since I've tasted real southern cooking. Ginger, she's my cook, looks down with disdain on that kind of food."

"Are you talking about blackeyed peas and cornbread, that sort of thing?"

She nodded. "And country ham and turnip greens."

"Fried okra?"

Shannon rolled her eyes. "And blueberry cobbler. All delicious and laden with calories. I guess it's a good thing I don't get that kind of food very often."

"But you obviously don't have any weight worries. Either that or you diet constantly."

"I never diet."

He grinned. "I know just the place. I discovered it some months ago when I was in Greenville on business. I think you'll love it, but don't get all gussied up, or you'll frighten the regulars. See you at eight."

Blake stood at the foot of the steps and watched as she walked to the car, slid behind the wheel and started the engine. Then she gave him a smile and a jaunty wave before wheeling the car around and driving down the path toward the road. He stood and stared long after the car had disappeared from view.

Never, not in his wildest imaginings, would he have thought seeing Shannon again would be like this. The disburdening effect was wonderful. Tonight he was merely going to have a date with a woman he didn't know very well, share dinner and a few laughs, then say good-night. Nothing momentous, nothing particularly memorable. Thank God!

But he was going to do his best to show her a good time. She looked as though she could use one.

CHAPTER FIVE

As she hurried about the motel room getting dressed, Shannon was as nervous as a teenager out on her first big date. It made no sense for a woman her age to let a little thing like having dinner with a man take on the flavor of a significant event, but it had been fifteen years since she'd had dinner alone with any man except Vic. Now that she considered it, this was the first time in fifteen years she would be with someone who hadn't even known Vic Parelli. The thought was accompanied by a reckless, devil-may-care feeling that was at once foolish and exciting and totally uncharacteristic of the conservative, sophisticated woman she had become.

It's only dinner, for heaven's sake, she scolded herself. *You've forgotten how to date.*

Yes, but who wouldn't have forgotten after so long? Especially since she and Vic so seldom went out, less and less as the years passed. He'd declared he was a homebody, that he hated going out in public to be gawked at, but Shannon had known that wasn't it. Vic hated for men to look at her, and men always looked at her. There was nothing she could do about it. She saw nothing remarkable about her face or figure, but men had been looking at her with varying degrees of interest since she was in her teens. Certainly she never sought attention. She avoided dressing provocatively, and she was quiet and self-effacing in public. She deliberately courted the friendship of women and, save for Jerry and Mike, showed other men only casual, passing interest. Still, they gravitated toward her, though she had often suspected they sought her out because she was Vic's wife and they were trying to ingratiate themselves with her in order to get to him. Sometimes their behavior had been so obvious it was laughable.

She'd never been able to convince Vic of that, though. Just let one man's gaze linger on her too long, and he would be sullen all the way home. It did no good to remind him of all the lovely women who fawned over him and bolstered his sometimes fragile ego. "That's different," he declared, and Shannon supposed that in Vic's mind it really had been vastly different. Sometimes he would clam up for days. Then she would have to be the one who would make all the loving overtures that restored harmony. Consequently, she'd never really mastered the art of being relaxed and mature in the company of men; she greatly envied women who could. Her anxiety over tonight's dinner date was the result of years of programming.

Enough of this! Vic wasn't around to scold her tonight. There would be no recriminations if her eyes roamed appreciatively over her dinner companion, which might very well happen, since Blake was so easy to look at. Crossing the room, she executed an almost-perfect pirouette, and laughter bubbled up in her throat. Not too bad, old girl. As she carefully applied her makeup, stroke by practiced stroke, she noticed an unusual sparkle in her eyes. Her lighthearted mood intensified, and she forgave herself for making so much out of an impromptu dinner engagement.

Blake hadn't forgotten how to date. He was prompt, and dressed immaculately in crisp dark slacks and an off-white sport shirt. When she opened the door in response to his knock, his reaction to the sight of her was a low whistle. The smile Shannon gave him was unusually shy. Accustomed to admiring looks from men, she was astonished that Blake's obvious approval pleased her so much. At the same time, she was shaken by her own reaction to his appearance—the kind of tingling sensation she hadn't felt since the days of Vic's courtship.

Her idea of casual clothes was the outfit she was wearing—a split skirt in a brilliant madras plaid and a royal blue shirt with small capped sleeves. She wore loopy earrings and a string of chunky beads around her neck. The effect was stunning, almost exotic. Blake's dark eyes glittered as they moved over her in frank appraisal. She took his breath away. For the first time that evening—by no means the last—he silently pondered the wisdom of spending several hours in this woman's company.

"Shannon, you're a picture," he said. "I'm sorry I'm driving the jeep. I hate to see you get windblown."

"I really don't mind the jeep, but my rental car is available. Why don't we take that? You drive."

When they entered the small, out-of-the-way restaurant half an hour later, every head in the place turned, for they made a striking couple. The restaurant was crowded and noisy, but it had a certain cheery ambiance that Shannon found appealing, and the food was delicious, reminiscent of her mother's cooking. She ate heartily, blessing the genes that allowed her to do so without gaining a pound. Her carefree feeling remained with her throughout the evening. Before tonight she had always been so uptight in the company of a strange man, but to her amazement, she was able to relax and respond to Blake's gentle questioning by talking freely about herself. It had been so long since anyone had seemed genuinely interested in what she thought about anything.

He asked her how she felt about a popular film that had recently appeared on cable. She wrinkled her nose disdainfully. "Oh... I was disappointed. That ending...ugh! Give me a happy one every time. I'm really not as fond of movies as I used to be. Guess it's age. I used to wonder why my folks weren't enthralled over the films I loved so, but now I know. Mom wanted to see Fred Astaire musicals, and dad longed for Jean Harlow and Carole Lombard. I like the kind of films they made when I was young."

He then asked her about a current bestseller, and her verdict was the same—the ending was awful. "When the hero and heroine walked off into the sunset...in different directions...well, I was depressed for days."

"You're a romantic!" he exclaimed, as though that was the most unusual thing in the world.

"I guess I am," she admitted. "Why do you sound so surprised?"

"There just aren't many of those around anymore. At least I don't run into them."

Over coffee and cobbler—peach, not blueberry— Blake finally asked the one question he had been itching to ask. How had she met and married Vic?

She smiled and toyed with her coffee spoon. "I landed a spot in the chorus line on his TV show—the thrill of a lifetime, believe me. This was the big time! I was on my way, I was sure of it. I didn't realize then just how insignificant one dancer in a company of ten can be. Nor did I have any idea how grueling a schedule a weekly show entails. Still, it was a long, long way from waiting tables at Papa Perone's."

"You waited tables?" Blake asked in surprise.

She nodded. "For over a year. You see, I didn't exactly take New York by storm, and I had to live. Papa Perone's was very popular, and the tips were great, better than what I made from the few dancing jobs I'd managed to get. But then I got the spot on Vic's show and...well, there's no way to describe the feeling. I was on cloud nine all the time. I guess I'd done a couple of the shows when I literally bumped into Vic backstage before the taping. I'd taken a wrong turn or something and was in a dead run. He turned a corner and splat...I almost knocked him down. when I saw who it was I was mortified. Everyone who worked on the show was a little in awe of him. But he was very nice. He asked if I was all right, then asked my name and if I was new, since he didn't recall seeing me before. Just quick small talk, and I scurried away and forgot about it. No one could have been more surprised than I was when he asked me to have dinner with him a few nights later. I was scared half to death, if you want the truth. He seemed so worldly and sophisticated, and I felt so gauche. We had absolutely nothing in common. There was the age difference to begin with. On top of that, I was a southern farm girl, and he'd grown up in a city tenement. His closest associates didn't approve of the relationship and neither did his children. But strangely, from that night on, neither of us saw anyone else.''

''As simple as that? Love at first sight. An attraction of opposites.''

''I guess so. I couldn't believe that a man like Vic would be interested in me. I'm still not sure what attracted him.''

''Aren't you?'' he asked with a sage smile.

She knew what he meant and took it as another compliment. ''Looks, you mean? Oh, Blake, New York is full of stunningly beautiful women, and Vic could have had half of them. I was warned by well-meaning friends that he probably was only having a little fling, that it bolstered his ego to be seen around with a young thing, but...'' Shannon paused and a thoughtful look crossed her face. ''But from the beginning I somehow knew it wasn't that way with Vic. I don't know how I knew, but I did. I trusted him completely. Yet, I was still dumbfounded when he asked me to marry him.''

''How long did you go together?''

''Before he proposed? Six months. Six incredible months.''

''I remember reading a lot about the romance.''

She grimaced. ''That was the bad part about it. The media. I never want to go through anything like that again.''

''I can imagine,'' Blake said idly.

''No, you can't, not really. Not if it's never happened to you. I once dreamed of 'being somebody.' Well, let me tell you that being somebody enough to focus the media's attention on you is awful, just awful. They write the silliest untrue things, yet you don't dare protest publicly for fear of stirring up an even bigger 'story.' Vic could handle it well, but I couldn't. All that fuss over the wedding squelched any desire I had to be a celebrity myself."

"Then you probably were never cut out for it."

"Probably not."

"Did Harry and Beth come to the wedding?"

"Oh, yes. Dad was so miserably uncomfortable in that tuxedo."

Blake chuckled. "Somehow I can't picture Harry in a tux."

She smiled wistfully. "The reception was enormous and lasted forever. Dad sat in a corner, drinking champagne and grumbling that he needed some sippin' whiskey. But mom loved it. She wore the most beautiful blue dress. I'm sure she'd never owned anything so elegant in her entire life. And she got to meet Frank Sinatra. I thought she was going to swoon. She could hardly wait to get home and tell everyone. I've always been glad she had that one glorious day."

The look on her face was so poignant that Blake decided to channel the conversation in another direction. "So... you got married, and..."

"Moved to Vic's house on Long Island."

"And lived happily ever after?"

She avoided that one. "Most of our friends and all of the press gave our marriage a year at best." In the short span of a few seconds Shannon clearly recalled the early happiness and her smug satisfaction later when the unconventional union had succeeded. Early skeptics came to point to the Parellis as living proof that show business marriages could endure.

Unfortunately, she also recalled the disillusionment that had set in when she realized she was the one making all the sacrifices necessary for its success.

She wasn't aware of the troubled look in her eyes until she caught the speculative gaze Blake had fastened on her. Straightening, she looked away. When she looked back again the troubled look was gone.

"There must have been a period of adjustment," he prodded.

"You mean, going from farm girl-cum-Broadway gypsy to mistress of the manor? Oh, there was!" That had been the scariest part of her new life—realizing that Vic expected her to run his beautiful house with aplomb. She hadn't had the foggiest notion how to do it. He'd also expected her to move about in his glittery, glamorous world with ease and poise. She hadn't known how to do that either.

"So, how did you manage?"

Shannon smiled. "Nicole, our maid. She'd been working for Vic for several years, four or five, and I'll swear she knew what he wanted before he did. For the first few months she followed me around, saying things like, 'Ma'am, this is the way Mr. Parelli likes this done,' or, 'If I were you, ma'am I'd do that this way.' Then my friend, Peg, took me in hand and taught me the ins and outs of functioning gracefully in that world. Her husband's with one of New York's top accounting firms, and he has a lot of famous clients, so Peg's had lots of experience in entertaining them. She was a storehouse of information. She's one of those fortunate people who's perfectly at ease anywhere with anyone. I guess Nicole and Peg saved me from many a faux pas.''

"But surely your husband knew you couldn't just move in and take over.''

Her eyelashes dipped briefly, and her voice was quiet. "Vic didn't like disturbances in his life—no hills or valleys.''

Blake had been studying her attentively as she talked about her life with Parelli. She'd tried to make it sound wonderful, but again some gut instinct told him it probably hadn't been all that glorious. What marriage was?

She sat across from him, her beautifully mani-cured hands resting on the table. That fabulous ring winked at him. She looked elegant and serene, like a woman of means who never worried about anything heavier than what to wear to such-and-such. Yet, she had managed to retain a refreshing innocence. She wasn't the total sophisticate. In fact, there was a haunting quality about Shannon that touched him. He attributed that to her losses. She had already lost everyone she cared about, and at a very early age. He sympathized with her, although he'd never had any-one to lose. He would have liked to reach across the table and take her hand, and had it been any other woman on earth sitting there, he probably would have done it.

But he cautioned himself against letting Shannon get to him. He sensed she could, very easily. He'd experienced an enormous sense of relief when they had parted that afternoon, and he wanted to leave it that way. Being obsession-free was a nice feeling.

"Did you enjoy your food?'' he asked casually.

"Enjoy it?" She chuckled. "You can look at my plate and ask that?"

"Was it all you'd longed for?"

"And more."

"Would you like another cup of coffee?"

"No, thanks."

"Then maybe we should vacate the table. I notice there's quite a crowd gathered at the door."

Shannon hated to see the evening end. Being with Blake had been a marvelous respite from the disquietude of the past few years, the loneliness of the last two months. It had been a release from all the restrictions of the past. He was thoughtful and attentive, refreshingly without pretense. He didn't try to dazzle her with his importance, something so many men did, especially the unimportant ones. Though outdoorsy, he had acquired a certain polish and self-assurance. She imagined he was able to handle himself well in any circumstance.

Odd how a person from such unpromising beginnings could have turned into this kind of an adult. It was impossible for her to equate the mature Blake with the boy she had known all those years ago. If she had stayed in South Carolina, would they have remained friends, she wondered, or drifted as far apart as they now were?

Regretfully she realized that they had spent the entire evening talking about her. She had learned almost nothing new about him. Was there a woman in his life, she wondered. Probably. If so, what was she like—innocent or worldly, lively or quiet? Had anyone ever broken his heart?

She would have liked him to stay with her and talk for hours. It had been so long since she'd enjoyed masculine company of her own age. But the most amazing aspect of the date was that it had felt completely normal to be having dinner with an attractive man she didn't know well. She hadn't felt self-conscious at all. And that, she decided, was due to Blake's personality. He was a comfortable presence.

What if I said, "You make me feel bright, animated and witty, all the things I never think I am?" What if I confessed that I don't want the evening to end? She didn't, of course, and the evening did end soon afterward.

Blake had given mometary thought to prolonging it. The cocktail lounge at her motel would be a likely spot. They could have a couple of after-dinner drinks. If there was a combo playing, they could dance. Holding Shannon in his arms, even platonically, was a delightful prospect.

All the more reason for refusing to act on the impulse. Each passing moment put his indifference in jeopardy. He simply drove straight from the restaurant to the motel and walked her to her room. She inserted the key in the lock, then turned to tell him a polite goodnight.

"Thanks for a lovely evening, Blake."

"I'm glad you enjoyed it, Shannon. So did I."

"It's been great seeing you again."

His face hovered over hers. "Yes...great." He always kissed his dates goodnight, and he knew he was going to kiss her, even though everything inside warned him against it. She just looked too kissable, and he'd never kissed her, hadn't even come close. A perverse, unmanageable part of his nature had to know what it was like to kiss Shannon.

Instinct told Shannon she was going to be kissed. They were standing very close; one of his hands rested lightly on her shoulder. Her luminous dark eyes fastened on him; her lips parted in expectation. A youthful excitement bubbled inside her as she watched his face bend closer to hers. It had been so many years since she had been kissed by a man she scarcely knew. She had only a second to wonder how she would respond before the first touch of his lips on hers.

The kiss was gentle and precise, without a hint of passion, but it was lengthy, and it took her breath away. Her body melted against his of its own accord, and a helpless sinking feeling overtook her. She managed an admirable restraint as she warmly returned the kiss, but all the while she yearned to clasp his head and hold it, so that the kiss could go on and on and on.

Her pliant response shook Blake, who had vaguely expected her to be stiff and uncertain. Instead, she came across as a woman badly in need of caring and affection, obviously the result of her widowed status. He could feel her body tremble. The sweet honey taste of her lips, the soft clean smell of her were an assault on his senses. Had it been any other woman, he would have pressed his advantage, but not with her. Never with Shannon. He didn't trust himself. He thought he was free of her, but he wasn't taking any chances.

By force of will he lifted his head and took a step backwards. In a low husky voice he said, "Goodnight, Shannon. See you tomorrow at two. Or better still, how about lunch? Then we can go to John's office together." Even as he issued the invitation, he wondered at his compulsion to see her, to be with her as long as possible.

Shannon's breathing was barely under control, and she was embarrassed that he'd been the one to break off the kiss. "Y-yes, that's fine, thanks."

"I'll pick you up at noon."

"Noon," she murmured. "Good night, Blake."

She opened the door and closed it behind her, then leaned against it for a moment before crossing the room to get undressed. She was shocked that a man's kiss could affect her so strongly, as shocked as she was by her too-eager response. He couldn't have avoided noticing; she had behaved like a sixteen-year-old.

As she wiggled out of her clothes, she paused to run her hands slightly over a slender, shapely body that seemed newly-awakened. Her sexuality had been submerged for a number of years, for Vic's passion had become now-and-then. Their lovemaking had lacked fire and spontaneity for quite a while. With a start she realized what a relatively chaste woman she was. It astonished her that Blake, with a touch and a kiss, could bring her desire bubbling to the surface so readily.

She slipped her nightgown over her head and went into the bathroom. Her nightly routine occupied her mind for a few minutes, but once in bed in the pitch-dark room she stared at the unfamiliar walls and tried to ignore the tripping of her heartbeat as she thought of Blake's kiss. It hadn't been all that much of a kiss really. *I'm too vulnerable,* she thought. *Blake could easily sweep me off my feet if he had a mind to. Thank goodness he doesn't appear to be sufficiently interested to try.*

Yet, she had read something in his eyes that went beyond simple masculine interest in a pretty woman. Another couple of days together, and . . . who knew what might happen? She could stay in Greenville for days, weeks if she wanted.

But she wouldn't. She'd been widowed only two months and hadn't stopped thinking of herself as Vic's wife. She'd meant it when she told Jerry there wouldn't be another man. Never again could she expend all that energy on adjusting to another man, to his whims and desires and notions of what a wife should be.

Abruptly, Shannon sat up and switched on the lamp. After consulting the phone book in the bedside table's drawer, she phoned the airline and made reservations on a late flight the following afternoon. That done, she felt better, more secure and in control. Then she called Jerry at home to tell him of her plans, which made them definite.

Tomorrow she and Blake would have lunch together. Nothing wrong with that. Then they would go to the realtor's office, sign some papers and say goodbye. By this time tomorrow night she would be back in her own room in the house on Long Island . . . *where I belong,* she added quickly.

She refused to entertain the notion that she was running away from a prospect too delightful to contemplate.

WHEN BLAKE CALLED FOR HER at the motel at noon the next day, Shannon was in the process of checking out of the motel. He wasn't surprised to learn she was leaving that afternoon. He knew he'd frightened the bejeepers out of her with that good-night kiss, which was ridiculous in one way and enchanting in another. During a wakeful period in the middle of the night he'd tried to recall the last time he'd scared someone with a kiss. He'd come up with Emmy Patterson in the fifth grade.

Yet, he knew it wasn't the kiss that had frightened Shannon so much as her response to it. Did she expect to go through life without feeling emotion again? Like most men, he couldn't help wondering what kind of lover her husband had been. With a twenty year difference in their ages, could they have been compatible in bed and out?

He imagined that she was eager to get back to the life she had shared with Parelli, even though it must be terribly lonely for her now. She was such a lovely, complicated creature, but though she intrigued him, this Shannon wasn't someone he wanted back in his life. He was glad she'd decided to go. If she hadn't, he didn't doubt for a minute that he would have asked her out again and again. He wouldn't have been able to help himself.

Lunch was a mildly strained affair, with conversation limited to general topics. Afterward they drove to John Foreman's office, where the ownership of the farm was transferred to Blake. Then they returned to the motel for Blake to pick up his jeep.

Shannon extended her hand. "Well, Blake, thanks for everything. You've been very . . . hospitable."

He clasped her hand and held it between both of his. "I've enjoyed every minute of it, Shannon."

"Lots of luck with the farm."

"Thanks. Have a safe trip home." He thought of kissing her goodbye, but then thought better of it.

"I hope the weather's good the whole way."

Blake released her hand and opened the car door. She slid behind the wheel, and he closed the door. Bending to bring himself to eye level with her, he asked, "Will someone meet you at the airport?"

"Yes, it's all arranged." Shoving the key in the ignition, she turned on the engine.

"Well, then...I guess this really is goodbye." Blake couldn't understand his reluctance to have her drive away. He wanted her gone, didn't he? Impulsively, he reached in his shirt pocket, withdrew a business card and handed it to her. "Maybe you should have one of these, in case something comes up."

Shannon took it and stuffed it into a side pocket of her handbag. Then she fumbled in the bag for a pen and something to write on. She had to make do with a deposit slip from the back of her checkbook. Hastily she scribbled while saying, "The address on this is the downtown New York office. I'll write my home address and phone number on the back...just in case there are questions...you know, about the farm or something."

"Of course." He took the paper, folded it and placed it in his shirt pocket. Now there really wasn't anything to do but say goodbye. Blake straightened. "Take care, Shannon."

"You, too, Blake." As she drove away she was appalled at her constricted throat and misty eyes. She glanced in the rearview mirror and saw Blake still standing in the motel parking lot, watching until her car disappeared from sight.

CHAPTER SIX

THREE MONTHS PASSED; it was mid-July. Shannon gradually had settled into a routine of her own making, for once having no one but herself to consider. Some days passed swiftly; others dragged on interminably. Although she would not have thought to express it in exactly such words, she was embarking on a courageous and oftentimes disconcerting quest for her own identity. The brief trip to South Carolina had kindled within her a burning desire to become a person in her own right.

Her first step after returning to the house on Long Island was to telephone Mike Erickson and offer her financial assistance with the dance school. The action, she suspected, was prompted by a kind of defiance, and therefore, it brought on brief stabs of guilt. Vic wouldn't have approved of her spending his money that way, but she was able to remind herself that it now was her money, and she could do with it as she pleased. Another milestone—in its way.

Then she sold the Florida home and managed to turn a nice profit. The sale was handled discreetly by a broker who specialized in such things. The beautiful, secluded house, with its hundreds of thousands of dollars' worth of recording equipment, was purchased by a twenty-six-year-old rock star who'd paid cash for it.

Still, Shannon balked at selling the Tudor mansion. Not too many steps too soon, her inner self cautioned. She wasn't sure yet just what it was she wanted to do with her life now that she was free of Vic's influence and domination. For so many years her entire being had been defined in relation to him. That self-image wasn't something that could be tossed aside like a worn-out shirt. She was intelligent enough to know that it would take time to find something that would give her life meaning and purpose.

Sadly but quickly she learned that Mike's dance school wasn't it. Her friend was like a kid with a new toy, and Shannon was delighted to be able to offer him financial backing, but the day-to-day running of the place left her unenthusiastic. Mike was disappointed that she didn't intend teaching a class or two, but she begged off, saying she no longer felt qualified.

And she'd always considered that school a special dream. Had it been a dream only because Vic had opposed it? Looking back, she could recall how rebellious she'd begun to feel. If he had lived, if the rebellion had grown, who could say what might have happened to their so-successful marriage?

So Shannon still struggled with her feelings, but she was beginning to find inner peace. She dealt with Vic's list on the first of every month and still hated it, but there were other, more enjoyable pursuits. Afternoons at the Post-and-Paddock, for instance, where she could linger long after Omar had been put through his paces and stabled. She "mucked around" in the garden all she pleased, and continued her mornings on the tennis court, which were much more fun now that there was no one to object to them. She lunched with old friends, and on a couple of occasions she'd allowed Jerry and Peg to inveigle her into dinner dates that included an extra man, whose company, she'd been able to enjoy and then forget altogether. One of the men, an extremely attractive insurance executive, had repeatedly called to ask her out again, but she'd refused, so the calls had stopped.

"Why?" Peg had asked her. "He's so disappointed."

"I guess...I'm just not up to dating yet," was the way Shannon explained it. Privately she was relieved to know she wasn't as vulnerable as she had feared. Not just any attractive man who came along could turn her head. The feeling of vulnerability she had experienced that night in Greenville had been prompted solely by Blake Carmichael, his presence and personality, and he was over seven hundred miles away.

Life settled into a smooth, restriction-free groove. Then, just when she thought she was more contented than she'd been in years, a certain edginess overtook her, a longing for something, but she didn't have the slightest idea what that something was. Not for the first time, she envied Peg and the rest of her friends who had children. Most of them were so busy with young teenagers that they had no time to wonder who they were or what they wanted.

SHANNON HAD JUST STEPPED through the den's French doors, coming in from the garden, when she heard the front door's chimes, then Nicole's quick footsteps in the foyer. She waited until the servant appeared at the threshold.

"Mr. Thorpe and another gentleman, ma'am."

Someone Nicole didn't know? A stranger indeed. "Please send them in, Nicole."

A minute passed, then Jerry and another man entered the room. Jerry embraced Shannon enthusiastically, then turned to his companion. "Shannon, I'd like you to meet Anthony Thompson. He's an old friend of mine."

"How do you do," she said, shaking his hand. "I'm always glad to meet a friend of Jerry's."

Anthony Thompson was a nattily-attired, urbane man of about fifty, slender, of medium height, with salt-and-pepper hair. Taking her hand, he said, "Mrs. Parelli, I can't tell you what a delight this is. Jerry's told me so much about you."

"Anthony is Editorial Director at Delphi press," Jerry said. "He has a business proposition for you, Shannon."

"For me?" She alertly noticed Jerry's broad grin and jovial attitude.

"Yes. Let's sit down and talk about it."

"Of course. Can I get you gentlemen something to drink?" The two men sat on the leather sofa, and Shannon took a nearby chair.

"No, thanks, dear. Anthony and I have just come from lunch." Jerry clasped his hands in front of him and regarded her earnestly. "I'm going to let Anthony tell you about his proposition, but I'll tell you this much—I'm very excited about it."

Intrigued, Shannon gave Anthony Thompson all her attention.

"Mrs. Parelli, to put it simply, I'm here to ask you to write a book for Delphi Press."

Shannon uttered a lilting little laugh. "You want me to write a book?"

Her laugh prompted a smile from Thompson. "Do you find such a project interesting?"

"Stunning, actually. That's the last thing I would expect someone to ask me to do."

"And if I told you the book would be about your husband?"

"Vic?"

"Yes, his biography. Celebrity bios are very popular these days, and it's occurred to me that Vic Parelli's life would make an interesting story. I mentioned it to Jerry, and he agreed. He also agreed that you're the logical one to write it."

"Are you serious?" she asked incredulously.

"Completely."

"Well, Mr. Thompson...I agree that Vic's life was interesting, with its rags-to-riches aspect, and naturally I'm flattered to be consulted, but..." She paused to laugh again. "I'm afraid I'll have to decline on the grounds that I'm no writer."

"I'm aware of that, Mrs. Parelli, but I don't expect you to write a good book. I'm only asking that you write down the facts. I'll get someone else to write the story well."

Shannon looked at Jerry, who said, "It's exciting when you think about it, Shannon. Vic would have been so pleased."

Yes, Shannon agreed on that point. Vic would have been very pleased over the biography, but she wasn't so sure he would have wanted her to be the one to write it. He would have wanted a pro.

Lifting her shoulders, she said, "I wouldn't know where to start. I can't imagine writing a book."

"You can simply jot down things as they come to you," Anthony said. "We can put them in chronological order later. We could do an 'as told to' story, but I think readers would be more interested in the book if they knew it had been written by Vic's wife. I realize that I'm asking you to take on a time-consuming task, but this is one project that has taken hold of me. I do hope you'll say yes."

"I...don't know. What if I say I'll do it, then find I can't?"

"I'm not the least worried that that will happen, Mrs. Parelli. Simply pretend you're writing a letter to a friend, someone who didn't know Vic but is interested in reading all about him."

"Do you realize that I know only bits and pieces about Vic's life before I met him?"

"I'll wager you know more about him than you think. Wives almost always do."

"Get Rosemary to help you," Jerry interjected. "Wasn't she the family chronicler?"

Shannon pursed her lips thoughtfully. Rosemary had faithfully kept up the scrapbooks that Vic's first wife had begun early in his career. On top of that, the young woman possessed an astonishing gift of total recall. Vic had often commented on it. "How does the kid remember all that stuff?" he would say. With Rosemary's help, she just might be able to do it.

Jerry leaned forward. "Shannon, a book would inspire brand new interest in Vic. It would sell his records to a new generation. It would keep him from being remembered as just another Italian crooner."

"Ever the money man, Jerry?"

"Ever the practical man, Shannon."

Given a dozen years, she couldn't have dreamed up such a project. On one hand, she considered it ludicrous that she would even think of writing a book. She simply wasn't qualified. On the other, however, Anthony Thompson was knowledgeable about such things, and he seemed to think she could do it. He seemed sure she couldn't write anything so dreadful that it couldn't be fixed.

He'd called it a time-consuming task. Hadn't she been looking for something like that? She could give it a try; it might even be fun. The world wouldn't stop if it didn't work out.

"Well..." she said uncertainly, "I guess I can try."

Jerry beamed, and Anthony Thompson rubbed his hands together with satisfaction. "Mrs. Parelli, we're going to set a deadline of December first on this, if that's all right with you. But if you find you have a problem with that, just give me a call. I'm sure something can be worked out. Jerry has a contract with him. If you've never seen one of these things they can be confusing. Let's just go over it together, point by point...."

For the next twenty minutes or so the three of them discussed the business part of the project. By the time the two men left the house Shannon had actually signed the contract and was experiencing some real enthusiasm for the book. She wandered from room to room, feeling as though she should start doing something, but she wasn't sure what. Finally it occurred to her that she needed a typewriter. She guessed she could still type. Wasn't that like riding a bicycle—once you learned how you never forgot?

So her first move was to go to a local office supply store to purchase a portable typewriter and reams of paper. Then, on her way home, she stopped in a bookstore she frequented and, with the bookseller's help, picked out a dozen recent celebrity biographies. The next few days flew by while she read and read and read.

THE LATE AFTERNOON SUN relentlessly beat down on Blake's neck as he hammered the last fencepost into the ground. Straightening, he arched his back and stretched his arms high over his head. In the distance he could see the painters loading their equipment into their van. Today they had finished up the interior painting. The two men shouted a goodbye to him. He waved them off, then focused his attention on the house.

Shannon's suggestion to paint it gray with white trim had been a good one. He wouldn't have thought of the combination, but it looked great. He'd taken some color snapshots of the house a few days ago; he just might send her one. There was still a lot to do to the inside, and the yard was a mess, but he'd accomplished a hell of a lot in three months. He hadn't intended devoting so much time to the farm so soon, but once he'd started, he hadn't been able to stop.

He dropped the hammer into the toolbox resting on the ground at his feet, snapped the box shut and picked it up. Tiredly he walked up an incline to the blue and white mobile home that he'd temporarily installed on the premises. Since he was spending more and more time on the farm, he'd needed a comfortable place to stay. The renovation had become anything but a weekend project. Sometimes he had to force himself to drive to Charlotte a couple of days a week to tend to business. But the business had become his "mother cow." It financed the farm.

Despite his fatigue, he was overcome by a feeling of well-being. He had found what he wanted to do with the rest of his life. Not since the fledgling days of his construction firm had he known such a sense of purpose. Challenges came at him from all sides, and he tackled them with enthusiasm. Only in more introspective moments did he admit there was something missing: another person to share it all with him.

He'd almost reached the mobile home when he heard a car swing off the main road and onto the lane leading to the house. He turned and squinted into the distance. The car was a late model compact, unfamiliar to him. He stood watching as it stopped not far away, and a young man got out. The man, too, was a stranger. Blake waved a welcome, and the man approached. He was on the short side, with sandy hair, a ruddy complexion and a quick, agreeable smile.

"Hello," he said.

"Hello," Blake replied.

"Mr. Carmichael?"

"That's right."

"I'm Reverend Tom Archer from the Community Congregational Church down the road."

Blake knew the small red-brick church. He stepped forward to take the minister's outstretched hand. "Good afternoon, Reverend. What can I do for you?"

Tom Archer's eyes swept his surroundings. "I've been meaning to get over and say hello. You've done wonders with this place. I've been watching the progress from the road.''

"There's still a lot to do.''

"Always is when you start something like this.''

"That's the truth, it surely is.''

The two men faced one another. The reverend, Blake was sure, was going to invite him to church on Sunday. He would tell him he'd sure try to make it, but he knew he probably wouldn't. "Would you like something cold to drink, Reverend? I have Coke and iced tea.''

"Now, a glass of tea would be nice, thanks. Heat's pretty bad this time of day.''

"Yeah, we're due for some rain to cool things off. Right this way....''

Blake ushered his unexpected guest inside and poured two glasses of tea. The two men sat at the kitchen table, drinking and making small talk for a few minutes. Then Tom Archer told him the reason for his call. It wasn't at all what Blake had been expecting.

"I came over here to ask something of you, Mr. Carmichael.''

"Oh?''

Tom nodded. "And I'm well aware that it's no small something. You see, our church sponsors a foster parent program in the area. It's a private organization; we don't receive any government money. We're funded by private donations. We work closely with the county adoption board, as well as with private attorneys who know of adoptive couples, but, unfortunately, adoptions are rare. Most of the kids who come to our attention are too old for us to reasonably expect adoption. Mostly we just try to find decent homes for them, and keep 'em in school until they're old enough to fend for themselves.''

"That's admirable work, Reverend. I was a foster kid myself.''

The minister brightened. "You don't say! Well, then, maybe you'll be receptive to this proposition of mine. There's this boy...his name is Randy. He's fourteen and, frankly, he's a difficult one. Not bad exactly. I mean, he doesn't run with a gang or use drugs or anything like that. Randy's problem is that there's never been anyone who's cared a flip about him. His folks split up right after he was born. The father left, and the mother's been married several times since. The latest stepfather doesn't want him around, and the mother doesn't want this marriage to go on the rocks, too, so Randy's become expendable.''

Blake shook his head sadly. "What a shame.''

"Isn't it, though? We've placed the boy in a couple of foster homes, but nothing's worked out. So many of our foster parents are older people, and Randy's just too much for them. The people who have him now are in their fifties. Everything seemed to be going fine until school let out for the summer. I guess the boy has too much time on his hands. Anyway, they've asked me to place him somewhere else. I heard about you and this farm.... Well, it got me thinking. A single man running a farm, lots of healthy outdoor work to do. You might be able to exercise more control over the boy.''

Tom paused and tried to gauge Blake's reaction to all this. He could read nothing in his expression. "I'm pretty desperate, Mr. Carmichael. I guess if you don't feel you can take him, I'll have no choice but to put Randy in a detention home."

That got Blake's attention. "Detention home?"

"I'm afraid so. There aren't many alternatives open to us."

A moment of silence passed. Finally Blake asked, "Where's Randy now?"

"I have him doing some chores at the church."

"And then?"

"Then I guess I'll let him bunk in my office tonight. He doesn't want to go back to the place where he's been living. Guess you can't blame him, knowing he isn't wanted and all. I'd take him home with me, but I have three children, and Randy's a loner. He would prefer the empty church to that madhouse of mine."

"Aren't you worried that he'll steal something?"

"There's nothing to steal," Tom said with a grin. "It's not an affluent church. But I think I could trust Randy with last Sunday's collection. He's not that kind of an incorrigible kid. He's surly, withdrawn, suspicious. He's wary of adults, and can't relate to his peers at all. But he isn't mean or dangerous. At least I've seen no signs of it."

It never occurred to Blake to issue a flat refusal, even though the minister's request imposed on his plans. But a young boy in need of a home was something he could empathize with. "I'm not sure I'm the man you're looking for, Reverend. I spend a lot of time shuttling back and forth between here and Charlotte, and once the boy's enrolled in school here..."

"These arrangements are almost never ideal, Mr. Carmichael. When you think about it, working parents usually have to rearrange their lives to accommodate their school-age children. Randy's certainly old enough to take care of himself for a few hours after school if you're otherwise occupied.'' Tom paused, then said, ''The worst of what you can offer him is a hundred times better than anything he's had before.''

Blake stared into his glass. This seemed to be one of those incidences that people later called fate. ''When can I meet Randy?''

The minister smiled. ''I can go to the church and get him right now. Be back in twenty minutes or so.''

Blake looked up and returned the smile. ''I'm not making any promises, but...why don't you do that?''

His name was Randy Sloan. He was gangly, all arms and legs, and reed-thin. Uncommunicative and defensive, he seemed as wary of Tom Archer, who had befriended him, as he was of Blake, a total stranger. He didn't make eye contact with either man; in fact, his gaze seldom strayed from the toes of his scuffed shoes.

Nevertheless, something about the boy touched a responsive chord in Blake. He guessed Randy reminded him of himself at fourteen, and the thought of a detention home made him shudder. That threat had hung over his own head when he'd been a youth. If it hadn't been for the Jamesons and this farm, there was no telling where he'd be right now. Prison maybe. There had been those who'd said he was heading in that direction.

He studied the boy with interest. Randy was young, but already he was trouble looking for a place to happen. Blake wondered if the old farm could work its magic on one more pitiful kid.

At first Randy expressed disdain for farming in general and this farm in particular. "Don't look like no farm to me. I don't see no cows or horses or chickens, and everyone knows a farm has animals."

"They come later," Blake told him. "I have other things to do first."

"Yeah? Like what?"

"Come on, I'll show you." Blake led the boy and Tom Archer to the creek bank at the rear of the property. "Look down there, Randy, and tell me what you see."

"Whadaya mean, what do I see? Water."

"See how it moves, swift and steady."

"Yeah, I guess so. So what?"

"One of these days that water's going to work for me. I'm going to harness all that energy and use it to run things."

"What things?"

"Oh, fans and lights and a refrigerator, things like that. What the water can't do, the wind and sun will."

"Heck, you're kiddin' me. You can't do that."

"Sure I can, and I will...someday."

"I'd like to be around to see it," the boy scoffed.

Blake and the minister exchanged glances. In the end, Blake told Tom that he would take Randy on a trial basis, but all the while he knew that unless the boy turned out to be completely hopeless, he would keep him until, as the minister had said, he could fend for himself.

NOT SURPRISINGLY, Peg Thorpe pounced on Shannon's new project with real enthusiasm, for Peg was enthusiastic about anything out of the ordinary. "Oh, Shannon, this is just what you've needed, something you can really sink your teeth into! I can hardly wait to read it!"

"Peg, I'm having misgivings. I'm...frankly, I'm not all that sure I can do it."

"Of course you can, Shannon. Of course you can!" Peg had no patience with misgivings.

Shannon was certain it was Peg's "of course you can" philosophy of life that had so drawn her to Jerry's wife in the first place. They had met at a cocktail party shortly before Shannon's marriage to Vic. Their personalities were totally dissimilar, but they had liked one another right away. "I have a feeling we're going to be friends," was the way the warm, effervescent Peg had put it that night, and they had. For the next few weeks it was Peg's enthusiasm that kept Shannon working at the book, even when her confidence sagged.

A short notice in Publishers Weekly, announcing that Delphi Press had contracted Shannon Parelli to write her late husband's biography, prompted a brief flurry of phone calls to the house. Friends were curious. A couple of newspapers wanted interviews, which she granted over the phone. Then things mercifully quietened down. Writing the book turned out to be a harder job than Shannon had bargained for. It was fairly easy in the beginning, when she related the details of Vic's early life. Rosemary had shown real interest in the project and had turned out to be a fountain of information about her father, his first family and early career, and Shannon was sufficiently detached from those events to be able to write objectively.

"What was he like as a father?" she had once ventured to ask her stepdaughter.

"Strict," Rosemary had answered without hesitation. "Very strict. More so with me than with John, of course, since I was a girl and Dad was ver-r-r-y old-fashioned. And that got even worse after Mom died. I went through the usual rebellious stage when I hated him."

"But then?"

"But then I grew up. He had to let go, and you came along, so he had something besides me to think about. I learned to like him. I never understood him, but I learned to like him."

"You and John... weren't exactly pleased when your father married me." It was a statement of fact. No use pretending she wasn't aware of the initial hostility.

Rosemary was only momentarily nonplussed. "Ah, Shannon, we were kids, and kids hate change. We soon came to see the marriage as a blessing... for us. I never thought it was a blessing for you, though."

"How's that?"

"He just transferred all his patriarchal tendencies to you. No one but those closest to him ever saw the rigidity beneath that so-smooth exterior. He was a... chameleon."

It had been an extraordinary moment and had heralded a change in her relationship with Rosemary.

Now, however, Shannon had reached the part of Vic's life that included her, and she was stymied.

Distractions were all around her. The slightest household noise interrupted her train of thought, a sure indication that she wasn't a writer. She realized that no one expected her to turn in a polished piece of work, but a certain amount of pride was involved.

It was difficult to write down the unvarnished truth, yet the really good celebrity biographies she'd read had been astonishingly frank. She didn't want her book to be a sugary tribute that sounded as though it had been written by the president of Vic's fan club, but she wondered how honest she could be, considering her ambivalent feelings about her late husband. Her surroundings didn't help. Memories of Vic abounded in every corner of the big house. Sometimes she could almost feel him reading over her shoulder, critical and disapproving.

But she had taken on the project and was determined to complete it. When it became increasingly obvious that the Long Island house wasn't the ideal workplace, she began thinking of somewhere she could go, somewhere peaceful and quiet with a minimum of interruptions and distractions. Then the letter arrived in the mail.

It was from Blake. The logo in the upper left-hand corner of the cream-colored envelope told her that. Carmichael Construction Company. Something having to do with her sale of the farm? For a moment Shannon was jolted by his unexpected, if remote, reappearance in her life. Her fingers trembled as she tore open the envelope. Inside was a photograph of the farmhouse, although she didn't recognize it as such at first. When she realized that the photo was of her childhood home she couldn't believe her eyes. Blake had indeed painted the structure gray with white trim; it looked charming and homey, the kind of place that invited you to come in and sit a while. The short note accompanying the photo, written in a bold masculine scrawl, said merely that he thought she might like seeing the old house now that the exterior renovation was complete. No red roses yet, but they would come in time. If she was ever back in South Carolina he hoped she would stop by and see it in person. He hoped she was well. Regards, Blake.

Regards, Blake. She smiled and blinked back a tear or two. She'd thought about him quite a lot during the past months. Their dinner date had been magnified many times over in her mind. She probably remembered it more clearly than anything that had happened to her since Vic's death.

And Blake must have thought of her occasionally; otherwise, why the note?

As impersonal as it was, the note started wheels turning in Shannon's head. Hadn't Blake said the farm would be only a weekend project for years? Would it be presumptuous of her to ask if she could stay in the house for a few months, just long enough to finish the manuscript? After all, he wasn't there most of the time; he might like having someone to look after the house for him. And what a perfect place it would be for her. There certainly weren't any memories of Vic at the farm. He'd visited it exactly three times during their marriage, once under protest that he really had other things to do, and twice to attend funerals.

She thought about it for several days. For some unknown reason the farm held an irresistible lure for her. She refused to admit that some of the lure might center around its owner. Only once did that thought consciously enter her mind, and she was able to push it aside, attributing all those queer feelings he'd aroused in her that night in Greenville to her mood at the time. Vacillating back and forth, she finally took Blake's business card out of her billfold and telephoned him at his office in Charlotte.

BLAKE'S EXISTENCE had become complicated because of Randy, but he welcomed the complication. It was just the shot in the arm his life had needed. Not that it had been smooth sailing all along. He'd wanted to throttle the kid a time or two in the beginning, but gradually the two of them had established a mutual rapport and understanding. The surly boy soon realized that, while Blake wasn't going to send him away, neither was he going to put up with belligerence or disrespect. Randy was expected to "clean up his act," and there would be no ifs, buts or maybes. In addition to making decent grades in school, he was going to display proper manners and use correct grammar. Their relationship reminded Blake of his with Harry Jameson. And since he wanted to give Randy as stable a home atmosphere as possible, he had leased his townhouse and moved to the farm on a full-time basis, going to Charlotte only a couple of times a week and taking Randy with him. Once school started, he planned to be gone only during school hours. It made for a lot of driving, but he was convinced it was worth it. Watching the transformation in Randy was worth anything.

Blake happened to be in his Charlotte office when Shannon telephoned. He was startled, to say the least, when his secretary informed him that a Mrs. Parelli was calling. Shannon? Tensing, he stared at the phone for the longest minute before picking up the receiver.

"Shannon?"

"Hello, Blake, how are you?"

"Well, I'm fine. And you?"

"Fine, thanks. I got your note and the picture. The house looks wonderful."

"I thought it turned out well."

There was a pause, an uncomfortably long pause, Shannon thought. But, of course, he was waiting for her to say something. After all, she'd called him. Suddenly she felt foolish, but she plunged ahead.

"Blake, I called to ask something of you. Now, if the answer is no, I want you to promise you'll say so."

"Of course."

"Well, it seems I've taken on this project and..." Hesitatingly, falteringly, she explained about the book, and the problems she was having. And when she had over-explained the situation, she got around to asking him if she could stay at the farm long enough to finish the manuscript.

Her request caught Blake by surprise, and for a moment he pondered how to decline graciously. He didn't want Shannon back in his life, even briefly. He'd sent her that photograph on an impulse...or so he'd thought. He'd never meant for it to open avenues of communication between them...or so he'd thought.

He knew all he would have to do was tell her about Randy, that the two of them now lived in the farmhouse, and that would be that. He was sure she wouldn't consider coming under those circumstances. Easy enough.

But then a vision flashed through his mind, a picture of Harry with his arm around a scrawny kid's shoulders, patiently explaining how and why something had to be done. And on the heels of that vision came another—the look of quiet desperation he'd seen in a lovely woman's dark eyes and the haunting quality that had touched him so. What an ingrate he was! The Jamesons had done so much for him, and now that one of them had asked him for something, he was trying to figure out a way to say no.

Quickly he decided to say nothing about Randy and the farm. "Shannon, you're welcome to the place for as long as you want to stay," he said simply.

"You're sure? I won't be imposing?"

"Not at all."

"Then, if you're sure, I'd like to come next week. Early. Say Tuesday."

"That's fine. I'll be looking for you."

"Will you leave a key somewhere?"

"No, I'll be there."

She wondered why he would be there in the middle of the week but didn't ask. "I'm sure I'll take the same flight I did last time. I'll be at the farm sometime in mid-afternoon. And, Blake...thanks so much."

When he hung up, Blake sat at his desk for a moment, grappling with the uneasiness that had seized him. His life was moving along so smoothly. He didn't want it disturbed. But why was he so sure Shannon would disturb it? Wasn't he rid of the old fascination? He pondered that for a moment or two, then left his office, rounded up Randy and drove back to the farm. Immediately he set about moving them back into the mobile home they had vacated only weeks before.

The boy was none too happy about the new turn of events, Blake could tell. He knew he had become Randy's entire world, and the boy had grown terribly possessive of him. That would have to be dealt with in time, though how he was going to do it escaped him completely.

"We don't need no girls around here," Randy fumed.

"Any girls," Blake corrected, "and she's not a girl. She's a lady, a very nice lady, and I hope you'll remember that and mind your manners."

"How come this happened anyway? Did you ask her to come?"

"Nope. She asked me. She needs a place to stay for a while."

"Tell her to go to a hotel."

"That wouldn't be very nice, would it?"

"Do you want her to come here?" the boy asked suspiciously.

"Well, Randy, to tell you the truth, I kinda like things the way they are, but she's an old friend, and you don't turn your back on old friends. This was her house long before it was mine, so she's welcome to it for awhile."

Randy acquiesced grudgingly. "Well, okay... but if she stays too long, will you ask her to leave?"

"She won't stay too long. A little while on this old farm, and I imagine she'll just be itching to get back to that fancy life of hers."

Was that the reason for his uneasiness over her visit, he wondered. His self-confidence, the sure knowledge that he was in control of his life, seemed to evaporate when it came to Shannon. He often thought of her, not with the old longing but with a new concern over how she was getting along. She had no family; was there anyone to comfort her? Probably not, or she wouldn't want to leave home.

Dear God, she'd soon be there for an unspecified length of time! He'd be seeing her every day. An absurd fear swept through him. There might still be enough of the old Shannon beneath her sophisticated New York veneer to entice him again, and under no circumstances did he want that to happen. She would be leaving; he had to remember that for his own good. He'd just have to make sure she didn't worm her way into his head and heart again.

CHAPTER SEVEN

SHANNON RETURNED TO SOUTH CAROLINA in early August. This time she handled all the details of the trip like a seasoned traveler. She arranged with Jerry to have Vic's list tended to every month. She thought to pack one suitcase full of linens, since there would be none in an unlived-in house. She made arrangements ahead of time to lease a car for an indefinite period, and it was waiting for her when she arrived at Greenville-Spartanburg. It was a late model Thunderbird, a gem of a vehicle. On the way to the farm she stopped at a supermarket and purchased several days' supply of groceries, along with some inexpensive dishes, glasses and cooking utensils, just enough to get by on until she decided what she really needed.

This time when she wheeled off the main road and onto the lane leading to the house, she experienced a strong sense of homecoming, though there had been changes. The wooden gate no longer sagged. The road had been black-topped and most of the over-growth had been cut down. Trees had been felled to increase the size of the clearing, and the fence had been repaired. The place had never looked so good to her, had never welcomed her so openly, not even when her parents had been alive and it truly had been home. Once she hadn't wanted to "waste" her life here; now it was like a haven.

But returning to the farm wasn't the only reason for her excitement and high spirits, and she knew it. There was a certain giddy excitement associated with the thought of seeing Blake again. She'd been aware of him at the forefront of her thoughts for days, and she could recall with amazing clarity that one moment of desire in his arms. Foolishness. It was a sad testimony to her life's emotional emptiness that she could remember one little kiss so vividly.

She had barely halted the car at the steps when the front door opened and Blake appeared on the porch. Lagging behind, to Shannon's surprise and curiosity, was a young boy. She slung her handbag over her shoulder and got out of the car. By the time she rounded it, Blake was standing at the foot of the steps. For a long wordless moment they stared at one another.

A funny feeling struck Blake in the pit of his stomach as he drank in the sight of her. She was dressed in a simple green cotton coatdress and looked very smart and stylish, very New York-ish. At least she fit his own notion of what New York-ish was. There didn't seem to be a thing he could do about his reactions to her, and he knew with absolute certainty that allowing her to return wasn't the wisest thing he'd ever done. "Shannon," he said quietly, "welcome back."

"Thanks. It's good to be back." And as good to see him as she thought it would be. Dressed in fresh khakis, he looked marvelous. His skin was a several-shades-deeper tan than it had been in April, which added to his potent masculine appeal. She tried to ignore the tripping of her heart when he bent to place a light kiss on her cheek. She had to forcibly restrain herself from slipping her arms around his waist and holding him to her.

Blakc liftcd his head and turned to the boy standing shyly on the steps behind him. "Shannon, I'd like you to meet Randy."

"Hello, Randy."

"Hullo."

"Randy's my foster son," Blake explained.

Shannon's brows lifted slightly. "Oh? Well…how nice. When did this happen?"

"We've been together…how long, Randy? Six weeks or so, I guess."

"How do you like Charlotte, Randy?" Shannon inquired amiably.

"We don't live in Charlotte," the boy said tersely. "We live here."

"Here?" Shannon quizzed Blake with her eyes.

"Out there, actually." He pointed to the mobile home on the rise of land.

"Moved up there a couple of days ago," Randy added pointedly.

"Moved? Oh, Blake, don't tell me you were living here in the house! Why didn't you say something?"

Blake shot Randy an admonishing glance, then turned to Shannon. "We'd barely begun moving into the house. We're used to the mobile home and are comfortable there. Really, Shannon, it's no big deal. I want you to stay in the house as long as you like."

He might have meant it; she couldn't be sure since his eyes were guarded. Her earlier high spirits plummeted. She was embarrassed by her intrusion and felt every inch the interloper, so perhaps she was being overly touchy, but she had expected a more effusive welcome from Blake.

Her gaze shifted to Randy, who was too young to have learned to hide his feelings. She would have had to be dense indeed to miss the message in his eyes. Hostility, pure and simple. He didn't want her there, and she correctly guessed that Blake was the reason. The boy was probably possessive and jealous and would have resented any third party.

Well, if this wasn't one damned mess! What should she do—turn around and go back home or stay and brazen it out? Blake's voice cut into her thoughts.

"Honestly, Shannon," he reiterated, "the house is all yours, and you're welcome to it for as long as you want."

She wanted to stay. She wasn't sure why, but she did. "I won't be in the way," she was quick to say. "If I'm to finish this project of mine, I'll have to keep to myself and to my work. You'll hardly know I'm on the place." This was said as much for Randy's benefit as Blake's. Her words implied, *I pose no threat to Blake's time and attention*.

"However you want it, Shannon," Blake said. Then he gestured toward Randy. "Son, let's see to Mrs. Parelli's luggage. Shannon, you lead the way."

The interior of the house had a brand-new smell, like fresh paint, and Shannon could see that the rooms had indeed received not only paint but new carpet in a soft shade of taupe. A wonderful color, she thought; so many accents could be used with it. But it didn't seem a color a man would think to choose. Who had done the house for him?

She couldn't resist making a hasty tour of the place. The furnishings, though spare, were eclectic, subdued and in excellent taste. Blake had kept her parents' oak dining room suite and her father's old stereo, but everything else was new. Her mother would have loved the way the house looked now, especially the kitchen, which is where Beth Jameson had spent most of her life. The appliances, countertop, cabinets and floor had all been replaced. The eating area had been wallpapered in a blue and white check, and some potted geraniums stood on the windowsill. It looked charmingly French Provincial... and decidedly unmasculine. There even was a copy of *The Joy of Cooking* resting on the counter.

"Are you a cook?" she asked.

"Afraid not. My secretary gave me that. She thinks I should learn."

"The kitchen is absolutely delightful!" she bubbled enthusiastically. "Don't tell me you did the decorating."

He shook his head. "My secretary again. She picked out most of the stuff."

His secretary seemed to have a lot of influence with him. Shannon tried to imagine the kind of woman Blake's secretary would be. For some reason, the picture that came to mind was of a comely young charmer who was enamored of her boss and eager to please. "How nice. Your secretary has good taste."

"And experience. She and her husband have spent five years renovating an old farmhouse. They have three grandchildren who love the country. Their advice has been invaluable."

Scratch the secretary, Shannon thought with some relief, and then wondered, why the relief?

"I'm afraid the upstairs isn't quite so livable," Blake went on. "The rooms have been painted, but that's about it. Randy's room has a bed and desk in it, and mine has a bed and dresser. We'll put your things in mine, since it's bigger."

She looked at him apologetically. "This is such an imposition. I never would have come if I'd known."

"I knew you wouldn't. That's why I didn't tell you."

"I meant it when I said you'll hardly know I'm on the place."

He looked away. "And we'll stay out of your way, too, Shannon. Promise."

"Are you here all the time now?"

"Not all the time. I spend several days a week in Charlotte, and Randy always goes with me. Once school starts I'll do my best to get home before he does, but if I don't make it, he knows how to stay busy until I do. He won't be bothering you."

"He wouldn't bother me," she said. "How...what made you decide to take in a foster child?"

He told her about Reverend Archer. "I found I couldn't turn him down."

"What a marvelous gesture!"

"I kept thinking about your dad, and...I guess I'm paying Harry back in a roundabout way."

Shannon now remembered that Blake had almost worshipped her father. It had taken him a while to cease being tongue-tied around her and her mother, but he had taken to her dad right away. "I suppose the boy's a lot of company for you," she said.

"Yes, he is. Randy and I get along just fine. We've worked out a nice routine for ourselves."

They left the kitchen, went through the dining room and into the foyer. Randy had carried most of her luggage upstairs, but a lone suitcase still stood at the foot of the stairs. They reached for it simultaneously; briefly their hands touched. Blake made a quick observation: she now wore that fabulous diamond-studded gold band on her right hand. "Here, allow me," he said, picking up the case. "After you," he added, and followed her up the stairs, mesmerized by the seductive movement of her trim hips and the smooth curve of her stockinged calves.

SHANNON HAD PROMISED HERSELF she would keep diligently to her work, and for weeks that was the way it was. Since Randy's bedroom had a desk, she arranged an office of sorts in there and slept in Blake's room, her parents' old room, which now was furnished with all the charm of an army barracks. At first she was content to do little but eat, sleep and work on the book. She awoke at dawn to all the unfamiliar sounds of country mornings—the first crow of a rooster on some distant farm, the lowing of calves and the cacophony of endless numbers of birds—and she marveled at the absolute quiet dark of country nights. She usually was in bed before eleven. Her one diversion was to take up cooking, which she did with enthusiasm. A little bit of housework and her own laundry had to be dealt with and were less entertaining. Thankfully Blake wasn't so hung up on his "back to basics" philosophy that he shunned dishwashers, washing machines and dryers. The house had all three, and she quickly learned how to use them. The days passed uneventfully but rapidly.

Eventually, however, she found herself with time on her hands. A person could only work so long and stand just so much solitude. She grew tired of her own company and thought it strange that Blake didn't even stop by to ask how she was doing. He seemed to need no one but the boy.

Occasionally she would see them coming and going. Soon she saw the school bus stop every morning and return every afternoon. Now, several mornings a week she would see Blake leave in the jeep, then return just before the school bus did in the afternoon. She often saw the two of them working around the grounds together, and she would have liked to join them but wouldn't have considered doing so without being invited. She clearly remembered Blake's remark about the nice routine he and Randy had established. Perhaps she was oversensitive, as she often tended to be where Blake was concerned, but at the time it had seemed he was obliquely asking her not to interfere with it.

Once, after an afternoon of grocery shopping, she was lifting the last of several heavy sacks out of the car when Blake pulled alongisde in his jeep.

"Need any help?" he'd asked.

It was an opening Shannon would have liked to grab, but it would have been ridiculous. There was only one sack and she obviously was holding it with no trouble. Though she'd tried, she hadn't been able to think of anything she needed his help with. "No, thanks. This is the last of it."

He'd hesitated a moment—she had thought, hoping he was going to say something—but he had merely touched a finger to his head in a little salute and driven on.

Another time she stepped out onto the back porch to stretch and soak up some sunshine. In the distance Blake saw her and waved. She guessed she should have called out "Hello, how're you doing?" or something. He would have had to call back and then maybe... But she had let the moment pass without a word.

She felt silly watching him and admiring him from afar, so she forcibly immersed herself in the book, which was going well. Away from the house on Long Island, she discovered it was easier to look honestly at Vic, herself and their marriage. She didn't like a lot of what she saw. She'd been so easily pleased, so malleable. A kind word or gesture from Vic and she forgave thoughtlessness and injustice. She always came around to him. But if I hadn't, she wondered, would the marriage have lasted?

Besides, the book wasn't about her. A lot of what she relived never found its way into those pages. Who cared about her perceived frustrations and disappointments? Reliving them, however, was an emotional catharsis of sorts. The longer she kept with the book, the more she wanted to write it well. She reread two of the best of the biographies and began to take the book more seriously than Anthony Thompson probably had envisioned.

Still, there were a lot of empty hours to fill, and while she'd never expected Blake to give her any kind of special treatment, she was a little hurt at being so thoroughly ignored.

SHANNON WOULD HAVE BEEN SURPRISED to know just how aware of her Blake actually was. He'd seen her far more often than she suspected. When he worked outdoors he glanced toward the house every few minutes, an almost involuntary action. When he was inside he sat either at the breakfast table or on the sofa. Both were situated near windows that afforded an unrestricted view of the house. He knew she emerged from the house about five-thirty every afternoon and took a short stroll, though never in the direction of the mobile home. Then she went inside and, he guessed, began preparing supper, for the light in the kitchen window would be on for the next hour or so. Afterwards, she'd walk to the trash bins behind the house. He found himself waiting for these brief glimpses of her. He knew she went to bed every night between ten-thirty and eleven, for that was when the upstairs light went out. She obviously wasn't a night person. He liked that; he was an early-to-bed, early-to-rise sort himself.

She was always well-dressed. Though her clothes were casual—slacks, shorts, sundresses and the like—she managed to look as though she had spent hours getting into them. Her figure was delectable. She had been a little too thin as a teenager, and though still on the willowy side, she had gained the few extra pounds necessary for a curvaceous, alluring body. And she still moved like a dancer, with ease and grace, head held erect.

What in the devil did she do all day alone in that house? Write that book and relive her life with Parelli? Wallow in her grief? What a depressing existence.

Much to his disgust, he thought about her all the time. Much to his dismay, he found she still excited him. He invented all sorts of excuses to go to the house, but all of them were pretty contrived, and she would know it. What the hell was wrong with him? If she needed anything, or if she was in the mood for company and conversation, she knew he was only a short walk away. The day she arrived she'd made it pretty clear that she wanted to be alone, and he definitely didn't need to be close to her. Just watching and admiring her from a distance aroused emotions in him that he'd thought—hoped—were dead.

So he stayed away. He wanted no lingering memories when she left again.

IT WAS A SCORCHER of an afternoon in early-September. Blake returned to the farm from his Charlotte office a little earlier than usual. As he approached the farmhouse he saw Shannon hurry out the front door, across the porch and down the steps. She appeared to have been waiting for him, for she ran to the side of the road and flagged him down.

"Something wrong, Shannon?" he asked.

She walked up to the vehicle. "Sorry to bother you, but the disposal seems to be jammed. I wondered if you could fix it, or do you want me to call a repairman? I'll swear I can't imagine what I put down it that would cause it to get stuck."

He switched off the engine and got out of the jeep. "Just happens sometimes. There's a little wrench under the sink. It came with the disposal. I'll show you how to use it in case this ever happens again."

Going into the house for the first time since Shannon's arrival was an assault on Blake's senses. The entire place seemed different, although nothing had been moved or changed that he could see. He guessed it was the woman herself who gave the house such an unfamiliar but pleasant atmosphere.

She, and the undescribably delicious aroma emanating from the oven. Something smelled like home cooking and made his mouth water. He and Randy existed almost solely on hamburgers, canned food and those boil-in-bag things. Throughout the long years of bachelorhood he had never bothered to learn to cook.

He retrieved the tool from under the sink, and in a couple of rapid motions he unjammed the appliance. "That does it. Come here and I'll show you how to use this thing."

A split second later he wished he hadn't. As she leaned over the sink a few strands of her silky hair brushed his cheek and the flowery smell of her overpowered the aroma of whatever was in the oven. He thought his heart had stopped beating for a moment; it definitely had skipped several beats. "Ah...all right...this part of the wrench fits right over the center. Then give 'er a twist. You don't have to muscle it, just a little twist. Works every time. Got that?"

"Sure. It looks simple enough."

He stepped away from her, and Shannon straightened to give him a tantalizing smile of thanks.

In spite of some lofty intentions, Blake couldn't take his eyes off her. She was wearing baggy white slacks with a drawstring waist, a simple blue-and-white striped blouse and funny little white sneakers with mesh insteps—comfortable, unspectacular clothes that on Shannon looked downright sexy. For a moment he caught a glimpse of his long-ago dream girl, and an unwanted, delicious sensation stirred inside him. Could it possibly be that in all the world there was only one woman who could make him feel this way? Was he doomed to be captivated by her forever? He could see he had been right to keep his distance.

But now they were together in the kitchen, and they had to make conversation of some sort. "I guess that does it," he said. "Those things just seem to have to get stuck every once in a while."

"Thanks so much, Blake. Now there's at least one home repair I can do myself."

"Does everything else in the house work?"

"Yes, I've been very comfortable."

"How's the book coming?"

She shrugged and laughed lightly. "Pretty good, I guess. Since I'm a rank amateur, I really don't know."

A moment of awkward silence followed. Shannon searched her mind for a way to keep the conversation alive. "You've done such nice things to the house, Blake."

"Thanks, but there's still a lot to do, not just in the house but all over the farm."

"I happened to notice you and Randy down by the creek yesterday afternoon," she commented. *Happened to,* she thought, *because I was standing at the window looking all over the place for you.* "You both looked so industrious. I wondered what you were doing."

"Why didn't you come down and find out?"

"I didn't want to get in the way."

"You wouldn't have been in the way. We could have used an extra pair of hands. We were measuring the creek's velocity, something I try to do every few weeks."

"Oh, yes, you mentioned something about that when I was here last spring. How do you do that? Or perhaps I should ask why you do it."

"Why do I do it? I have to know the swiftness of the current, along with a couple of other measurements, in order to convert it into kilowatt hours."

Shannon blinked. "Oh."

"As for how I do it . . . well, that's kinda complicated to explain. It would be easier to show you than to tell you about it. If you're really interested, I'd enjoy showing you exactly what I'm doing."

"It sounds fascinating," she said. "I'd like that."

"I guessed you wanted to be alone."

"Not all the time."

"Then take this as an open invitation. You're welcome to join us anytime." Now why had he said that? The words just seemed to pop out of his mouth of their own volition. He wondered if he would live to regret issuing that invitation.

"Thanks, Blake. I'll probably take you up on that."

Blake tried to think of what to say next. To his pleased surprise, Shannon didn't seem in the least anxious for him to leave. "Something sure smells good," was what he came up with.

"It's beef burgundy. My cook at home makes it frequently, and now I'm trying my hand at it." She paused, then added, "I'd love to have you and Randy for supper . . . if you don't have other plans."

"Well, I . . ."

She indicated the cookbook lying on the counter. "I'm afraid my expertise in the kitchen is limited to following a recipe verbatim, and it seems all of them make six servings. I always end up with so much food.''

The aroma was driving him crazy. Her invitation was irresistible. ''Thanks,'' he said, ''we'd enjoy that. I'm not sure Randy knows what real home cooking is like.''

''Remember, I'm a novice.''

''What time are we expected?''

''I usually eat around six-thirty, but if that isn't a good time for you, the beef can wait.''

''Six-thirty's fine.''

At that moment their conversation was interrupted by the sound of Randy's voice. He was outside, calling Blake's name.

''I didn't hear the bus,'' Blake muttered, glancing at his watch. He walked to the kitchen door and opened it. ''In here, son,'' he called, and a second or two later Randy shuffled uncertainly through the door.

''We're in luck, Randy,'' Blake told him. ''Shannon's asked us to have supper with her. No soup and sandwiches tonight. Just smell what's in store for us. Isn't that great?''

''Yeah, guess so,'' the boy said indifferently. He didn't notice the aroma of beef burgundy. He was too busy looking at Blake looking at Shannon.

THE MOMENT BLAKE AND RANDY left the house, Shannon turned down the heat under the beef, set the table as nicely as she could with her limited stock of dishes and placemats, then went upstairs. For the next forty-five minutes or so she treated herself to a full beauty routine, something she'd seldom bothered doing since coming to the farm. She dressed in tan slacks and an ecru linen-look blouse. She felt clean and fresh and energetic. Tonight would be such a nice change from eating alone and reading until bedtime.

THE BEEF WAS DELICIOUS, Blake told her two or three times. Randy said nothing, but Shannon noticed that he gobbled down every bite. In fact, they both ate like they hadn't had a decent meal in months. She didn't bother asking if they wanted seconds; she merely filled their plates again and watched them devour the contents.

Throughout the meal she valiantly tried to converse with Randy, but her questions were awkward, and he answered in monosyllables, so she concentrated on Blake, who was more talkative. His construction firm had just begun building a complex of luxury townhouses, and he enlightened her on all the details such a project entailed, as well as the problems. Mealtime passed pleasantly for Shannon, in spite of the hostile youngster seated across from her. She'd be damned if she was going to let a fourteen-year-old intimidate her, which is what she suspected Randy was trying to do. At the same time, it bothered her that she couldn't get him to warm to her. As a woman who'd always wanted children, she'd rather imagined she would be good with them.

She got to her feet and began clearing the table. Blake immediately stood up and offered his help. "Randy and I are old hands at KP duty, aren't we, son? We'll clean up, and the cook can rest."

"Oh, no," Shannon said. "I like to move around after I eat."

"Then, tell you what, I'll help, and Randy can get on up to our place and do his homework."

Randy protested. "Aren't you coming?"

"In a bit. Get on with it, and no TV until the homework's done."

"I don't have all that much to do. I can wait for you."

"Randy!"

"Oh, okay." Glumly he shuffled toward the back door.

"Hey, Randy, haven't you forgotten something?"

The boy turned. "Huh? Oh, yeah...." His gaze reluctantly shifted to Shannon. "Thanks for supper."

"You're welcome, Randy. We'll have to do it more often." She was glad she didn't have to rely on Randy's enthusiasm for encouragement and self-esteem.

Once Randy was gone Blake turned to her with a defensive smile. "Don't mind Randy, Shannon. He doesn't know how to relate to people. He's had a rough life."

"Any rougher than yours was?"

"About the same, I guess." His brow furrowed. "No, worse. I don't remember my folks at all. I don't remember if they were loving or indifferent or what, but Randy remembers his mother all too well. The memories aren't pleasant ones, I assure you. From what Tom Archer's told me, Randy's mother makes a sweeping statement in favor of planned parenthood."

The moment he'd uttered the words he wanted to retract them. That he of all people could say such a callous thing appalled him. An image of Norma passed through his mind. He sometimes wondered how life had subsequently treated her, just as he wondered why he couldn't erase the guilt feelings that swept through him every time he thought of her. Why the guilt? Why couldn't he forget? She'd done what she wanted to do. He'd had nothing to do with it.

But then, he'd never been very good at forgetting, had he? The lovely woman in the kitchen with him was a perfect example of that.

Oblivious to the dark thoughts in Blake's mind, Shannon sighed. "It doesn't seem fair, does it? Women have children they don't want, and so many want them and can't have them."

"That bothers you, doesn't it? Being childless, I mean."

The question caught her by surprise. Was she that transparent, or was Blake simply more astute an observer than most? "Yes, it bothers me," she said truthfully, and it crossed her mind that this was the first time she'd admitted that openly. "I think I would have liked being a mother."

And she probably would have been a good one, he thought, only he didn't know why he thought it. "Then why don't you adopt?"

"At this late date?"

"Sure, why not? I'm going to try to adopt Randy."

"Blake! Really? I've heard that it's so difficult. Do you think you'll have any luck?"

"I don't know, Shannon. Randy's not your average adoptable kid. I doubt anyone else would take him, and Tom Archer agrees. He's paving the way for me. I think the people in the foster parent program would like to point proudly to one legal adoption. I'm banking on that.''

"Well, I wish you all the best. The boy certainly seems taken with you. I guess that's a sign he hasn't suffered any permanent emotional damage.''

"Yeah," Blake agreed, "we get along pretty well, but what he really needs is some kind of relationship with kids his own age.''

"How's he doing in school?''

"No complaints so far.''

Blake glanced around the kitchen. Shannon had been busy all the time they were talking. He'd done nothing, but suddenly the kitchen was clean. He propped one hip against the counter and crossed his arms over his chest. "I was a lot of help, wasn't I? You're really fast and efficient. Funny, I wouldn't have imagined you were domestic.''

"Domestic?'' She smiled, for that wasn't a word that had ever been associated with her. "How would you have imagined me?''

"Oh, the quintessential socialite, I guess. Running from social event to social event, with time out for 'good works' in between.''

Shannon closed the dishwasher and turned it on. She recalled the sameness of her days, when her time was spent on meaningless pursuits. Her "good works'' had consisted of allowing Peg to get her involved in all sorts of charities and causes. Social events had centered around Vic's friends and associates, his career. The afternoons at the Post-and-Paddock, and a few mornings on the tennis court had been the only times she'd engaged in activities simply because she enjoyed them, and she'd been made to feel guilty about those. "I've discovered I enjoy cooking and puttering around a house," she said. "I never had the chance to before. I was never a socialite, Blake. We didn't lead that kind of life."

"What kind of life did you lead?" he asked with interest. He couldn't help himself; he longed to know more about her life with Parelli. She'd never tell him everything he wanted to know, so he'd probably be first in line to buy that damned book. And that wouldn't tell him everything he wanted to know either.

"Rather sedate. It was nothing like the popular image of show business life. Very few of our friends were celebrities. Vic liked to play golf, and he was crazy about sports of all kinds. If there was any kind of game on TV, you could be sure he'd be in front of the set. We entertained about six times a year, tops. Oh, there were breaks in the routine, of course. Vic had personal appearances and TV specials, recording dates. Sometimes I went, sometimes I didn't. Sitting in on a recording session has to be the most boring way to spend a day if you aren't one of the participants. But at home we pretty much lived an average life." She didn't bother to mention that they were seldom alone, that Vic had liked being surrounded by his pals. Her husband's need for constant companionship had surfaced in the book, and she still wasn't sure if it should stay in or not.

"How long did you dance after you were married?"

"A year."

"Why did you quit?"

"Well, I quit Vic's show because after our marriage I wasn't one of the bunch anymore. I was the star's wife, an outsider. The other dancers no longer asked Mrs. Parelli to have lunch at Walgreen's, and I hated that left-out feeling. Afterwards I did a few commercials and one off-Broadway show that folded after six performances. Then I quit altogether.''

"Why? You were awfully good, as I recall.''

She flushed with pleasure. "You saw me dance?''

"I watched the show as long as you were on it, yes.''

"Really, Blake? Where were you?''

"Lackland Air Force Base in Texas. I watched it in the NCO Club every Saturday night. Stopped when you left, though. Variety shows weren't really my favorite form of entertainment. In those days I went heavily for the macho things with screeching tires and gun play.'' He paused, then said, "I can understand why you might not have wanted to dance on your husband's show, but why did you quit altogether?''

"Oh...two careers in a family caused conflicts. Sooner or later everyone has to establish priorities, and I discovered Vic was number one.''

"He wanted you at home,'' Blake said. It wasn't a question.

"Yes.''

"Are you putting that in the book?''

She wondered if he could see inside her head. That morning she had written a couple of paragraphs about her decision to quit dancing at the ripe old age of twenty-two. Then she had torn them up. Upon re-reading them she'd decided they made Vic sound manipulative and possessive.

But he *had* been manipulative and possessive. It was the hardest part of writing the book—deciding what went in and what didn't. The list, for instance.

Did that go in? How would it read? Would it come across as a gesture of enormous generosity...or as a power play? She realized she could put down anything that crossed her mind and let the editor do the deleting, but she wanted it to be as much her book as possible. It was a project that was uniquely hers. "No," she told Blake. "No one cares what I did or why. The book is about Vic's life."

"I think it's a shame you quit. You might have ended up on Broadway. That's what you wanted. You used to talk about it all the time."

She smiled wanly. "Look at you. All you ever talked about was a wife and a big family. Life takes funny twists and turns."

Blake's arms dropped to his sides and he pushed himself away from the counter. "So it does, Shannon, so it does. Well, much obliged for the supper."

Shannon didn't want him to leave, not yet, but there was no good reason for him to stay. Not unless he just wanted to talk to her, which apparently he didn't. "Don't mention it," she said. "I enjoyed the company."

"Guess I'd better go see if Randy's actually getting his homework done."

"Yes, I...guess so."

"Parenting is damned hard work. Oh, by the way, I've been meaning to tell you...there's a vegetable garden out back."

"Yes, I know."

"You're welcome to as much of the produce as you want. I've been giving away a lot of it."

"Thanks. That will be a real treat."

"I've started a compost bin, too. You'll see it, or smell it. If you have vegetable peels or trimmings, I'd appreciate it if you'd put them there instead of throwing them down the disposal.''

"Of course. I'll try to remember.''

"Good night, Shannon.''

"Good night, Blake.''

She went out onto the back porch with him and watched as he walked up the incline toward the mobile home, noticing in particular his swift, sure stride. He was a splendid man, she thought, potent and vital, the kind of person people referred to as "salt of the earth." Yet, she would have proudly walked into any drawing room in the world on his arm. She imagined he would look splendid in a tuxedo.

She tried comparing him with Vic and found that little comparison was possible. They both were handsome, successful men, and both their lives had the up-from-nothing aspect, but that was about it. There was a feeling of power associated with Blake that had nothing to do with money or influence. All of Vic's power had derived from money and influence. Offstage or away from the cronies who were indebted to him, Vic had often displayed the insecurities that were holdovers from his bleak childhood and were the reason for his jealousy and possessiveness, of course.

But no one could have had a more miserable childhood than Blake. Where were his insecurities? Well-hidden, if they existed at all. A soft smile touched her lips. She had a feeling that Blake's wife, if there had been one, could have played tennis, ridden, painted, danced, chaired a committee, done anything she wanted, and it wouldn't have disturbed his ego one whit. He was vital and energetic and magnificently masculine, unlike anyone she had ever known.

Face it, she liked him . . . a lot.

CHAPTER EIGHT

THE AFTERNOON SUN WAS HIGH in the sky. Shannon wore a big floppy hat to shield her skin from the worst of its rays as she sat cross-legged on the creek bank. In her hand she held Blake's stopwatch. Earlier he had tied strings across the stream at two locations twenty feet apart. Now he was standing some distance upstream from her, holding a cork in his hand.

"Ready?" he called.

She nodded. "Ready."

Blake tossed the cork in the water, and it began moving downstream. Shannon kept her eye on it, and the moment the cork moved under the first string, she activated the watch. When it passed under the second string, she cried, "Mark! Ten seconds exactly!"

Blake then made his way down the bank to her. "That jibes. I guess I'll go with that."

She handed him the watch, and he put it in his pocket. "Now, tell me what we just did," Shannon requested.

"We measured the stream's velocity. That's the sixth time I've done it, so I guess ten seconds is pretty accurate. Thanks for the help."

"I held a stopwatch. That doesn't seem like much help."

"But it is. I couldn't very well drop that cork up there, then scamper down here in time to see it pass under the other string."

"This is all very mystifying to me," Shannon confessed.

He squatted on his haunches beside her. "It isn't, not really. You see, in order to find out how much power this stream can deliver, I had to know three key measurements—head, velocity and the cross-sectional area. Head is the difference in elevation between the water's source and the point over there where I intend putting the turbine. Velocity, of course, is how fast the water flows, and the cross-sectional area is the width and depth of the stream. When I got those figures, I multiplied head times velocity times area, then divided by twenty-three."

"Why twenty-three?" she asked.

"That's the formula used to make the answer come out in kilowatts."

"Oh."

"Then you multiply that by 720, the number of hours in an average month."

Shannon looked up at him. "How come you know all this?"

"The turbine dealer told me how to do it."

"So, what did you come up with?"

"If my measurements are accurate—and I've taken 'em enough times to be sure they are—I figure this stream will deliver about nine-hundred kilowatt-hours for me. Meaning, I can use it to run everything in the house but the central air-conditioning and heating unit."

Shannon lowered her head and stared down at the stream rushing by her. "Fascinating. But I can't help wondering why you're going to all this trouble. Why not just pay your electric bill every month and be done with it?''

He grinned. "Now, if that doesn't sound exactly like someone from the city. It's my independent streak, I guess. I've been alone most of my life, and I don't like depending on anyone or anything. That includes the utility companies. When you generate your own power, you're less likely to waste it. No one has the right to over-consume. Besides, it's part and parcel of the whole thing; that is, keeping the ecological balance.''

Ah, yes, she had heard him speak of the "balance" many times. Bringing your life into mental and physical harmony with the world around you, he called it. He wanted a return to self-sufficiency. He was going to turn the farm into something you read about in *Mother Earth News*.

To Shannon it all sounded terribly romantic, and very Thoreau-ish, until it collided with day-to-day reality. The vegetable garden was a case in point. With all his heart Blake believed in organic gardening. No pesticides, no chemicals allowed. Instead, a special birdhouse had been built to lure purple martins, and the garden had been stocked with beneficial insects like ladybugs and praying mantises. Unfortunately, Blake's balance also included a black garden snake named Homer. Shannon, who had taken it upon herself to care for the garden before she learned all this, had almost fainted the first time she encountered Homer. Her scream had brought Blake hurrying to her side.

She'd pointed a trembling finger. "Bl-Blake...there's a s-snake in there!" She handed him her hoe. "Dad used to kill snakes with one of these, but...I c-can't."

"That's Homer," he'd explained casually, putting down the hoe. "I'm sorry I forgot to warn you about him. He's in there on purpose. He's perfectly harmless to humans, but he feeds on insects that feed on plants. Homer does more good than a truckload of pesticides, and he doesn't upset the balance one bit."

Try as she might, Shannon simply couldn't get used to Homer. Fortunately, the snake was no fonder of her than she was of him. The moment she entered the garden, Homer slithered away to curl around the base of a nearby crape myrtle, where he patiently waited for her to be gone. Still, she always worked with one eye over her shoulder, and the only way she would have gone into the garden after dark was at gunpoint. Homer, she thought, carried organic gardening too far.

Yet the snake was so typical of Blake's approach to everything. No half-way measures. She was certain that if a bull elephant had been good for the balance, Blake would have had one of those, too. When she'd first expressed interest in the things he was doing around the farm, he had presented her with a stack of books that, he'd told her, would help explain some of the things he hoped to do. The books hadn't constituted everyday light reading. She had thumbed through most of them, everything from *Biological Control of Natural Enemies* and *Cheap Energy for the Home* to *Grandmother's Household Hints*. He had how-to books on a wide range of subjects—how to raise everything from bees to goats, how to make everything from furniture to soap.

Amused, she had asked him if he actually intended making his own soap.

He'd answered the question seriously. "Of course. If I'm going to raise pigs, and I am, I'll have a lot of lard after fall slaughter. I don't want to cook with it—too much cholesterol—so why not make soap out of it?"

If she'd had to sum up his personality succinctly, she guessed she would have had to say that Blake simply looked at life differently than most people did. A lot of her father had rubbed off on him. Harry Jameson had been a kind, gentle man who had expected to find beauty and goodness all around him, so he had. Blake was a lot like that.

And he was a solitary sort. He could work alone hour after hour and never seemed to get bored or restless. How different from Vic, who had needed people around all the time. She'd often wondered what on earth her husband would have done if he'd ever found himself absolutely alone for one hour.

"When is this water power thing going to become reality?" she now asked.

"As soon as I can afford to build my power station."

"When will that be?"

"Who knows? As soon as I sell a couple of those new townhouses, I guess."

"How much will it cost?"

He pursed his lips. "Oh, somewhere in the neighborhood of twenty-five thousand. Too much for me to spend right now. My money's tied up in the townhouses, and the interest on the builder's loan is eating me alive. So, the power plant has to wait. I never over-extend financially. Never. I'm convinced that's the chief reason I've succeeded when so many builders have gone under.''

Also typical, Shannon thought. She wondered if he'd ever done a headstrong thing in his adult life. It was on the tip of her tongue to offer to lend him the money. She would have liked to help his ambitions along, and money seemed to be the only thing she had in great abundance. But a prudent part of her mind cautioned against it. Blake was a fiercely independent sort, and they weren't that close. She felt they had only a tenuous hold on a very fragile friendship. There was a part of him that just couldn't be reached.

But so much had changed since that evening over beef burgundy. Shannon still spent her days alone, which was good for the writing, but she turned off her typewriter in the afternoon and joined Blake and Randy at whatever they were doing. Then the three of them had supper in the farmhouse kitchen, and clean-up was a joint affair, with Blake and Randy handling the lion's share. It was a routine they had just fallen into, one which Shannon thoroughly enjoyed.

But in all this time Randy hadn't spoken a direct word to her if he could help it. The boy made no pretense of accepting her, which was refreshingly honest if nothing else. Shannon tried to understand. Now that she knew about Randy's background, she imagined he was very insecure and frightened to death of losing, or even sharing the only adult who had shown him any loving kindness.

She wished she could understand Blake so readily. She sensed there was something about her that put him on edge—she couldn't imagine what it was—

and it bothered her enormously. She wanted them to be friends, so she had adopted a chum-buddy attitude, hoping it would make him feel more at ease around her. She wanted someone to talk to at the end of the day. Sometimes he seemed to want that, too. During those times Shannon felt they were coming close to the warm rapport of their youth.

There were other times, though, when he could be so aloof. One seemed to follow the other, as if he couldn't quite make up his mind how he should treat her. She wondered if he was one of those men who was simply uncomfortable around women. After all, he'd never married.

Still and all, she found her new routine more pleasing than the old. She worked at her writing, she kept house and cooked and worked outside. Back home she'd always seemed to be looking for something to occupy her time; but on the farm she was busy constantly. She'd discovered she enjoyed puttering around a house, especially a kitchen. This domesticity was a facet of her personality never before revealed. She no longer felt alone; she felt useful. She ate heartily. At night she slept like a baby. She awoke with the sun and bounded out of bed, eager for whatever the day held in store. She'd never felt better in her life!

Blake glanced at his watch. "It's about time for the school bus," he commented. "I think I'll drive down and intercept Randy. I need to go into town for a few things, and I'll take him with me." He paused, then added, "Want to come along?"

Shannon would have liked to go, but Randy resented her presence so much. She could always feel the strain between Randy and herself, so the prospect of the three of them in the cramped confines of the jeep wasn't very appealing. "No, thanks," she said. "I have some things to do."

He shrugged. "Okay. Need anything from town?"

"I don't think so. Blake, have you heard anything more about the adoption?"

"Not a word. These things seem to take forever." He got to his feet and helped her up. She stumbled and fell against him. The body contact was a shock to Blake's nervous system. His hands clutched both sides of her waist to steady her. For a moment they stood face to face, and Blake experienced an outlandish urge to tell her she was the most beautiful woman he'd ever seen. He wouldn't, of course—his good sense hadn't left him completely—but the urge was there, and that alone appalled him.

Shannon was overwhelmed by the intensity she saw in his eyes. He was looking at her in the strangest way. She was aware that his hands at her waist felt warm and strong. She'd felt herself tremble when she fell against him; had he felt it, too? She would die of embarrassment if he ever suspected that her thoughts about him sometimes took strange and dangerous turns.

"See you at supper," he finally said, releasing her.

"Sure," she said. "See you at supper."

He turned to go, then stopped and turned back. "I'm going to Charlotte in the morning. Would you like to come along, just for the change?" The invitation was spontaneous. He had correctly surmised that Randy might be the reason she never wanted to go anywhere with them.

Shannon didn't hesitate a minute. "I'd love to," she said. She was elated at the prospect of being alone with him, and it gave her a curious sort of thrill to know he wanted to spend the day with her.

"Okay," Blake said. "Good." He shoved his hands in his pockets and walked away, despising himself for wanting her company so badly.

THEY LEFT THE FARM at nine-fifteen the following morning. It was a typical day in late summer—bright and hot—and they made the drive to Charlotte in a little over two hours. Along the way they had casually talked about mundane things. Shannon noticed there were no awkward lapses in the conversation, but all the while she had been acutely aware of his presence beside her, conscious of being alone with him for a long stretch of time. She was beginning to acknowledge a powerful attraction to him, which disturbed her and fascinated her at the same time. Odd that she couldn't be indifferent to him, as she was to most men. The attraction strengthened her determination to foster friendship between them. Anything more profound was too impossible to consider.

Shannon had been to Charlotte maybe twice in her life, many years ago, but she remembered it as "the city with all the trees." Now as they drove into the city, she could see that her memories had been accurate. They went straight to Blake's offices, where Shannon was introduced to his employees, most of whom were unabashedly curious about her. Afterwards they had lunch at a Chinese restaurant where Blake was obviously well-known, and then they drove to the construction site where the townhouses were being built. While he tended to more business, Shannon walked through and admired several of the units that were in later stages of construction. When Blake was finished, they stopped for ice cream cones on the way out of town. They were back at the farm before Randy returned home from school.

The trip to Charlotte had been a pleasant interlude, nothing extraordinary, yet as Shannon moved around the kitchen preparing supper that evening, she experienced the strangest mixture of emotions pulling at her. She decided the day had somehow been momentous, even though nothing unusual had happened.

Still, she felt different, closer to Blake in some obscure way. He had been wonderfully compatible all day, a bit on the talkative side, and he had smiled and laughed frequently. Once, when they had started to cross a busy street to his office, he'd taken her hand in his, and she recalled how warm and right it had felt there. Later, their eyes had happened to meet over the table at the restaurant, and the look that had passed between them . . . well, she couldn't explain it adequately. It had conveyed a certain special rapport.

For the first time she admitted that becoming emotionally involved with a man again wasn't the most preposterous thing in the world. It could happen.

SEVERAL DAYS LATER Shannon was startled by the sound of the doorbell in mid-afternoon. It was the first time she'd heard it since she moved into the house. Blake and Randy always used the back door. She turned off the typewriter and hurried downstairs to answer it.

Two elderly women stood on the porch, both of them dressed neatly in tailored suits that looked much too warm for the summer afternoon.

"Mrs. Parelli?" the taller one asked in a soft, cultured Southern drawl.

"Yes." Shannon couldn't imagine how the two strange women knew her name. Come to think of it, how did they know she was there?

"I'm Mary Hatcher, and this is my sister, Mildred Prentiss."

"How do you do."

"We wanted to stop by, introduce ourselves and have a word with you, if we may."

"Of course." Alive with curiosity, Shannon stepped back and held the door open wider. "Please come in."

"We're not interrupting anything?"

"No, no. Please come in."

The two women stepped into the foyer, and their eyes darted about in a quick inspection. Then they fastened sweet smiles on Shannon as she led them into the living room.

"May I get you ladies something cold to drink?"

"No, thank you, dear. We can't stay but a minute," Mary Hatcher said.

"Then, please have a seat."

Mary and Mildred sat down on the sofa, crossed their legs at the ankles and primly folded their hands in their laps. Shannon had the uncomfortable feeling that she was being placed under a microscope. "Well," she said uncertainly when neither of her visitors said anything, "what can I do for you?"

"Why, we've simply come calling, Mrs. Parelli." Mildred finally opened her mouth.

"How...very nice," Shannon said. "I'm surprised you knew I was here. I've not contacted anyone since I returned to South Carolina."

"Returned?" Mary asked in surprise. "You've been here before?"

"I was raised here, Mrs. Hatcher. Right in this house. My maiden name was Shannon Jameson."

Mary's and Mildred's eyebrows raised in unison. "Were you Beth Jameson's daughter?" Mildred asked.

"Yes."

"Lovely woman. Her death was such a tragedy."

"Yes, it was," Shannon agreed.

"I'm sure I knew you when you were a child, dear, for I visited Beth many times. Yes, I remember you now. You wore long dark pigtails."

"When I was very young, yes."

"Then...." Mildred's hand went to her mouth. "Oh, good heavens! Parelli! Now, why didn't that name register with me? You're the widow of the singer. Oh, my dear, another tragedy. Such a loss."

"Yes, ma'am, it was." Shannon paused to clear her throat. "May I ask how you knew I was here?"

It was Mary who explained. "The boy, Randy."

"Randy?" Oh, God that could mean anything! How did these women know Randy, and what else, pray, had he told them?

"Yes, he told Reverend Archer, and the reverend told us."

"Then you're members of the reverend's church."

"No, Mildred and I both live in Greenville. We know Randy in another respect. You see, we serve on the adoption board that's considering Mr. Carmichael's request."

Shannon's stomach did a flip-flop. "Oh?" she said weakly.

"We've called on Mr. Carmichael many times, but he never seems to be at home. He does own this house, doesn't he?"

"Yes, he bought it from me. Blake's very busy, you see. He spends some days in Charlotte on business . . . but he's always back before Randy comes home from school," she added quickly.

"This is his house and you're staying here?" Mary's disapproval was quite evident.

"Yes, but Blake and Randy aren't living here in the house right now. Well, of course they aren't, because I'm living here temporarily. They're staying in the mobile home up on the hill."

"I see." Mary exchanged a quick glance with her sister, then looked at Shannon. "We try to make several calls on prospective parents. We feel it's best to meet them on their home territory, to actually see the home the child will live in."

Shannon waved a hand to indicate the house as a whole. "As you can see, Blake is in the process of redoing the entire place. I think it's going to be lovely, a very nice home for a young boy. Randy loves it here, he really does." She stopped when she realized she was chattering.

The women glanced around noncommittally. Then Mary said, "We've especially wanted to meet Mr. Carmichael because . . . well, frankly, Mrs. Parelli, Mildred and I are generally opposed to adoption by single persons."

"Really, Mrs. Hatcher? Why?" Shannon asked bluntly.

"Experience has taught us that a child is better off with a nuclear family."

"But isn't one parent better than no parent at all?"

"Not always. Once, several years ago, the board granted the adoption of an infant girl by a young woman whose husband had died unexpectedly. She had been thoroughly investigated and seemed like such a fine lady. She was financially secure, had a lovely home, and there was no doubt that she wanted a child. We later discovered that the woman had taken a young man into her house and lived with him openly without benefit of marriage. It was strongly suspected that the liaison had been postponed until the adoption was official."

Mildred leaned forward. "It seems young people don't want to get married anymore. They like to live together, like dogs in a pack," she sniffed.

"Mildred!" Mary admonished.

"Well, it's true," Mildred defended.

"Let's just say that we've learned to be overly cautious," Mary added.

Shannon would have liked to ask some pointed questions, such as, was there any evidence that said child was neglected or unloved? But looking at the two characters across from her, she thought better of it. She immediately had them pegged as self-appointed arbiters of social conduct. "Mrs. Hatcher, Mrs. Prentiss...I'm sure that if you could meet Blake and see him with Randy you wouldn't have any qualms about the adoption. They are devoted to one another, and Blake is a totally responsible man."

"Have you known him long, Mrs. Parelli?" Mary asked.

Shannon hesitated, but only for a fleeting second. "Since I was sixteen," she answered blithely.

"So long. You're very old friends, then."

"Yes, very. More than friends actually. You see, Blake is, ah, my foster brother."

"Ah!" Mary exclaimed. "I guess that explains why he would just move out and let you use his house." She looked enormously relieved.

"I guess so. He's a nice man."

"He's never married, has he?" Mildred asked.

"No." Shannon's teeth clenched together tightly. God, where did people like this get their information? Then she reminded herself that the adoption board would be privy to all sorts of facts about Blake. Oh, she wished they would just leave! She hated talking about Blake without his knowledge. Her mind whirled. She would have to remember everything she told the sisters, so she could relate it to him.

"Doesn't it strike you as odd that a man his age hasn't ever married?"

"Not particularly," Shannon said. "Back home I have many friends in their thirties who've never been married."

"Where's home?" Mildred asked.

"I live in New York."

"Well, ah, New York is...different, I imagine. Much different from here. Don't you find that, in most cases, these older, unmarried parties are...ah, they're..."

Mary interrupted. "What Mildred's doing a poor job of saying, Mrs. Parelli, is that one of the problems associated with single adoptive parents is...well, we have to be absolutely sure they're heterosexual."

Shannon glanced from one woman to the other and held back the laugh bubbling in her throat. "How on earth can you be absolutely sure of that?"

Mary looked taken aback. "Well, I . . . word gets around about those people, doesn't it? They can't hide it forever. No one could withstand our investigation without being found out. I'm sure of it."

"You don't have to worry about Blake in that respect, Mrs. Hatcher."

"Oh? How sure are you of that?"

Shannon gulped back her dismay. This meeting was not going well. She was trying to think of a way to answer the question when she heard the sound of the back door opening and closing. Footsteps crossed the kitchen and dining room. Shannon hoped and prayed it was Blake arriving in the nick of time.

It wasn't. Randy appeared in the foyer. "Blake in here?" he asked succinctly.

Shannon swiveled her head in his direction. "No. Isn't he home?"

Randy shook his head. "Don't guess so."

"Well, I'm sure he'll be along any minute. Randy, I'd like you to meet Mrs. Hatcher and Mrs. Prentiss."

"Hello, Randy," the women chorused.

"Hi," the boy said awkwardly, then looked at Shannon. "Guess I'll just hang around and wait for Blake to get home." He twirled around and was gone.

"Good heavens, is the boy a latch-key child?" Mildred asked.

"Oh, no. Blake is almost always here before Randy gets home. He must have been detained in Charlotte, but Randy's perfectly capable of taking care of himself, Mrs. Prentiss. He's fourteen, after all.''

A moment of strained silence followed; then Mary got to her feet and her sister did likewise. ''We'll be going now, Mrs. Parelli. Please tell Mr. Carmichael we tried to contact him... again.''

Shannon stood up. ''If you'll leave a number I'm sure he'll call you. Perhaps you can make an appointment.''

''No, we prefer to call unannounced,'' Mary said as the two women left the house.

SHANNON INTERCEPTED BLAKE when she finally heard the jeep arriving. He stopped beside the house and turned off the engine. ''What's up?'' he asked, seeing the strange, anxious expression on her face.

''Of all days for you to be late!'' she fumed like a scolding wife.

He frowned. ''What's going on?''

''I had two visitors this afternoon. A Mrs. Hatcher and a Mrs. Prentiss.''

He uttered an oath under his breath. ''Those two! What did they want?''

''I'm not sure. To find out what I'm doing here, I think.''

''How in hell did they even know you're here?''

''Randy told Reverend Archer, and he told the two women.''

Blake's mouth compressed tightly. ''What did you tell them?''

''The truth, what else? I guess they're satisfied that we aren't...er, co-habitating. I told them I'd known you since I was sixteen and that you're my foster brother.''

"I guess that's the truth, sorta. Stretched a bit, but the truth, nevertheless."

"They informed me that they generally oppose adoption by a single persons."

"I know," he said worriedly. "Tom Archer's warned me about them. Seems the sisters are holding up the adoption proceedings solely because of that. Apparently they have a lot of clout since they've been serving on the board for years."

"This wasn't the best day for you to be late. Randy showed up before you did, so our moral watchdogs have branded him a 'latch-key child.'"

"So? I'm late once in a blue moon. There are thousands of latch-key kids, a lot of them younger than Randy. You can't sweat the small stuff, Shannon. What else?"

She took a moment to think over her conversation with the sisters. A mischievous twinkle appeared in her eyes, and a sly smile crossed her face. "Not much. They just wanted to know if you're heterosexual."

His eyes widened. "God a'mighty! What did you say to that?"

"I told them I was sure you were." A little giggle escaped her lips. "Then they wanted to know how sure I was."

Blake shook his head in disbelief.

"Fortunately," Shannon went on, keeping a straight face with some difficulty, "Randy walked in about then, so I was spared the necessity of answering that one."

In spite of the grim news, a little smile quirked the corners of Blake's mouth. "Well, suppose Randy hadn't walked in just then. What would you have said?''

She pretended to give it serious thought. "I guess... I guess I would have had to confess that I have no idea what your sexual preferences are. How would I know?" She stepped back and smiled again. "See you later."

Blake watched the seductive movement of her hips as she strode back to the house. She had the sexiest walk he'd ever seen, and it wasn't an affectation. He swallowed the ridiculous urge to go after her, sweep her into his arms, carry her into the house, and show her just how heterosexual he was.

God, if he didn't get her off his mind he was going to be a basket case!

CHAPTER NINE

BLAKE STARTED UP THE JEEP and drove on to the mobile home, where he found Randy sitting on the front steps, reading a comic book. "Hi," he said.

"Hi," the boy answered, his face breaking into a grin. "Where'ya been?"

"I got tied up in Charlotte."

"Did you get the basketball hoop and backboard?"

Blake snapped his fingers. "Sorry, I forgot. I'll get it tomorrow and set it up, for sure."

The boy couldn't hide his disappointment. "Okay."

"Haven't you got something more productive to do than read a comic book? Homework, for instance?"

"Just a little."

"Well come on inside and get it done before supper."

"Do I have to? I'd rather do it later. There's nothing to do after supper anyway, since you always stay down there and talk to her."

Blake glowered at him. "Don't argue with me, Randy. Get the homework done, now!"

Uttering a subdued sound of resignation, Randy did as he was told. While the boy spread out his work on the kitchen table, Blake opened the newspaper he'd had no time for that morning. He quickly scanned the first three pages, then turned to the sports section. But within minutes he realized he wasn't paying any attention to the paper; he was staring out the window, down toward the house. His mind was on Shannon, as it had been all day and the day before and the day before that. Ever since the day in Charlotte. Why was that, he wondered. Nothing out of the ordinary had transpired, yet he sensed a change.

That friendly, good-natured routine of hers had totally disarmed him. He was trying his damndest to put things into perspective, to remember that she was the young widow Parelli who lived in a grand mansion in New York, so far removed from the world he knew that they might as well have lived on different continents. But no amount of self-warning could prevent him from falling for her all over again. The one thing he had vowed wouldn't happen had happened, and he knew he was courting trouble.

He no longer tried to stay away from her. On the contrary, he gravitated to her like a bee to clover. No luscious detail of her escaped his avid gaze. He felt like a lovesick schoolboy half the time, and all he got in return was that "best friends" attitude. One moment he wished she would leave; the next he wished she would finish that damned book, stop thinking about her husband and notice him.

She wouldn't, though. Why did he dwell on it? She was committed to being Mrs. Parelli, and her interests in South Carolina were negligible. That was so obvious. Every time he'd asked her about the book he'd noticed a certain wistful quality creeping into her voice. He guessed she still longed for Parelli, which was only natural, but it turned his gut inside out.

He stared at the sports page and sighed with disgust. He'd been in a foul mood for days, and there was no need to wonder at the cause. Unrequited love had played hell with his disposition. He'd gotten into an uncalled-for argument with his painting contractor that afternoon, one reason he'd been late getting home. The next time he saw the man he would apologize. No real harm done, but that kind of thing had happened too often lately, and he wasn't the argumentative sort.

"Oh, cripes!" Randy's voice snapped Blake out of his miserable reverie.

He hadn't been aware that the boy had left the table. Looking up, he saw Randy at the kitchen sink, staring with dismay at an overturned glass of milk.

"What the devil are you doing?" he barked.

"I was getting a glass of milk, and I knocked it over with my elbow," Randy said.

"Well, get it cleaned up!"

Randy tore several paper towels off the roll and mopped hurriedly, glancing at Blake with a dark frown. "I will, I will! It's only spilled milk."

"Watch what you're doing from now on."

"Why're are you being such a grouch? You've been like this for days."

"Your imagination," Blake growled. "Get that mess cleaned up and finish your homework."

"It's done." Pouting, Randy finished mopping up the spill and wiped the counter with a wet cloth. "If it's all right, I'm going outside again."

"All right. Don't stray."

Randy walked to the door, then turned to Blake, fuming. "I know what's got you in such a bad mood. It's her!" He jerked his head in the direction of the farmhouse. "You never got like this before she came along. You know what I wish? I wish I could do something that would make her so mad she'd leave in the morning!"

"Randy, that's enough!" Blake exclaimed, but the boy was gone.

SHANNON STOOD at the kitchen sink, idly peeling the potatoes she had boiled for potato salad. She paused long enough to glance over the recipe once again. She'd never made potato salad in her life, but the recipe sounded like what Ginger served. It had been a warm day, and though the house was comfortably air-conditioned, the weather didn't seem to call for a hot heavy meal. She would serve cold cuts, the salad, ice cream and cookies, and she hoped that was hearty enough for the "boys." They weren't finicky eaters; they ate anything she set before them.

Occasionally her gaze wandered out the window to the mobile home, and she speculated on how Blake and Randy spent their time indoors. Whatever it was, they never seemed to lack for something to do.

They were so fortunate to have each other, she thought with a sigh. Watching them together made her long even more for a child. If she and Vic had had a baby, she would be about Randy's age now. Yes, she, for she would have wanted a daughter—a little dark-haired delight who would rush in from school, eager to tell her mother everything that had happened during the day. Someone to share intimate chats about feminine concerns. A daughter who would have become a woman, a mother, a friend.

But, Shannon conceded, it might not have been all that cozy. She recalled the words of a friend in New York whose oldest child, a daughter, was fifteen. "My God, Shannon, a fifteen-year-old girl is the strangest creature alive! That kid of mine might as well have dropped down from another planet for all I can communicate with her. Count yourself lucky to have been spared teenagers." And the friend hadn't considered that a callous remark in the least.

Besides, Vic would have wanted a boy and been horribly disappointed if he hadn't gotten one.

Just then Shannon's eyes caught some movement in the yard outside the mobile home. Was it Blake? Her heart gave an erratic beat. The sight of him always caused queer stirrings inside her, and that had intensified since the day in Charlotte. She had tried very hard to place him in a comfortable niche, but he refused to stay there. As a woman she found it impossible to conveniently label him "friend" and nothing more. Though she'd thought there were distractions back home, she had discovered Blake to be the biggest distraction of all. Earlier, before the sisters arrived, she'd been having a difficult time with the manuscript. Her concentration had been at an all-time low. Her mind kept wandering from Vic and his life to Blake and his. Could she ever write a book about him! Except, she quickly amended, there would be some blank spaces.

She guessed Blake might be the luckiest person she knew. Some people never found what it was they wanted to do, but he had, and he loved every minute of it. She liked simply following him around, observing the man and the way he worked with self-assurance and absorbed interest. She thought about him all the time. There'd never been anyone to dream about before. She was acutely aware that she slept in his bed night after night. Lately her dreams had taken a softly erotic turn. When morning came, she would wonder how a woman of such limited experience could even think of those things.

There was another movement in the yard. Shannon saw a figure moving down the incline toward the house. It wasn't Blake; it was Randy. He was walking in a dejected way—thumbs hooked in the pockets of his jeans, shoulders slumped, head down. He shuffled on, kicking at the ground as though he was angry.

Shannon frowned. She couldn't imagine why the boy was coming to the house without Blake. Then she saw him change direction. He wasn't coming to the house at all. He was heading for the vegetable garden, which was even more curious. Randy never went near the garden.

Her interest arrested, Shannon watched as he carefully stepped between the neat rows of vegetables, then came to a halt at the row of tomato plants. For a moment he stood still. Then he glanced around furtively, and in an instant she thought she knew what he was up to. The knife she was holding fell from her hand and clattered in the sink. Uttering a cry, she raced for the back door.

For days Shannon had been watching one particular beefsteak tomato on the vines. The entire crop had yielded beautifully all summer, but this one fruit looked like something on the cover of a seed catalog. She had proudly announced that she was waiting for the perfect moment of ripeness to pick it, and she thought the moment was about upon them. She'd talked about that one tomato so much that Blake had made a joke of "Shannon's tomato," and he gave her nightly progress reports when he came in for supper.

She stepped out on the back porch in time to see the damage done. It happened in the blink of an eye. Randy picked that particular tomato off the vine, held it aloft as high as his arms could reach, then dropped it and watched it splatter on the ground.

At first Shannon couldn't believe her eyes. What a spiteful, hateful thing to do! Her disbelief quickly turned to rage, and she marched toward the boy in the garden. That did it! They were going to have it out! She'd bent over backwards trying to win his friendship, but she was through coddling him. "Randy!" she called angrily. "You stay right where you are!"

His head jerked up, and he turned as if to run.

"Don't you move!" Shannon barked, advancing on him.

Apparently Randy realized that running would do no good. He'd been caught in the act, dead to rights, without a leg to stand on. He stood rooted in place, mouth set grimly, and watched her approach.

For once Shannon entered the garden without first checking on Homer's whereabouts. Her eyes were flashing. She came to stand in front of Randy, chest heaving, hands on hips. "All right, young man Suppose you tell me why you did that."

"D-did what?"

"You know what I'm talking about! Why did you pick that tomato?"

"A squirrel did it. It . . . was an accident," he said lamely.

"The devil it was an accident! There was no squirrel. I saw what happened. Why did you do it?"

Shannon was livid, and it showed. Randy's defiance crumbled somewhat under the onslaught of her temper. "Because," he said glumly. "Because I hate that dumb tomato."

"That doesn't even make sense, Randy, and you know it. Why do you hate that tomato?"

"Because it's yours. Because Blake's been snapping at me all week, and it's all your fault."

"That's ridiculous. Why would it be my fault?"

"It just is. I know it is."

"That's not true, Randy, and I think you know it deep down inside. You just use me as the reason for everything that displeases you. I'd like to be your friend, but you make it impossible. Tell me why you don't like me."

"Because you're here!" he blurted out and without hesitation. "We didn't want you to come, and Blake's been in a bad mood ever since you got here."

Shannon stepped back as though he'd slapped her. "We?" she asked. "Blake didn't want me to come?"

Randy shook his head. "Before you came, I asked him if he wanted you here, and he said he liked things just the way they were. He said you wouldn't stay very long, but you have!"

A rush of color diffused Shannon's face. The thought of being an unwanted guest mortified her. Why hadn't Blake said something when she called? Any excuse, no matter how contrived, would have been preferable to letting her come when she wasn't wanted. Come to think of it, he was always asking her how the book was coming. Was he really asking when it would be finished, when she would be leaving? Well, she damned sure wouldn't stay now.

Then she took a moment to study the pettish expression on Randy's face, and she thought again. She didn't trust the boy to tell her the truth about anything. The only way to get to the bottom of this was to talk to Blake. She'd confront him point-blank. He wouldn't have time to think of a lie. She thought she'd know if he was telling the truth.

She took a deep breath. "All right, Randy. Run along, and we'll forget this. No use crying over spilled milk."

"Funny you said that. Are you gonna tell Blake?"

"Probably," she said truthfully.

"He'll whop me!" the boy cried.

"Has he ever 'whopped' you before?"

"N-no."

"Then I doubt he will now. Go on."

Randy turned and fled like a spooked rabbit. Shannon watched until she was satisfied he had gone down to the creek, then she marched purposefully to the mobile home and pounded on the front door.

Blake answered, and when he saw who it was standing on the front stoop his mouth dropped, and he gaped in astonishment.

"Shannon! What..."

"May I come in?" she asked icily.

"Of course." His heart thumped against his ribs. He stepped back as she entered, and swept by him, overpowering his senses with her sweet scent. What on earth? Shannon had never visited him before. He watched as she walked to the center of the room and stood with her back to him. Her body was abso-

lutely rigid. She was good and upset about something, which further surprised him. He'd never seen
her in anything but the best of moods.

She glanced around. The mobile home had probably been purchased furnished. It had that look
about it. Everything was too well-coordinated. She
moved to the bar that separated the kitchen and dining area from the living room. Propping one hand on
it and the other on her hip, she faced him squarely
and said, "It seems we won't be enjoying 'Shannon's tomato,' after all. It met an untimely death."

Blake was completely confused. "What?"

Succinctly she related the incident of Randy and
the tomato. Blake listened in disbelief. That's what
had brought her here? Naturally he was upset that
Randy would do such a thing, and he certainly intended speaking to the boy about it, but . . .

Dear God, all his thoughts had been centered on
her most of the day. Now she was before him, snug
in those well-fitting designer jeans, propelling him
further into a mindless state of arousal, and she was
only concerned about that damned tomato!

"I'm sorry, Shannon, and Randy'll get a good
piece of my mind, but . . . aren't you over-reacting to
the loss of a tomato?"

She straightened and threw up her hands. "It's not
the tomato. Don't you see that? It's Randy's jealousy of you and resentment of me. I'm sick of it!"

Blake's lips compressed tightly. He'd wondered
when all this was going to come to a head. He
thought Shannon had been remarkably patient up
until now, and he'd hoped time would take care of it.
It was easy for him to understand the boy, since he'd
been in his shoes. He wouldn't expect Shannon to.

"You probably don't understand kids, especially not kids like Randy. He's had more trouble in his short life than you'll have had when they bury you. I know he's difficult, but I don't think it's personal. He's difficult with everyone but me. He'll come around. Be patient with him."

"Patient?" she cried. "I've bent over backwards with that boy, and all he does is stare at me as though he wishes I would drop dead."

"It's probably not that bad."

"Oh, no? Believe me, it's that bad. But I'll give him credit for one thing: he's honest about it, which is more than I can say for you."

"Now, what's that supposed to mean?"

"He told me that...that neither one of you wanted me here in the first place, that you liked things just the way they were. Is that true?"

Blake felt a lump stick in his throat. Her blunt question caught him off-guard. "Yes, I guess so...in the beginning," he admitted.

Shannon's face grew hot. Well, she'd wanted the truth, and she'd gotten it, in spades! What did she say now? "Wh-why didn't you tell me when I called and invited myself here?"

"A lot of reasons."

"Give me one."

"Chiefly, your dad. I remembered all the things he'd done for me."

Her father? She almost choked. What an idiot she'd been, thinking she had made such great strides in fostering his friendship. And all those fantasies of hers, dreaming about him in a romantic sense! Thank goodness she was the only one who knew about them. "Dear God, do you mean you let me come here because of some misguided sense of loyalty to my father?''

"I told you . . . that was in the beginning."

"And now?"

Blake took a deep breath. "Now, it's different."

"In what way?"

"Now . . . I want you to stay."

Shannon took a step toward him. Her eyes were clouded with bewilderment. "Are you telling me the truth?"

"Yes."

"What made you change your mind?"

"It wasn't a mind change so much as . . . It wasn't that I didn't want you here, Shannon. I just didn't think it was . . . a good idea, that's all."

"Why?"

"Dammit, stop asking so many questions!"

"Then give me some answers. Why didn't you think it was a good idea for me to come here?"

"Because I was afraid what's happened would happen!"

Shannon frowned. "You're not making any sense. Why are you so mad? I'm the one who should be mad. My beautiful tomato was pinched."

"I'm not mad!"

"Of course you are. Tell me . . . what's happened?"

"Nothing!"

"You just said something's happened. I want to know what it is."

Blake was not at his dead-level best. In fact, he thought he might be at his dead-level worst. He'd had a lousy day; he was in a foul mood. Had he been more his usual collected self he might not have said what he said. As it was, the words just popped out. She might as well know. What he had to tell her probably would send her fleeing back to New York, but that might be best all the way around. "I've fallen in love with you all over again!" he growled. "And it just isn't right for a man to have to go through that twice in a lifetime."

A few seconds passed before the full implication of his words hit Shannon. She was stunned, too stunned to realize that he had, after a fashion, told her he was in love with her. "Blake, I...I don't know what to say. Again? I don't think I understand."

"You wouldn't. You never noticed how lovesick I was."

"Are...are you talking about when we lived on this farm?" A vision of the shy boy he'd been crossed her mind. She'd thought him simply quiet. Could he really have been lovesick?

He brushed past her, walked into the kitchen and got a can of beer out of the refrigerator. Popping the top, he took a hefty swallow, then set the can on the counter. "Yeah, a long, long time ago. My first love. It was more like senseless worship. Unfortunately, unlike most first loves, this one didn't fade quietly into memory. I never forgot you."

Shannon's hand went to her forehead, and a tiny laugh escaped her lips. "Blake, that's the most... incredible, romantic, and...far-fetched thing I've ever heard!"

"You're right. I'd kept this mental picture of you in my head all those years. Then the day I met you here, the day before I bought the farm—I didn't just happen to be here. I'd been waiting, hoping you'd come. And that afternoon I discovered that my infatuation with Shannon Jameson had come to an end because she no longer existed. I can't tell you how relieved I was. I was free of you at last. No more memories.''

Shannon was a little taken aback. He'd confessed himself in and out of love with her in the same breath.

He lifted the can to his mouth and took another drink. "Then you called. I knew, I knew I shouldn't let you come back here!"

"That's the reason you didn't want me here?" she asked breathlessly. "You...thought you might...fall for me...again?"

"That just about sums it up. I'm right back in the same goddamned mess." He slammed the beer can down on the counter. "There's something basically wrong with a man who stays obsessed with one woman for eighteen years."

She gave a little cry. "Oh, Blake, do you have any idea how that stuns me? Or how absolutely wonderful it sounds?" In a burst of emotion, propelled by an exquisitely warm feeling that ran from her toes to her spinning head, she swept around the bar, crossed the kitchen and slid her arms around his waist, burying her face against his chest.

For a moment Blake simply stood with his arms at his sides, startled. Then, as if he suddenly remembered what one was supposed to do in a situation like this, his arms went around her and tightened. Her hair brushed against his chin. His heart was pounding so frantically he was sure she could hear it; to his own ears it sounded like the beating of a dozen drums. The reality of Shannon in his arms surpassed all his dreams. In a minute, if he could gather his wits, he guessed he would kiss her, but right now he just wanted to hold her, feel her. . . .

It was a shock to Shannon's love-starved body to feel his firm masculine length pressed tightly against her. Her hands inched up his back, rubbing and petting. He felt wonderful, all strong and sinewy. His warmth seeped into her veins, and she felt strangely weak and strong at once. Her petting movements stopped. She withdrew her arms from under his; her hands crept up the hard wall of his chest and locked behind his neck. She lifted her face, arched her neck, and their lips met.

This was nothing like the restrained kiss they had shared that night in the motel. This one began almost brutally, with pent-up hunger, and ended in the sweetest kind of passion. Wild, breathtaking, wonderful.

When they parted, they stared at one another with eyes full of astonishment, as though they had just discovered some marvelously innovative way of expressing desire. "Oh, Blake . . . ?"

"Shannon . . ." His voice was thick with emotion. "You'd damned well better think this through. I've waited over eighteen years to get close to you, and if you think I'm going to be satisfied with hugs and kisses, think again." One hand went to the nape of her neck, and his thumb traced her jawline. He used the back of his other hand to stroke her breasts as lightly as the brush of a butterfly's wings, more thrilling than overt fondling could ever have been.

"Blake . . . there's so much I'd like to tell you . . . things I've thought about . . . I just don't know how." She leaned forward and touched the pulse point at the base of his throat with her lips, then the underside of his chin. She heard his breath catch. Her arms went around him again, and they stood locked in a powerful embrace, content for the moment with one another's nearness.

Shannon propped her chin on his shoulder and pressed her cheek against his, loving its rough texture. Her gaze traveled to a short corridor that led to a bedroom. The door was open, revealing an unmade double bed. Blake's, she was sure. A shirt she recognized was slung over the foot of it. Lost in a sensuous fog, she thought that untidy, rumpled bed was the most inviting sight she'd ever seen. All her previous romantic fantasies came unbidden to mind. Had it been physically possible for her to do so, she would have liked to sweep him up in her arms, dramatically carry him down that hall, toss him on the bed and ravish him! The picture in her mind's eye was so tempting—and hilarious—that she couldn't suppress a chuckle.

Blake held her away from him slightly, giving her a quizzical look. "Something's funny?"

She nodded, her eyes bright, her mouth smiling provocatively.

"Then let me in on the joke."

At that moment there was some noise at the front door. Shannon jumped back so far that her rump hit the bar. Blake's eyes flew to the door. It opened, and Randy stepped inside. He glanced apprehensively from Blake to Shannon and back to Blake. Both of them stared at him with weird expressions.

He stood for a silent moment, eyes resting on some point between them, apparently steeling himself for whatever was coming. The silence lasted another few seconds.

Then Blake cleared his throat. "Shower before supper, son."

Relief washed over the boy's face. "Yeah, sure," he said and bolted for his bedroom and bath in the front of the trailer.

Once the boy was gone Shannon looked at Blake with yearning. "I...I guess I'd better get to the house and finish the potato salad," she said. "It'll be time for supper... soon."

"Yeah, I guess so." He took a step toward her, remembered Randy and stepped back. "See you down at the house in a bit."

"Sure." She pushed herself away from the bar and walked to the front door. Just as she reached for the knob she heard his voice behind her.

"Shannon."

She turned. "Yes."

A smile twitched the corners of his mouth. "Today's just begun."

She gulped and nodded. "I ... guess it has."

"Do me a favor, will you? Take that thing off." He pointed to her right hand.

Shannon glanced down at the sparkling ring. She hadn't thought of it as a wedding ring in a long time. "All right," she said, then opened the door and left. She half-ran, half-skipped all the way to the house, like a child. As she passed the vegetable garden, Homer uncurled his body, hissed and made for the crape myrtle.

"As you were, Homer," she said, not breaking stride. "This afternoon I even love you."

SUPPER THAT NIGHT was a palpitatingly strained occasion. Randy was even more uncommunicative than

usual—he was still pouting—and this was one time
Shannon would have welcomed even his monosyllables. Far too much silence lay over the table. She and
Blake valiantly strived to make casual conversation,
but every time their eyes made contact, sensual vi-
brations sizzled between them like electric currents
and words died in their throats. Shannon's nerves
were stretched to the snapping point.

She was certain Blake intended coming back to the
house as soon as Randy was asleep for the night.
Today has just begun, he'd said. There was the long,
lovely night ahead of them. The thought brought on
such a feeling of heady excitement that she had some
difficulty conducting herself with informal decorum
during the meal.

It still was a bit unreal to her. During all those
years with Vic, both the early golden ones and the
later restless ones, there had been someone thinking
about her, caring for her! Her mind could hardly as-
similate it. The man she had dreamed about lately
had dreamed about her years ago!

Blake and Randy left immediately after the dishes
were done. Shannon passed the hours after supper as
best she could. She didn't watch television and she
didn't read, although she tried to do both. Her eyes
strayed to her watch so often that the evening passed
with agonizing slowness. She knew Randy was supposed to be in bed by nine-thirty, but she wondered
how often that schedule was adhered to. And how
long did it take him to actually fall asleep?

Nine o'clock came and went. Shannon's pulses
were galloping. She left the kitchen door unlocked
and went upstairs. She turned bathing into a leisurely, luxurious experience, shampooed and dried

her hair, and afterwards she took time to study herself in the mirror over the sink. A high rise of color suffused her cheeks; her face seemed to glow from within. She walked into the bedroom and slipped a diaphanous nightgown over her head, then got into bed and waited.

This was something brand new to her, and she was unsure of everything but her desire. That she was very certain about, but everything else...

Should she have waited for him downstairs, she wondered. Was waiting expectantly in bed a bit much? Should she leave the bedside lamp on? She thought a moment and decided against it. There was a full moon, and its light bathed the room in delicate shadows, creating a dreamy, romantic effect.

What would he say when he came to her? How did one go about conducting an affair? Was everything left to instinct or were there rules to follow? There had been no affair before she married Vic. In fact, they'd only been completely alone a dozen times before they married, for he'd had an entourage that followed him wherever he went. On her wedding night she'd lain with stiff, locked muscles, waiting for her new husband to relieve her of her virginity. It wasn't an experience she recalled with pleasure.

She was acutely aware of her limited expertise. She had read enough racy novels and had listened to enough of her friends' uninhibited gossip to realize that marrying a man twenty-one years her senior had caused her to miss something. Maybe many somethings. She'd told herself that sex wasn't all that important, but maybe she'd been wrong. Maybe it was life's pounding core.

Her entire body tingled and hummed. A primitive excitement roared through her, then quickly died as a new doubt entered her mind. *What if he doesn't come at all?*

THIS IS NO ILLUSION, Blake thought incredulously, overcome with the intensity of his emotions. Shannon and tonight were real. He wasn't going to wake up in the morning and find it all had been a damned dream.

He glanced at the kitchen clock. Almost nine. God, it had been a long evening! His gaze shifted to his companion on the sofa. Randy was sprawled, immersed in his favorite TV show, some godawful, noisy police thing that Blake was watching solely to pass the time. The hero, a young cop, was single-handedly, and with very little trouble, solving an international crime that had baffled the FBI and Scotland Yard for years. Nonsense.

But, he conceded, no more nonsensical than the stuff he'd been addicted to at fourteen.

His mind wandered, and he missed the show's climax. The announcer told them to stay tuned for more, and a commercial came on. Blake reached for the remote control and switched off the set. "Enough of that," he said. "Go on and get ready for bed."

"Aw, I'm not sleepy," Randy complained.

"You will be at six in the morning. Go on now." Getting to his feet, Blake went into the kitchen for yet another drink of water.

Randy eyed him quizzically. "How come you're so fidgety?"

"I'm not fidgety."

"Sure you are. You must'a gotten a hundred glasses of water tonight."

"Oh, I guess I've got a lot on my mind."

"Yeah? Like what?"

Blake set down the glass and looked at him squarely. "Like why this kid who I thought had so much good sense would do something as stupid as picking that tomato."

Randy stared morosely ahead. "I was wondering when you were going to get around to that."

"It really was dumb. More like something a six-year-old would do."

"Yeah." For a moment the boy looked properly chastised. Then he displayed the hint of a smile. "Boy, was she mad!"

"That's not funny!" Blake snapped, and Randy's smile quickly vanished. "Tomorrow you're going to apologize to Shannon."

"Aw, Blake..."

"Do it! I should have had you do it tonight, but I...forgot. And I'm going to ask you to do something else for me."

"Like what?" the boy asked.

"I want you to be nicer to Shannon, Randy. She'd like to be your friend, and if you'd give her half a chance, I think you'd like her."

"Why should I? You like her enough for both of us."

Blake chose to ignore that for the time being. He thought carefully before he spoke. "Son, there'll always be people I like and like to have around. That doesn't mean they'll affect our relationship. I want you to remember that. Now, go on and get ready for bed."

"Oh, all right." Randy reluctantly got to his feet and ambled to his room. Blake again glanced at the clock. Randy dawdled at bedtime, just like any kid, but once his head hit the pillow he usually fell fast asleep. He could only hope that would hold true tonight. His heart was thumping with anticipation.

He walked into the living room and turned off the lamp over the television set. As he passed through the kitchen he paused to close the curtains, but not before looking toward the house. The bedroom light was on. Molten lava pumped through his veins. Was she waiting for him shyly, expectantly, apprehensively, what?

He went into his bedroom, undressed and headed for the shower. Sharp needles of water pummeled his skin but did nothing to cool his heated body. He washed his hair, towel-dried it, then shaved, using a blade instead of an electric razor. A splash of aftershave, and he returned to the bedroom to dress in clean jeans and shirt, not bothering with underwear. When he walked back into the kitchen he couldn't see a light coming from the front bedroom. Checking, he discovered Randy was in bed. He waited in the doorway a minute until he was satisfied that the boy was asleep. Soundlessly he opened the front door and closed it behind him.

As he hurried across the moonlit grounds toward the house he noticed that the upstairs light was off. What if she'd gone to sleep? What if he'd misread all those smoldering looks during dinner? What if it all turned out to be just another of his wishful fantasies? He was going to feel like the biggest fool ever if that kitchen door was locked.

CHAPTER TEN

IT WAS TEN AFTER TEN when Shannon heard the back door open and close. She knew because her eyes had hardly strayed from the bedside clock. A mixture of relief and apprehension swept through her as Blake's footsteps echoed through the house. Then she heard his heavy tread on the stairs. Her breath hung in her throat; she felt as though she were strangling.

After what seemed minutes but could only have been seconds, he stood silhouetted in the doorway. Moonlight streaming through the bedroom window illuminated the angles of his face. Sparks glittered in his dark eyes. Shannon sat up in bed, her own eyes wide, spellbound at the sight of him. Tremors raced along her spine. A tormenting sensation began in the bottom of her stomach and spread between her thighs. Still Blake didn't move. He stood as if paralyzed, one hand clutching the doorjamb. When she could stand it no longer, she held out one beckoning arm to him.

That gesture galvanized him into action. To Blake the distance from the door to the bed seemed like a yawning mile. He couldn't cross the space fast enough. Currents of energy surged inside him. But something happened when he sat on the edge of the bed and took her in his arms. He suddenly felt as uncertain, inexperienced and shy as he had at seventeen, when he'd adored her silently. Thunder-struck with emotion, he thought, My God, it's really going to happen!

How did one go about making love to an idol? All his previous experience with women counted for nothing, for she was no ordinary woman. In his mind she even transcended the extraordinary. For reasons unfathomable to him, fate had decreed that she was the only one. He still couldn't believe they were there together. It had taken half his life to get to this point, and he wished he could stop the hands of time and make the night last forever.

Pulling inches away from her, he touched her face gently, as though it were made of spun glass. He studied her features, he caressed her cheek, brow, mouth and chin. Her thick lashes dipped briefly under his unabashed scrutiny, and for a moment she looked exactly like the young girl he had fallen in love with all those years ago. His heart seemed to swell to twice its normal size. To think that in all the world she was the only one! It boggled his mind.

He bent his head and his mouth touched hers. Her lips were parted, cool and soft. He remembered now; they tasted like honey. Deepening the kiss, he was delighted by her spontaneous response. Their lips clung, parted, clung again. Then he gathered her to him and nestled her head on his shoulder. He closed his eyes and explored the gentle sweep of her shoulders, and the soft curves of her back with his hands. He was appalled that they trembled so.

Shannon simply melted against him. He smelled like soap, aftershave and shampoo, a very special scent that clung to her nostrils and made her light-headed. The hair at the nape of his neck was damp;

he must have showered and shaved just before coming to her.

For a long time she held him, waiting breathlessly for his first overture. It wasn't immediately forthcoming. His exploring hands stopped and rested on her back. He was so still, so absolutely still. It came to her in a flash of insight that he would be at least as awed and uncertain as she was, for he had waited such a long time. So, summoning up a boldness she wouldn't have dreamed she possessed, she fumbled with the buttons of his shirt, her nimble fingers releasing each from its hole. She pushed the shirt off his shoulders, down his arms, and flung it to the floor. Her restless hands then had free access to the satisfying warmth of his heart.

Shaken by a thrilling sensation he'd never before experienced, Blake allowed her a moment of examination. They shared quick, light, nibbling kisses as her roaming fingers tantalized him. His senses flared, and he responded by closing a hand over the fullness of one breast. Gently he massaged until he heard her soft moan. Then he pushed himself away from her slightly, and bent to take off his shoes and socks. Standing, he unzipped his jeans.

Shannon watched in fascination as he undressed. She stared at him as though she'd never seen a naked man before. Had she been a man she thought she would have envied him his physique. He was a perfect specimen of masculinity, like a prize bull in the very prime of is power. "Blake," she murmured, "you're beautiful!"

It was such a simple, heartfelt remark. Her words, coupled with the look on her face, sent Blake's mind reeling. There was so much he would have liked to say to her, soft words of love that he uttered so fluently in his fantasies. Now, however, he was as nonverbal as he'd been in his teens, when the mere sight of her had been enough to tangle his tongue.

"Thanks." He managed that one choked, unremarkable word. Then he was beside her under the covers.

His hand rested on her thighs, then moved up her hips, deftly carrying her nightgown past her breasts and over her head. To his gratification, she raised herself slightly to facilitate its removal. Then she laid her head back on the pillow and allowed him to feast his eyes on her.

Dear God, she was as gorgeous as he'd always known she would be! Her breasts were as firm as a girl's. There were no marks, scars or other imperfections to mar what to his mind was a flawless body. With an expression of lust tempered by wonder, he curved her against him, and the sensation of her warm flesh pressed to his sent tiny eruptions exploding through him. His arousal was complete, and he wanted to take her, make her his; he deserved that after all these years. He thought he could be forgiven a little ravishment.

But tonight had to be perfect, or as perfect as a mere mortal man who was full and pulsating with longing could make it. He nuzzled her neck, buried his head against her breasts and teased a rosy bud grown hard with desire. She slithered along his hard length and pressed her thighs to his. He thought everything inside him had shattered into a thousand pieces.

"Blake," she whispered on a suspended sigh.

"Oh, Shannon, I feel such a need to make up for lost time." He wanted to murmur endearments in her ear seductively, but words which should have flowed got garbled in his throat. What came out sounded like "sweet, sweet, sweet."

Shannon arched her body; her hips wiggled seductively. She ran her fingers down his back to his buttocks, loving the doeskin-like texture of his skin and the roughness of the coarse hair on his chest and legs. She found the niche of his body where she fit so perfectly. All this sensitive foreplay was new to her, and she wanted it to go on and on. His hands, lips and tongue worked together to entrap her in a magical spell. She wrapped her arms around him and bound him sleekly with her legs. The fire burned out of control.

She wanted this man to take her so that she could give him the greatest pleasure he had ever known. If he had loved her all those years he would have fantasized about her; now she wanted all those fantasies to come true. Was she capable? She drifted into a haze of pure pleasure and urged herself to hold back nothing, to give herself fully and completely as she had never done before.

Finally there was nothing to do but to give in to the tumult raging inside them. He covered her body with his own, cradled her in his arms and smiled down into her upturned face. He took her with unbridled passion; then they fell into sweet, intense lovemaking with the ease of long-time lovers. Though he was almost wild with emotion, Blake took pains to make sure his possession was sensitive and caring, not demanding and obsessive. He showed as much concern for her longing and desire as for his own. He took the time to make her feel she deserved to experience joy, too. As incredible as it was, Blake seemed to sense her need to prolong the enchantment.

Suddenly his movements stopped; he stilled in her arms. "Blake?" she cried in desperation, her body urging him to continue.

"God...I forgot. Shannon, do you use anything?"

Oh, Lord, she'd forgotten, too. She'd never used birth control in her life. "No...I'm sorry..."

"Then I'm going to have to interrupt this, and it's damned near going to kill me." He thrust again. "Relax...don't worry. Just enjoy. I'll be careful."

That lovemaking could be expressed as this kind of mutual union was an extraordinary revelation for Shannon. Before she had always felt the giver of pleasure, never the receiver. She almost reached the summit, teetered, then took the final step. Golden fire spread out from the core of her femininity.

Blake had waited to see the first mark of ecstasy cross her face before giving in to his own clamoring need. He withdrew from her, and their lovemaking ended in one finite moment, overwhelming in its intensity. They clung together long after the fervor ceased. Shannon lay in the fierce domination of his arms, stunned and sated, lost in the bewitchment of the first real fulfillment she had ever known. It had been a glorious adventure, a voyage of discovery, and she hated for sleep to come. She didn't want to lose the magic.

SLEEP DID COME, however, and when they awoke some hours later they were two astonished people who were dumbfounded over what had happened to them.

"I'm tempted to believe we just discovered something rare and wonderful," Shannon murmured, "something the rest of the world hasn't caught onto yet."

Blake chuckled.

"It's a cliché, I know, but…it really was never like that for me before." Her fingers played lightly with the mat of hair on his chest. "I didn't even know it could be like that. You are magnificent."

"It's very gratifying to hear you say that. There's not a man alive who doesn't like to be told he's the best ever."

"Well, before your chest puffs up too much, I think I should be honest and tell you that you're only the second man I've ever been to bed with."

"I suspected as much," he said seriously. "There's an innocence about you that I wouldn't normally associate with a woman who's been married fifteen years."

"I feel as though there's someone else in this bed with you, someone I don't even know."

"Well, if you knew her, you'd like her."

Blake propped himself on one elbow and looked down at her. He brushed her hair away from her face and kissed her gently on the forehead. The force of what he felt for her staggered him. There had been so many women before her, but she was the only one who had possessed him. Now he'd never be free of her. He didn't want to be free of her. And even in his present state of contentment, that knowledge frightened him more than anything every had. "May I tell you something, lovely lady? In my fantasies I've made love to you about a thousand times. But the reality far outshone the fantasy."

She traced the outline of his mouth with a fingertip. "Were you really in love with me all those years ago?"

"Besotted."

"That seems so incredible," she sighed. "To think I never noticed."

"I worked hard to keep you from noticing. I was such a kid, and you were the first soft, beautiful thing that had ever come into my life. I was in love with you and scared to death of you at the same time."

She recalled how shy he'd been, how little he'd talked. "I just thought you were the silent type. I wonder what would have happened if I had noticed."

"You probably would have shied away from me. You were more interested in dancing than in boys. I hated every fellow who ever came to take you out, but you really didn't give them much attention. At least we were friends."

"I was kind of a misfit, you know."

"No, I didn't know. You, a misfit?"

"Not an oddball or outcast or anything like that. Just different. I was more interested in dancing lessons than in trying out for cheerleader. I had my mind set on Broadway, and all the other kids had theirs set on the Friday night game. Just different."

"I wouldn't have noticed. I thought you were perfect."

"These past eighteen years, Blake . . . I did think about you from time to time, wondered how you were, if you were married, that sort of thing."

"I would have been pleased to know that."

"I've thought of home and my childhood a lot in the last few years," she confessed.

"Why?"

"Age maybe."

Blake chuckled. "I doubt that."

"Then I don't know why," she said rather wistfully.

His head went back to the pillow, and it was Shannon's turn to prop on an elbow and stare down at him. He looked utterly blissful, almost boyish. "Blake, you said...when I was here in April that you were relieved that the attraction was gone."

"That didn't last long, did it?"

"When I came back this time, you seemed so...oh, hostile is the word, I suppose."

"Hostile? Really?"

"And stand-offish."

"How else could I fight the attraction?" It was a simple question that didn't require an answer.

"You know, we've talked a lot about me but almost never about you. Tell me about the last eighteen years, Blake."

"You know about most of them. Hard-working years. That's about it."

She smiled. "I know that isn't so. A man who looks like you do? There must have been women. A lot?"

"Why do women always want to know that?"

"Do we?"

"Always."

"That tells me you've known a lot of women."

"Oh...some. A few."

"Anyone special? Did you ever come close to marrying?"

Blake hesitated. A slight frown creased his forehead. Had he ever come close to marrying Norma? He'd thought about it, but she'd taken care of that before they'd actually come close to the altar. "No," he told Shannon. "Not really."

Shannon had noticed the hesitation and the frown. There had been someone; she was sure of it. "Forgive my feminine curiosity, Blake. I shouldn't have asked. There's no reason for you to tell me anything."

He slid an arm beneath her shoulders and pulled her to him. "I really don't mind talking about it. It was a long time ago. Her name was Norma."

"How long ago was this?"

"Oh . . . fifteen years. I was twenty-two and fresh out of the service."

"If you remember her name and how old you were," Shannon said softly, "then she was special."

"Special? Yes, I guess you could say Norma was special."

"Don't tell me about her . . . unless you want to," Shannon said, alive with curiosity, dying to know everything about Norma.

"It might do me good to talk about her."

"Why? Is there a hangover of some sort?"

"Yeah, I guess there is."

Shannon snuggled against him and listened alertly while Blake told her about the woman named Norma.

"I'd been in business just a few months when I met her at a party in Charlotte. I guess we'd been going together about six months when she told me she was pregnant. At first I panicked...that was the only way to describe it. I really liked her, but I knew I wasn't wildly in love, and I was terrified of getting married. However, I started scraping together all the money I could. I don't know exactly what I planned to do with it, just get it together in order to take care of her and the baby. My mind wouldn't go any further than that. I'd managed to come up with about five thousand dollars when I showed her my savings book. I remember...she had the funniest look on her face when she asked me what it was for.''

He paused and frowned thoughtfully. It had been a long time since he'd dredged up the facts all at once, and the picture he recalled wasn't pleasant. ''I told her it was for whatever we needed...doctor bills, hospital, whatever. I hadn't exactly mentioned marriage, but somewhere in the back of my mind I thought it was inevitable. Then Norma said that marriage scared hell out of her. I didn't blame her; it scared hell out of me, too. I...told her as much.''

Shannon tensed as she waited for him to continue his story. She knew he'd never been married and had no children. What had happened to Norma?

Blake heaved a heavy sigh. ''What she really wanted, she told me, was to go back home for a while and think things through. Home was...oh, I forget, some little burg up near the Virginia border. Of course, she'd have to quit her job, and she didn't have any money...Norma never had any money. So I gave her some, almost all of it, in fact. I expected to hear from her in a few days, but a couple of weeks went by.''

Shannon noticed that his voice sounded more burdened with each passing sentence. She lay very still and listened as he poured out what had obviously been kept bottled up for years.

"I didn't get a telephone call, which is what I expected. I got a letter. Funny, I can still remember it word for word. 'Dear Blake,' it read, 'Thanks to the money you gave me, I got rid of my problem. You've been a dear, and I'm sure you'd do the 'honorable' thing. But I'm only twenty-one, and I don't want to get married. I know there are places in this world where an unmarried mother isn't at all scandalous, but my hometown isn't one of them, and I've decided to stay here. Take care. Love, Norma.' That was it."

Shannon raised herself up to look at him. "You never saw her again?"

He shook his head.

"And it still bothers you. Why, Blake? You didn't do anything."

"Didn't I? What if I hadn't given her so much money? What if I'd only given her gas money and a couple hundred bucks to tide her over?"

Shannon shrugged. "I don't know. What if?"

"She probably knew I didn't really want to get married. What if she thought…that by giving her so much money I was suggesting she…do what she did?"

Shannon gave careful thought to what she was going to say. "I think she did what she wanted to do. I think she would have done it under any circumstances, whether you'd given her money or not. She would have found a way. This isn't the 1950s, you know. There are places to go. Women almost always make the choice themselves. And it doesn't sound to me as though Norma was any crazier about the idea of marriage than you were.''

"I've often wondered about that, too. There was such a look in her eyes when we talked about it. Disappointment, I think, although at the time I was too rattled to see it as that. All her talk about not wanting to get married...maybe she just wanted to set my mind at ease.''

"Maybe, maybe not. You'll never know, will you? Why the guilt?''

"I don't know. I was terribly depressed for days after getting that letter. I kept thinking of how much I'd always wanted a family. But I also felt an enormous sense of...relief.'' He sounded deeply troubled.

"Ah...it was the relief that made you feel guilty.''

"I had bought my way out of an unpleasant situation.''

"No. You gave her some money, and she used it the way she saw fit. You learned about it after the fact. Don't waste your time on guilt, Blake. It'll almost kill you if you do. There was nothing you could have done to prevent the abortion.''

"I wonder. I was careless, and she suffered for it.''

"Well, she was careless, too. Certainly a woman has to share the 'blame,' if it can be called that. You both were terribly young, and we all make mistakes—do things in our twenties that we'd never do in our thirties.''

Shannon was truly moved. Somewhere in her feminine psyche she had harbored the belief that affairs of the heart never touched men as deeply as they did women. Men enjoyed women easily, and forgot them just as easily...or so she'd thought. Yet here was Blake, disturbed over a youthful indiscretion. It spoke volumes about his nature, she thought.

Several moments of silence followed. Blake gently stroked her hair, kissed her temple, and then asked, "What about you, Shannon? Did you make mistakes? If you were twenty-one again, would you do the same things all over again?"

She quietly laid in the circle of his arms and thought before answering. What he was asking was if she would marry Vic again, and that wasn't an easy one to answer. The resentment hadn't always existed. There had been so many good times. If he had dominated her, if she had lost her identity somewhere along the way... well, that might have been more her fault than Vic's.

A picture of herself at twenty-one came to mind. Living in that godawful walk-up with Marianne Henderson and Sara McCall, pinching pennies, skipping breakfast, praying the new hose didn't get a run, eating all that calorie-laden Italian food in the kitchen at Papa Perone's because it was free. Looking back, it didn't seem she'd had a care in the world then, even though she had lived at near-poverty level. But she was sure there had been difficult moments she didn't remember. That kind of life probably was carefree only in retrospect. If she hadn't landed the spot on Vic's show, she no doubt would have endured the gypsy life for another year or two, then gotten discouraged and come back to South Carolina. That usually was the pattern. Marianne had come back, married an accountant and moved to Tennessee; Sara had gone home to Ohio. How could that existence compare with the life Vic had given her?

"Probably," she said finally, truthfully. If she were twenty-one, she would again be dazzled by Vic Parelli and all the "good things" he'd dangled in front of her. She wouldn't be able to help herself.

Blake flinched. He hadn't wanted such a pat answer. He'd hoped she would open up, tell him exactly how she felt about her life in New York. He'd hoped she would tell him her deep-down feelings about her husband. He wanted to know what he was up against. At least he thought he did.

Oh, what the hell? He rolled over, pulling her beneath him. His strong body covered every inch of hers. "Why are we talking about such somber things?"

"I can't imagine. How did the conversation even get started?"

"Womanlike, you were curious about my past."

She smiled seductively. "I'm not curious anymore," she whispered. "It doesn't matter. I don't care about anything but right now."

His hands sculpted her flesh, moved over her throat, her shoulders, and down to her breasts. He kissed her over and over and murmured her name in a litany of love. When he entered her Shannon was once again astonished at the force of passion he unleashed in her. She rejoiced in his possession. She felt deliciously wanton, wicked, insatiable . . . and wonderfully young, desirable and free. He made her aware of the joy she was bringing him, and she wanted to think that in all the world there wasn't another woman who could make him feel this way. If he truly had loved her for eighteen years, maybe she was right.

BLAKE SLIPPED AWAY sometime during the night in order to be properly in his own room when Randy awoke in the morning. It was all he could do to stumble out of bed when the alarm clock rang, but once up he felt wonderful. While Randy dressed for school, he fixed his breakfast, whistling all the while.

"How come you're in such a good mood this morning?" Randy wanted to know.

"Oh, I don't know. Looks like it's going to be a gorgeous day."

The boy squinted out the window beside the dining table. "Looks to me like it's going to rain."

"That's what I mean. We need some rain."

And Randy shrugged away unpredictable adult behavior.

When the boy was finally on the bus, Blake sprinted across the grounds, into the back door of the farmhouse and up the stairs, shedding his clothes along the way. Slipping into bed beside the still-sleeping Shannon, he stretched full-length beside her, his body glorying in the satin warmth of hers. For once he wasn't going to think about any one of the dozen things he needed to do. His mind was focused only on the reality of the woman beside him. Smiling contentedly, he fell asleep to relive last night's ecstasy...but not before making a mental note to visit a drugstore before the day was over.

Shannon slept until eight. Awakening by slow degrees, she was first aware of Blake beside her. The warmth of his body seeped into her veins, giving her life. Energy surged through her, as though a switch had been flipped on. Turning carefully, she looked into his blissful face and a soft smile curved her mouth. Resisting the urge to capture his lips with hers, she slid out of bed, dressed and made for the kitchen, stepping over Blake's hastily discarded clothes on the way. She was ravenous! The coffee was made by the time he ambled downstairs. She prepared a breakfast worthy of two lumberjacks, and they ate every bit of it. Afterwards they drove into Greenville and stopped first at a drugstore, then at a sporting goods store to purchase basketball paraphernalia. It rained intermittently throughout the morning, but by noon the sun was out. Blake treated her to another visit to the soul food restaurant she'd enjoyed so much in April. They were back home by two o'clock that afternoon. When Randy returned from school Blake had the pole, backboard and hoop in place beside the drive. The boy's reaction was the nearest thing to uncontained glee that Shannon had ever seen. From that moment to dusk, interrupted only by supper, Randy was too preoccupied with his new basketball set to notice the private looks that passed between Shannon and Blake.

But any less occupied person who cared to observe could have seen that here were two people engaged in a celebration of life.

THE DAYS THAT FOLLOWED were dreamlike in their rapture, the nights even more so as their budding desire burst into full bloom. Every night Blake went to the farmhouse after Randy was alseep. His lovemaking captivated Shannon, who had discovered there was an entire world of emotions she'd never before experienced. The intimacy she had shared with Vic paled by comparison.

She wasn't sure what she was feeling was love, but it was an honest passion that made her glad she was alive and female. She felt limp, glutted with happiness. Blake had unearthed a taproot of sensuality in her that staggered her and delighted him. When they were together, every part of her came alive. She didn't waste a moment's time thinking about the future; she lived only for now. As the days passed, she began to feel something like the person she'd always wanted to be—someone daring enough to allow herself to be loved with carefree abandon.

On the farm it was easy to hold the world at bay. They took long walks in the woods, as they had done as teenagers. They sat by the stream and talked about everything under the sun except the future. They even made love there one golden afternoon, capriciously, almost furtively. It had been a delightful sexual romp; afterward they had rolled in the grass and laughed like children. My God, Shannon had thought, where has this wanton side of me been all these years?

They saw virtually no one except each other...and Randy, of course, who was the only jarring note in the idyll they'd created. As young as he was, he still seemed to sense that the relationship between Shannon and Blake had turned a corner. He dealt with that by withdrawing from Shannon more than ever, by demanding more of Blake's attention, by being hurt over any real or imagined slight. He was maddening and exasperating, yet his affection for Blake was so real and touching that she couldn't help liking him a little. What she felt more than anything was a sense of inadequacy over not being able to reach the boy. And she worried because Blake was being torn this way and that.

Blake loved Shannon, and he loved Randy. It distressed him that the boy remained so openly hostile to the woman he loved. "This thing has to be resolved, Shannon. I can't imagine what's going on in the kid's head, but I'm going to have a long, serious talk with him."

"I wish you wouldn't," she said.

"Why not, for God's sakes?"

"What would it prove? There's no doubt in my mind that Randy will do anything you ask him to, even pretend to like me. No, love, his acceptance, if it comes at all, will have to be heartfelt."

Having never had brothers or sons, she knew nothing about boys Randy's age. But somehow, some way she would win him over. For Blake's sake and for hers. Randy became a challenge, and she'd discovered, to her surprise and satisfaction, that she could rise up and meet challenges. Something obstinate inside her wouldn't rest until she had won Randy's friendship.

CHAPTER ELEVEN

THE TELEPHONE'S SHRILL RING interrupted Shannon's thoughts. She switched off her typewriter and hurried into the bedroom next door to answer it.

"Hello."

"Shannon."

"Jerry!"

"What in the devil are you doing down there?" Jerry's voice boomed from the other end of the line. "No one's heard a word from you."

"Sorry, Jerry, I've been meaning to call, but..." Shannon let the sentence die. She hadn't stayed in touch with anyone but the household staff, who assured her that all was going well. She didn't even have to be concerned with their salaries or the bills, for Jerry took care of everything. Regretfully, she realized how negligent she'd been not to have called him, once or twice at least. "I've been working," she said.

"Well, how about staying in touch? I saw Anthony Thompson yesterday, and he'd like you to give him a progress report."

"All right, I'll call him today, promise."

"When are you coming home?"

"I'm...not sure."

"You've been gone two months!"

"I realize that." She hadn't, though. The idyllic days followed, one after the other, and time had gotten away from her. The manuscript was nearing completion. She could have it finished in a couple of weeks if she worked diligently. But it was so easy, too easy to set it aside and do whatever Blake had on his mind for the day. She confessed to herself that she was dawdling, prolonging the rapture.

"It won't be long now, Jerry," she'd said. And it wouldn't be. She had to go back.

"Here's Peg."

"Shannon!" a very familiar feminine voice trilled.

"Peg, it's so good to hear from you."

"I'm dying of curiosity. How's the book coming?"

"Pretty good, Peg. Yes, I think it's coming along nicely."

"Finish it quickly, will you? I'm expiring of boredom without you."

Shannon laughed. "What's the matter? Did you find yourself with an idle half hour last week?"

"Much more than that," Peg said. "Oh, Shannon, I must tell you something! Remember Susie Cunningham? Well, let me tell you what happened to her in Chicago...."

For the next few minutes Shannon listened in amusement while Peg filled her in on all the local gossip, and there was an astonishing amount of it. It often had amazed her that her friend knew so much private information about all their acquaintances, but Peg's gossip was only frivolous, never malicious. She simply seemed to possess unusual interest in people and the things that happened to them. There were some in their social circle who regarded

Peg's chatter as artificial and shallow, but Shannon never had.

Couldn't I give her an earful, she thought. *Peg would be agog if she knew about Blake.* But all along Shannon knew she would never tell even Peg about the affair. It was the most glorious, most private part of her life. She didn't want to share it with anyone.

Shannon listened while her friend chatted away until Jerry reminded his wife that the call was long distance. Once she and Peg had hung up, she consulted her address book for Anthony Thompson's number and called him. For the next twenty minutes or so she did more listening than talking. The publisher was full of plans for the promotion of Vic's biography—radio and newspaper interviews for syndication, autograph parties around the country, an extraordinary thirty-six-copy floor display for bookstores, and—the publisher paused for dramatic emphasis—an appearance on the Johnny Carson show!

Shannon didn't know what she was feeling—disbelief, dismay... a little excitement? It hadn't occurred to her that she would have to publicize the book, and it wasn't the sort of thing she would look forward to doing. She certainly balked at the Carson show.

"Please scratch that, Anthony. I'd be very bad at that sort of thing. Besides, authors are usually treated like stepchildren on those shows."

Anthony sounded disappointed. "Well, let's say the Carson show is negotiable. You might feel differently once you've had a taste of all the publicity."

"Oh, Anthony, how wrong you are!"

SHANNON LET THE SCREEN DOOR close behind her and stepped out onto the front porch. Blake was sitting sprawled in a wicker rocker, watching Randy as he dribbled a basketball up and down the driveway, sank a basket, dribbled, and sank a basket.

"Want some coffee?" she asked.

"No, I don't think so, thanks."

Shannon pulled another rocker next to his and sat down. Breathing deeply of the soft evening air, she closed her eyes for a minute. This was the time of day she'd grown to love best, when the heat of the day was replaced by the coolness of night and earthy aromas permeated the air. It had rained most of the week, but tonight was clear, and the smell of humus was even more pronounced, for Blake had spent a good part of the day tilling beds around the house in anticipation of the fall planting season. He'd ordered hundreds of dollars worth of shrubs and ornamentals. "The plants are something I can afford," he'd said, making reference to the power station that was still a future dream. "This time next year these grounds are going to be something to see."

Her thoughts abruptly braked. Where would she be this time next year? Flitting around the country promoting her book? She couldn't imagine herself actually doing something like that, but if it had to be done, she supposed she would do it. It would mean becoming Mrs. Vic Parelli again, day after day— something else she wasn't particularly looking forward to. She had been existing in a kind of euphoria, where the past was forgotten and tomorrow would never come. The euphoria had been shaken up a bit by Jerry's call and the conversation with Anthony Thompson. They had reminded her of her obligations.

Shannon opened her eyes and let her gaze wander around her surroundings. The farm was a warm, hospitable retreat, but she wondered if it was the place for her. She spent most of every day writing about Vic and the life on Long Island and had suddenly realized that she'd lived in New York almost as long as she had lived on this farm. There she had a home and friends, a sophisticated sort of life so alien to this bucolic existence. And who could predict what new avenues of interest would open up with the publication of the book?

So why am I so drawn to this place? Giving Blake a sidelong glance, she had her answer. Caught up in the thrill of the first genuine love affair of her life, she wanted to believe their idyll could go on forever, even while a sensible part of her acknowledged that it couldn't. Reality was going to rear its head one of these days, and she would have to make a choice. Blake was the kind of man who would want a commitment. Some day soon he was going to ask her if she would stay here with him, and she honestly didn't know what she would answer. She was happier than she'd ever been, but their lovemaking was only partly responsible. Another part of the happiness stemmed from her newfound sense of freedom.

I don't know what I want, she thought. *I guess I want my elegant, easy life and my earthy lover all at the same time. I wonder what Blake would think of the Tudor mansion. Not much probably. No one there gives a hoot about the ecological balance, and everyone over-consumes to the hilt.*

Why couldn't they carry on a long distance romance for a while? Was that unreasonable? She could spend part of every week here, part in New York. She knew of far more unorthodox arrangements. Why not?

Because something told her Blake wouldn't stand for it.

She glanced sideways again. Thank goodness he hadn't pressured her so far, not at all. For the time being he seemed only committed to loving her ardently, and she reveled in every second of it. Let the future take care of itself. She wasn't going to go looking for conflicts.

Blake was watching her out of the corner of his eye. Sometimes, like now, she would withdraw from him, crawl off into some private corner of herself where he didn't belong, and an old fear would clutch at him. He knew he should be content and satisfied—he had more of her than he had ever dared dream he would—but he wasn't. Having sampled heaven, he wanted it with a red ribbon tied around it and his name on it. Something told him he wasn't going to get it, not that easily, and that twisted his stomach into a painful knot.

You're a greedy bastard, Carmichael. Why not just enjoy, enjoy?

"You're awfully quiet," he commented.

Her head jerked in his direction. "Oh, I was just watching Randy," she lied. "He never seems to get tired of that, does he? I wonder what the fascination is."

"I don't know, but it's there. I'm just glad he has it."

For a few minutes Shannon idly watched the boy, her mind drifting and returning. Then she found herself studying him with some interest. She was more knowledgeable about basketball than most women. Vic had been an avid Knicks fan, so like it or not, she had watched untold hundreds of hours of the sport and had learned to enjoy it. No one could spend all those hours watching and listening without learning plenty about the game.

Just then Randy made a particularly difficult shot, and she applauded enthusiastically. "Way to go!" she cried.

Randy stopped dead in his tracks and stared at her in absolute disbelief. For a moment Shannon thought he was actually going to smile at her. He didn't, but he did look directly at her, and there wasn't a hint of hostility in his expression. She was absurdly pleased over that victory of sorts.

Then something snapped in her head. She'd been searching for something, anything that would thaw the chill between them, at least a little. The something had been right before her eyes all the time. Randy loved basketball, and she knew a lot about the sport, apparently more than Blake did. What brought people together quicker than a common interest?

"You know," she commented to Blake when Randy resumed his play, "that was one heck of a hard shot to make."

"Yeah? How come you know that?" he asked, shifting his position to look at her.

"Why do men think sports are their prerogative? I'll bet I've watched more basketball than half the men in this country. Randy's awfully good, take my word for it. He has all the right moves.''

''Really?'' He re-focused his attention on the boy in the driveway.

''Really. I wonder if he's ever thought about trying out for the team at school.''

''I doubt it. Randy's not a joiner, Shannon. He's never had any close friends, so he doesn't feel at ease around kids his own age.''

''Ah, but take a few kids with a common interest and you get instant friendship. I think you should encourage him to try to play in competition, Blake. Fourteen seems to me about the right age to develop his ability, and if interest counts for anything, he's a shoe-in. Wouldn't it be something if he could play for Clemson or South Carolina one day?''

Blake rubbed a forefinger across his mouth and frowned in thought. ''It'd be something, all right, but I don't think he's going to be tall enough.''

''Oh, no? Look at him, all arms and legs. I'll bet he's going to be a lot taller than you are.''

''Think so?''

''It would be awfully good for him to have some sort of extracurricular activity, something other than school and this farm. He might loosen his grip on your shirt tail.''

Blake said nothing. He found Randy's devotion impossible to resist, as anyone would, yet he was intelligent enough to realize the danger inherent in such devotion. Shannon was right; the boy needed other relationships, other interests. Now he studied Randy with more than average interest until darkness forced basketball to be abandoned for the day. He thought about what Shannon had said, and the next day he put the idea to Randy.

"I've never played on a team before," the boy said.

"I know that, and it's something everyone should try once."

"Aw, Blake, I'll never make the team."

"And why not?"

"I'm new. All the other guys have known each other since the first grade. They have it all sewed up."

"Listen to me, Randy. That coach wants a winning team, and if you're good, he's not going to care if you've been there fourteen years or fourteen days."

"I'm probably not good enough."

"You won't know until you try, will you?"

"Guess not."

"If I go with you, will you at least go to the tryouts?"

Randy shrugged. "Okay."

BASKETBALL TRYOUTS were in fact being held after school that week, which meant Randy would miss the bus and need a ride home. Blake had planned to meet him in the gym, but something came up at the last minute. "Some sort of holdup on building the road to those townhouses," he told Shannon. "They were supposed to start today, but my foreman says no one's shown up. I'm going to have to go to Charlotte and see what the problem is. Obviously I'm not going to sell those things if people can't get in to look at them. Do you mind picking up Randy?"

"Of course not. Just tell me how to get there."

She arrived at school before tryouts were over, so instead of waiting in the car, she went inside the gym and took a seat in the bleachers. There was a lot of activity down on the court. All the milling and scuffling looked terribly disorganized to her, and it was several minutes before she spotted Randy in the crowd. She sized him up in comparison with all the other boys; he was taller than most. It bothered her a little that he was hanging back, not participating in any of the adolescent horseplay going on around him, but then he was a very shy, quiet boy. Only with Blake did he open up to any degree.

She glanced around at the spectators in the bleachers. Most were women, mothers of the hopefuls, Shannon guessed. She wondered how competitive these tryouts actually were. Did everyone stand a good chance? If Randy failed to make the cut, what on earth would she say to him on the way home?

Apparently the boys had already been put through the paces and were waiting for the names to be announced. Shannon noticed Randy scanning the bleachers, looking for Blake, she was sure. She waved and caught his eye. He waved back, but his eyes continued to dart around. When he didn't find who he was looking for, his disappointment was evident.

Finally, a tall, slim man took center court—the coach, Shannon correctly assumed—and a hush fell over the gymnasium. The man introduced himself as Fred Jenkins, then informed them that the day's tryouts had been preliminaries, that the team would be selected after a week of after-school workouts. He began reading a list of names. There was a smattering of applause as each boy's name was announced. When Randy's name was called, Shannon burst into such enthusiastic sole applause that several spectators turned to look at her. When the last name had been announced, the crowd dispersed. Randy scampered up to Shannon. "Congratulations!" she cried, and resisted the urge to give him a big hug, something she felt certain he wouldn't welcome.

"Thanks. Where's Blake?"

"He couldn't come, Randy. He had to go to Charlotte, but he's going to be so proud of you."

"Aw, I haven't made the team yet," he said modestly.

"You will, I just know it. You'll probably end up in the NBA someday."

"Heck," he scoffed. "Not comin' from this little ole school, I won't."

"And why not? Larry Bird's from French Lick, Indiana. How big can French Lick be?"

Randy eyed her quizzically. "How come you know that?"

"I'm a fan."

"Yeah?" His voice implied that was the strangest thing he had ever heard.

"Yeah."

"Why would a girl like basketball?"

Shannon smiled. "A lot of women like the game, Randy. What about those cute cheerleaders who jump and yell and cry?"

"They don't do that 'cause they like basketball. They do it 'cause they're girls."

Shannon got to her feet. "Well, I'll bet some of them do it because they really are excited and interested. Come on, let's go home. I'll bet Blake's there by now, and he'll be itching to hear the news."

As she and Randy walked to her car, it occurred to Shannon that the two of them had just carried on a conversation.

RANDY SAID HARDLY A WORD during the drive back to the farm. His lone comment was about the leased Thunderbird. "This really is a neat car."

"It is, isn't it. Strange you've never been in it before."

He fidgeted and twisted in his seat, drummed his fingers on his knees, untied and retied his shoes. Shannon could tell he was about to burst with excitement. The minute she turned onto the road leading to the house he spied the jeep parked in front of the mobile home. "Blake's home!" he shouted. She braked, and he jumped out of the car and ran up the rise. Shannon followed at a slower pace. When she opened the door and stepped into the living room, Randy had already spilled his news.

"Well now, that's great, son, it really is." Blake beamed and winked at Shannon over Randy's head.

"Gee, Blake, I don't know how to thank you. It's really going to be great if I make the team. What made you think of it anyway?"

"It wasn't my idea, Randy. It was Shannon's."

The boy looked at him blankly for a second. "She thought of it?" he asked incredulously.

Blake nodded. "Seems she's a fan, and she mentioned that you had all the right moves."

Randy turned to Shannon. "Well, I'll be! Th-thanks."

"You're welcome. It was the least I could do for the future of the National Basketball Association." Her eyes lifted to Blake. "How did things come out in Charlotte?"

"Not too good. The rains have turned the place into a quagmire. There won't be any roads right away."

"That's too bad."

"Yeah, a temporary setback. The power station will have to wait a bit longer. But we won't let that put a damper on our celebration, will we? I'll take you two out to dinner."

"I can fix something here," Shannon said. "Anything our future basketball star wants. What would you like for supper, Randy?"

"Thick crust pepperoni pizza with onions and extra cheese," he said without hesitation.

"We'll go out," Shannon decided.

SHANNON FAITHFULLY ATTENDED every one of the workouts that week, since Blake was occupied in Charlotte until four or five every afternoon, and someone had to drive Randy home. By the time Friday rolled around and Randy was selected for the team, she wasn't the least surprised. She thought he was darned good, better than any of the other rookies and almost as good as the best of the two-year veterans.

She listened carefully as Coach Jenkins spelled out the rules. There would be workouts every day after school until the season started; illness was the only excuse for missing one. Every boy was required to maintain a C-plus average; there was no excuse for failure to do so. Several of the boys exchanged nervous glances over that one. At least, Shannon thought with a smile, Blake shouldn't have any trouble getting Randy to do his homework.

A curious sort of maternal pride swelled inside, which was absurd. The truce she and Randy had entered into had been in effect only a matter of days. One thing she'd say for the boy—now that he'd accepted her, he accepted her completely. He called her by name and looked directly at her when he spoke. He complimented her cooking and read the sports page to her. Naturally, Blake noticed.

"Do I detect a dramatic change in your relationship with Randy?" he asked her.

Shannon nodded. "Nice, isn't it?"

"May I ask what brought on this sudden reversal of attitude?"

"Apparently a woman who likes basketball is impossible to dislike."

"You're something else, Shannon, you really are. I..."

He tried to think of a way to convey his appreciation. How many people would have expended so much effort on winning over an unpleasant boy? "Thanks...for your patience."

He adored her. She had fascinated him as a young girl, and now she captivated him as a woman. The girl of his dreams had turned into a woman beyond his wildest imagination.

It could be so good, he thought. The three of them had become almost like a family, and that's the way he wanted it. Three people who had no one coming together to make a family—the thought pleased him enormously. For a man who had been alone all his life, he was unusually family-oriented.

One day soon he would ask her if she would stay, if she would marry him. He hadn't done it before now because, frankly, he feared her answer. He knew how she felt about their lovemaking, yet she hadn't said a word, not one, that indicated she was ready to commit herself to him and his life.

He was well aware that by forcing her to say "yes" or "no" he was leaving himself wide open to rejection, but it was a chance he had to take. After waiting for her so long, he'd never forgive himself if he didn't.

CHAPTER TWELVE

IT WAS TIME TO HARVEST all the produce left in the garden. Blake and Shannon spent one day bringing in the vegetables and cleaning out the garden, and Homer went into hibernation for the winter. Another day was spent preparing the bounty for the freezer. The weather forecast predicted a slow-moving cold front would pass through any day, and first frost wouldn't be far behind. When Shannon stepped outside the house that Friday morning she could feel the first nip of fall in the air, right on schedule. It was the middle of October and there, at the foot of the Great Smoky Mountains, seasons more or less arrived when expected.

She glanced up toward the mobile home in time to see Randy step out the front door and head down the lane to meet the school bus. This morning he carried a small suitcase, for he was leaving with the team to attend a basketball clinic in Columbia over the weekend. He'd been beside himself with excitement over it, the first real adventure of his life.

Being part of the team had done wonders for him. Daily, Shannon had watched his self-confidence grow, and she took considerable pride in her own part in the transformation.

As he neared the house, she waved and called, "Have fun."

"Yeah." He grinned broadly and waved back. "See you Sunday."

She watched until he disappeared from view, then went back into the house, poured another cup of coffee and went upstairs to her "office." The stack of typewritten sheets resting on the desk now was an impressive one numbering four hundred pages. Who would have thought months ago that she would have four hundred pages in her?

It was about finished, could be finished with a couple more days of steady work. She was dragging her heels, and she knew it. Yet, she had to get busy. She had an appointment with Anthony Thompson in New York the first week in November. The last time she'd talked to him he had asked her to set a date, so she had, but that had been several weeks ago when the first of November had seemed far away.

The time had passed so quickly, too quickly. She wasn't ready to leave. She wondered if she ever would be. The farm had become a haven of peace and privacy. She had—by a sort of osmosis, she guessed—absorbed some of Blake's love of the natural forces surrounding them.

Staying, however, meant compromising her independence, and she wasn't ready for that, either.

She was completely happy with the status quo. She was busy and free of all the petty criticism that had, it seemed, in retrospect accompanied her every action for too long. She felt desirable, and loved; it was a heady experience. At this point in her life she needed nothing else.

Blake did, though, and that troubled her. He'd been hinting in a not-too-subtle fashion that it was time they talked about the future. So far she'd man-

aged to evade the issue, but that couldn't go on in-
definitely.

Oh, why couldn't he be satisfied with things the
way they were? Was it even reasonable to expect him
to understand her need to expend energy on herself...just for a while? Probably not. How could she
ask him to believe that her yearning for freedom had
nothing to do with her very real feelings for him?

Clearing her mind, she sipped her coffee and sat
down at the typewriter. She was proud of the book.
She didn't know what the pros would think of it, but
she, the amateur, thought it was pretty good. And it
was the first important thing she'd done all on her
own since the day she'd auditioned for Vic's show.
That alone filled her with a kind of self-satisfaction
she would have found difficult to explain to anyone,
especially Blake, and she easily talked to him about
everything.

Or almost everything. She rarely discussed Vic
with him. She'd never revealed to him her ambivalent feelings about her husband and their marriage.
Blake knew as little about the real Vic Parelli as the
general public did. Of course, the book would
change some of that.

The book was something else she never discussed
with Blake unless he brought it up first, and he seldom did. He no longer asked how it was going or
when it would be finished. He seemed to hate the
whole idea of the biography.

She rolled a sheet of paper into the typewriter and
typed at the top "Chapter Twenty-Two", the final
chapter. In it she would have to cover Vic's death,
but she wasn't going to make it maudlin or milk it for
readers' tears. Just the facts, ma'am, and then it

would be over. The project had been an emotional experience, to say the least.

She began typing. Despite her firm resolve to the contrary, it wasn't long before a king-sized lump had formed in her throat.

She had been working for three hours, writing and rewriting, when she heard Blake's footsteps on the stairs. Then he appeared in the doorway. "Hey, sweetheart, I just had an idea. I..." He stopped abruptly when she turned to look at him. "Why're you crying?"

"I'm not crying," she sniffed. "I've got tears in my eyes. There's a difference."

"Over that?" He inclined his head toward the typewriter.

"Yes. I'm on the last chapter."

"And you're the one who dotes on happy endings."

"I know, but this one can't very well have a happy ending, can it?"

"I...I guess not." Blake hated himself for what he was thinking, that the ending was a happy one for him. If Parelli weren't gone, he wouldn't have Shannon. He looked again at her sad face and wondered if he actually had her at all.

Shannon switched off the typewriter and folded her hands in her lap. "This will have to wait," she muttered, more to herself than to Blake. She could ask Anthony Thompson to have whoever whipped the manuscript into shape write the ending, but would that be honest? She was so proud of having written all those words herself. Inevitably, she imagined, there would be people who would ask, "Did you really write that book?'' She wanted to be able to tell them truthfully that she had.

She lifted her eyes to Blake and managed a credible smile. "So, tell me about this idea you just had."

"I need some things from town. I thought we might go in together, do some shopping and grab a hamburger somewhere. This is the first weekend we've had all to ourselves. I'll buy a couple of steaks and cook them tonight. A bottle of good wine. Make it an occasion. How does that sound?"

Shannon slipped the cover over the typewriter. "That sounds great. Let's go."

THEY RETURNED TO THE FARM at three that afternoon. The temperature had been dropping steadily all day. Shannon shivered in her lightweight clothing as she and Blake carried groceries into the house. "I'll take my stuff on up to my place," Blake said, "but I'll be back in a bit to light the pilot in that old furnace. We might need some heat before the night's over."

"Okay. Oh, Blake, there are some logs stacked out by the back porch, not more than six or seven of them. Would a fire in the fireplace be a bit much this early in the season? I love a fireplace."

He shrugged. "No telling how long those have been there. They'll probably burn like kindlin' wood, but what the hell? If you want a fire, we'll have a fire."

Shannon put away the groceries, then went upstairs to change out of her jeans. Blake had said he wanted to make this an occasion, so she whimsically decided to dress for it. Trouble was, the wardrobe she'd brought in sweltering August wasn't exactly appropriate for the sudden weather change. And she'd certainly not brought anything for an "occasion."

Her eyes roamed over the clothes hanging in the closet, then fell on one particular garment—a jade green hostess gown. Just why she had packed it she couldn't remember, but it had proven to be much too warm for the southern climate. Tonight it would feel good, though, and it was a rather spectacular gown. It had long sleeves, a scooped neckline that revealed just a bit of cleavage, and it fell to the floor in shimmering folds. The fabric tended to cling to her curves and felt sensuously soft when it swished around her legs. Smiling delightedly, Shannon threw it across the bed, then went into the bathroom to take a quick shower.

Ten minutes later, after applying her makeup, she slipped the green gown over her head and stood at the bathroom mirror to do her hair. Though she was wearing it shorter, there was still enough of the glossy stuff to twist into a French knot. But after completing the hairdo, she thought it was too severe, so with a fingernail she freed several tendrils to fall around her face and the nape of her neck. That, she decided, was better.

She heard the back door open and close, and the clatter was followed by the sounds of Blake's movements downstairs. There was some banging and clanging. She was screwing gold studs into her earlobes when a blurted "goddammit!" wafted up the stairway. He obviously was having some trouble. Chuckling, she gave herself a couple of quick sprays of cologne, then went downstairs to see what was going on.

The door to the furnace compartment in the hallway was open. Blake was kneeling on the floor, his head inside the closet. Though his voice was muffled, she could clearly hear his expansive cursing. "Something wrong?" she inquired.

"Whoever designed these things must have had sadistic tendencies. One, you can barely reach the pilot light because it's behind a thingamajig, and two, when you do reach it, the damned thing won't catch. I've used half a box of matches, and it's still not lit."

Shannon stood behind him and watched him try one more time. "How's the weather?"

"Clear and getting colder by the minute."

At that moment she heard a distinct whoof, and Blake muttered, "Ah, at last. At least if we need heat tonight we'll have it."

Getting to his feet, he closed the closet door and turned. His eyes widened and raked her from head to foot. "Well . . . look at you!"

"Like it?" She slowly turned for his benefit. "Just a little something I threw on at the last minute."

"Like it? How could I not like it?" He moved toward her. "Shannon . . . sweetheart, you look gorgeous!"

She slid her arms up the broad wall of his chest and clasped her fingers behind his neck. "You said you wanted tonight to be an occasion, so I decided to dress for it."

"I've never seen you like this before." A little ripple of trepidation swept through him as his eyes feasted on the sight of her. It occurred to him that this breathtakingly lovely sophisticate probably was the real Shannon, not the jean-clad woman who dogged his footsteps, hoed the garden, canned tomatoes and didn't mind getting dirt under her fingernails. He swallowed hard, then drew her to him and planted a firm kiss on her mouth before saying, "You'd make a room full of ugly people average out pretty good just by walking into the place. And look at me . . . in my Paul Bunyan garb."

He was still dressed in the clothes he had worn to town—plaid shirt and faded jeans. "Well, I happen to think you're fairly gorgeous in those clothes, too."

"But this is an occasion. These clothes won't do at all." His dark eyes glittered mischievously. He slid one arm around her waist and led her into the living room. "Tell you what. You sit here while I go up to my place. I won't be gone long at all."

"Blake, there's no need for you to change clothes."

Gently he pushed her down to sit on the sofa. "Just wait here, okay?"

She shrugged. "Sure. Where would I go?"

"Give me ten minutes, tops."

"Take all the time you want. I don't think we have to be in a hurry for anything."

He left the room. Shannon heard the back door close. After a minute or two she got to her feet and closed the drapes to block out the late afternoon sun. She saw that Blake had stacked the wood in the fireplace. The logs were so old and dry that she had no trouble setting them alight. Next she fiddled with her dad's ancient stereo until she found an easy listening station. The sound of a hundred strings filled the air. She turned down the volume, took a look around the room, then returned to the sofa and waited, humming and tapping her foot in time with the music. A short time later the back door opened and closed again.

Blake spent a moment or two in the kitchen; then he walked through the dining room, crossed the foyer and stood on the threshold of the living room, arms poised like a symphony conductor. In one hand he held two goblets. In the other was the bottle of Cabernet Sauvignon they had purchased that afternoon. He smiled the smile of a man who was enormously pleased with himself.

Shannon drank in the sight of him, gasped and clapped her hands together delightedly. "Oh, Blake!" she cried, laughing. "A smoking jacket!"

"I'm asking . . . is this class or isn't it?" He made a slow turn, inviting her inspection.

Shannon placed one hand at her throat as an uncontrolled giggle escaped. He was wearing black trousers, a crisp white shirt and an elegant maroon velvet jacket with black satin lapels. He looked absolutely divine, urbanely handsome, a far cry from the earthy man she knew him to be. "A smoking jacket!" she cried again. "What are you doing with a smoking jacket?"

He ambled into the room, his grin broadening. With an exaggerated flourish he set the wine bottle and glasses on the coffee table. "Just a little something I threw on at the last minute. Nothing really." Then he snapped his fingers. "Oops, forgot something. Don't move, my sweet." Loping across the room, he went back to the kitchen and returned in seconds, carrying a corkscrew and a napkin.

Shannon rested her elbows on her knees and propped her face in her hands, watching in amused fascination as he wrapped the napkin around the wine bottle. With the finesse of a maitre d' he presented the label for her approval. "Does the vintage please you, ma'am?"

"I picked it out, remember?"

"Ah, yes, so you did." After two aborted attempts, he opened the bottle and poured wine into each goblet. Tiny bits of cork floated on the surface of the burgundy liquid. "Sorry about that," he muttered. "I'm used to pop-tops." He handed her one of the glasses, took the other one and lifted it ceremoniously. "To us, my dear."

Shannon tried to take a sip of the wine, but another giggle escaped, and the liquid trickled onto her lips. Her tongue darted to catch the wayward drops, but Blake alertly relieved her of the chore. His head bent, and his tongue traced the outline of her mouth, licking up each drop. "Much more efficient than a napkin."

Shannon's breath fluttered against his mouth. "Oh, Blake, this is positively decadent at four in the afternoon!"

"Nice, huh?"

"You know, this is a side of you I haven't seen before."

"Ah, fair flower, you inspire me to be the man I've always wanted to be."

"Fair flower? My sweet? You sound like something out of an old Cary Grant movie. This is the man you've always wanted to be?"

"Unimpressed, I see. Ah well, the attempt was well-meant, if a bit clumsy." He set his glass on the coffee table, removed hers from her hand and set it beside his. Then he stood up. "I gather I'll be forgiven for removing this stuffy jacket."

"I want you to be comfortable," she cooed, "but the jacket really is beautiful. Though somehow I can't see you shopping for such a garment."

He slipped it off and threw it across the room. It landed half-on and half-off an arm chair. "I had to buy it for a bachelor dinner I once attended. Last time I wore it, as I recall." Hitching his trousers at the knee, he sat down beside her. He cast a glance toward the fireplace as he did. The logs hissed, popped and blazed cheerfully. "That fire's going to last about thirteen minutes, you know."

She nodded. "Still, it's nice. Makes the room seem so cozy."

Smoothly, he gathered her into his arms. "I know a way to make it seem even cozier."

She snuggled against him. "Love in the afternoon?"

"Uh hmm."

"This is an occasion then."

"You better believe it."

With one arm encircling her shoulders, holding her close, Blake slid the other under her knees and swung her legs over his lap. He rested his hand on the curve of her hip for a moment before moving down to remove her slippers, then to grasp the hem of her gown and inch the silky fabric up until her knees were exposed. Her bare legs were firm and smooth to his touch. His restless hand slipped under the gown and rested between her thighs.

An intense, warm, fluid feeling surged through Shannon, and all her senses leaped to life. Her stomach knotted into a tight coil of need. It was gratifying to know it soon would be assuaged. She lifted her face to him and received his mouth, clamping firmly and insistently on hers. She parted her lips to give his probing tongue easy access to the warm hollows of her mouth.

Lifting his head, he smiled down at her. Shannon placed her face against the V of exposed skin where his shirt was open. His coarse chest hair tickled her cheek. "You know," she said with a contented sigh, "I think I'm living all my wildest fantasies."

"I know I'm living mine," he said huskily, "every one of them. They always were centered around you...always...every damned one of them." His hand moved further up, clutched at her bikini panties and tugged. Considering the position they were in, he removed them with surprising ease. Shannon kicked them to the floor.

"Anything else but you under here?" he asked.

"My bra," she said dreamily. "It's strapless...hooks in front."

It was little more than a wisp of lace. Dispensed with quickly, it joined her panties on the floor. By now the gown's hem was twisted around her waist. Blake took the time to make a leisurely one-handed exploration of her body, petting and massaging until he heard her moan softly. Satisfied that he had brought her to the pinnacle of desire, he pulled the gown over her head. Then he deftly slipped from beneath her, maneuvered her into a prone position and stood up to divest himself blindly of his own clothes.

He hovered over her for a second, long enough for her to reach for him, to close her fingers around him. He almost collapsed upon her. Her legs bound him like loving chains, and she welcomed his powerful thrust.

SOMETIME LATER, dovetailed against his body, Shannon announced, "I'm freezing."

Blake reached behind him and groped on the floor for her gown. "Here, put this on."

She did so awkwardly, since there was barely room on the sofa for both of them. She wiggled the garment down to mid-thigh, then snuggled against him again. "Are you cold?"

"Nope. Warm as toast." A silent minute passed. "Shannon, don't you think it's time we talked?"

Her heart stilled, then started up again. This was what she had been dreading. "About what?"

"I think you know. About tomorrow, and the day after that and the day after that. You know how I feel about you. You must know what I want."

"I have to go back...." She started to say "back home." She left it at "back."

"I know that, but for how long? A week? Two?"

"I don't know, Blake." Briefly, she told him about Anthony Thompson's plans for promotion of the book. "I guess I'm obligated to do whatever he wants."

"How long will it take?"

"I have no idea. I'm a novice at this, remember? But I have to guess it'll be a year or more before the book comes out. In the meantime . . . well, planes fly back and forth every day."

Blake swallowed hard. A dismal picture was forming in his mind—one of Shannon flitting in and out of his life as the whim or opportunity struck. Six months ago he would have been delighted at the thought of having her in his life at all, but now he wanted more. He wanted everything. He wanted her to make a permanent break with the New York life, but she had all sorts of obligations back there. God only knew what would happen when that damned book came out. What if the thing turned out to be really big? What if Shannon herself became famous?

His heart sunk. Did he honestly think for a minute that a woman in her position would want to settle down with him and turn to homesteading?

"Then let's talk about the more immediate future," he said. "What about Christmas?"

"Oh, Blake, I'd love to spend Christmas here!" she breathed, hoping that would satisfy him. "Let's plan on it!"

He dismissed his worries and frustrations. This was no time to be dwelling on what might be. Enjoy the moment, his mind implored him. Lower your expectations. Take what she can give and relish it. Don't ask her for a certified guarantee. "Well, I guess that's something."

For Shannon it was more than just something. It was enough, and she regretted that it wasn't enough for Blake. She was feeling very alive and free, and Christmas would give her something wonderful to look forward to. Anticipating it would keep her going during the time they had to be apart.

"We'll do it up splendidly!" she bubbled. "We'll have every Christmassy thing you can imagine! The prettiest tree in South Carolina, a wassail bowl, a big wreath on the door. I'll bake cookies with all those little colored sprinkles on them, and we'll have turkey and stuffing and... Oh, Lord, I don't know how to stuff and roast a turkey! But I'll find out. Think of Randy! Do you suppose he's ever had a Christmas like that in his entire life?"

Blake smiled against her hair. "I doubt it. Come to think of it, the only Christmas like that I've ever had were the two I spent with your family. Of course, the Air Force puts on a pretty big spread at Christmas, but a mess hall, even a crowded one, isn't the best place to have Christmas dinner."

"I can imagine," she said, though she couldn't, not really. She recalled all the lavish holidays on Long Island. Vic had always hired a decorator to "do" the house. Then they would throw their annual Christmas cocktail-buffet for hundreds of gowned and tuxedoed guests, who could be counted on to comment that "no one does this sort of thing as well as the Parellis." The affair had snowballed to gigantic proportions through the years. And on Christmas morning there were dozens of outrageously expensive gifts for her under the tree. It all had been an orgy of superabundance, yet something had always been missing. For want of a better word she would call it . . . joy.

But this year would be different. This year the three of them would have a real country-family Christmas, and she wished Blake would absorb some of her enthusiasm. With a little difficulty, she turned until she was facing him. "It's going to be so wonderful, Blake!"

"Yeah, if it really happens, it's going to be great!"

"If it happens?"

He smiled a sad smile. "Shannon, I'm not stupid. There's a very good chance you won't come back . . . not after going . . . back . . . there."

"Oh, Blake, how can you think that? Of course I'll be back. Nothing's going to prevent that. I'm already looking forward to it."

"But you'll only leave again."

She sighed. "Why must you dwell on that aspect of it?"

"I want you with me all the time."

"And I want to be with you . . . as often as can be managed. Please accept that for now."

"Do I have a choice?"

They faced each other solemnly for a moment; then Shannon's mouth curved into a slow, seductive smile. "Nope. Enjoy me while you can, or send me packing."

"I have a life-sized mental picture of myself doing that," he said facetiously.

Their gazes locked intimately. They shared several rapid kisses, content simply to lie in each other's arms. At such moments, Shannon could easily imagine herself staying on the farm forever.

Just then the doorbell pealed loudly. The sound startled both of them. "Ignore it," Shannon whispered.

"Suits me," Blake agreed. But when the chimes sounded again, he sat up and fumbled for his trousers. "Oh, hell!" he muttered.

Shannon stretched and purred like a kitten. "What's the matter?"

"Emil Larson, the fellow who owns the farm down the road. I'm sure that's who it is. He stopped me yesterday and asked if he could borrow my post-hole digger today. I'd forgotten all about it."

"He can get it tomorrow," Shannon protested.

"Your car's out front, and mine's up by the mobile home. He probably went up there first. He'll know I'm around somewhere." He zipped his trousers and grabbed for his shirt, slipping into it but not buttoning it. "I'll tell him the digger's propped up against the barn. This won't take but a minute, love."

Reluctantly Shannon sat up, pulled her gown down to a more decorous length and ran her fingers through her disheveled hair. She watched Blake stumble toward the foyer and open the front door.

"Oh!" she heard him exclaim. "Ah . . . hello."

"Hello. Are you Mr. Carmichael?"

The voice sounded familiar to Shannon. She leaped to her feet, hitting the coffee table with her knee and almost knocking over one of the half-filled wine glasses. A wave of panic swept through her, and she frantically, uselessly smoothed at her gown, her hair, her face.

"Yes, I am," she heard Blake say. "But who . . ."

"I'm Mary Hatcher, and this is my sister, Mildred Prentiss. May we come in, Mr. Carmichael?"

Blake recognized the names immediately, and he stifled a groan. "Well, I . . ."

"We can only stay a minute," Mary Hatcher said. "We've had the most difficult time getting in touch with you."

What could he do? He had no choice but to invite them in. Helplessly he stood back and allowed them to enter. He fumbled with the buttons of his shirt and said, "I, ah . . . how do you do, ladies. I'm afraid . . . you see, I wasn't expecting company."

"We prefer it that way, Mr. Carmichael."

The women's backs were to the living room, where Shannon stood in a state of shock. Even so, she had her wits enough about her to make a rapid survey of the room. The sight sent her heart plummeting to the pit of her stomach. Smoldering fire, soft music, a bottle of wine and two half-filled goblets. Added to all that were some rumpled sofa cushions, Blake's shoes and socks on the floor and...

Dear God! Her bra and panties lay against a coffee table leg, in plain view of anyone who entered the room. Shannon's face grew hot. One foot shot out from beneath her gown as she tried to kick the incriminating bits of nylon and lace underneath the sofa. She didn't succeed. Unable to think of any other solution she stepped over the undergarments, effectively hiding them with her gown. She ran trembling fingers down her hips and managed a shaky smile just as the sisters turned toward the living room.

"Oh, my goodness...Mrs. Parelli," Mary Hatcher said, "I didn't realize you were here. How nice to see you again, my dear."

"Thank you, Mrs. Hatcher, it's nice to see you, too. Hello, Mrs. Prentiss." To her own ears her voice had a false ring to it. She tried not to imagine how she must look. Behind the two women Blake stood, rolling his eyes toward the ceiling. To her dismay, Shannon saw that he looked as if he had just crawled out of bed.

Mary and Mildred began to move toward the living room, but they stopped abruptly at the sight confronting them. Both women blanched slightly; then their faces set into pinched, accusing expressions. Shannon swallowed hard. Apparently the sisters had immediately jumped to all the right conclusions. The scene had "seduction" written all over it.

A ghastly silence fell over the room, until Blake mustered the presence to say, "Please come in, ladies. May I get you something to drink?"

"No, thank you," Mary said in a tight voice. Her face had turned the color of pink grapefruit. "I'm afraid we've come at a bad tme."

Shannon couldn't deny that. She was sure she'd never been so mortified. She stood like a statue, not daring to move for fear of exposing the lingerie at her feet. "N-not at all. Please come in."

"I...I think not, Mrs. Parelli. We didn't realize how late it is, did we, Mildred?"

"No...it is late," Mildred murmured.

"But didn't you want to see me about something?" Blake asked. By this time he had buttoned his shirt, but there was nothing he could do about his bare feet. Unlike Shannon, he wasn't especially embarrassed over the intrusion, and he was a little surprised that she was. His eyes sent her a message: relax, this is no big deal.

She read it loud and clear. Oh, God, she thought, he doesn't realize the seriousness of this!

Mary Hatcher leveled a stern look at Blake. "I think our business with you can wait, Mr. Carmichael. Forgive us for...interrupting you. Come, Mildred...."

"Please don't bother to see us to the door," Mildred sniffed. She looked as though she had suddenly smelled something fetid. Both women turned and walked in stiff, mincing steps to the front door.

Despite Mildred's request, Blake hurried to open it for them. "Tomorrow then?" he suggested. "It's Saturday. I should be around all day."

"Perhaps." Mary all but pushed Mildred out the door. "I assure you, Mr. Carmichael, you will be hearing from us." Then they were gone.

Blake closed the door behind them, then leaned against it for a moment, his shoulders heaving. To Shannon's dismay she realized he was laughing. His laughter stopped, however, when he pushed himself away, turned and saw the expression on her face. "Sweetheart, what's wrong?"

"What's wrong?" she cried incredulously. "Those two women! Look around you! You'd have to be a ten-year-old simpleton not to realize what's been going on here!"

"So?" He chuckled. "You said they wanted to be sure I'm heterosexual."

"I wish I could laugh with you, but it isn't funny. Crying would be more appropriate. I neglected to tell you something else they want—a nuclear family, no live-in lovers, no co-habitating." Her hands went to her face. "Oh, Blake, if I've jeopardized your chances with Randy..."

"Hey, hey...." He crossed the room and took her in his arms. "You haven't jeopardized anything. I'm sure even Mary Hatcher and Mildred Prentiss realize that people make love."

"You don't know those two! They, or rather the adoption board under their leadership, once granted an adoption to a young woman whose lover later moved in with her. You and I might not see a thing wrong with that, but Mary and Mildred are still incensed over it. And they're determined to see it doesn't happen again."

"Oh, how ridiculous!" Blake muttered, but worry began building inside him. He wasn't going to let

Shannon see it, though. "I told you...you can't sweat the small stuff."

"I'm afraid this isn't 'small stuff.'"

He pressed his cheek against her hair and hugged her to him reassuringly. "Let's not conjure up problems. Tonight was supposed to be an occasion. There's wine to be drunk, steaks to be eaten. Stop thinking about those two and concentrate on us."

She slipped her arms around his waist and rested her head on his shoulder. "Oh, all right," she said. "There's not much I can do about them, anyway."

They stood locked together, swaying slightly to the music coming from the radio. It was a second or two before Shannon recognized the tune—Vic's recording of "Just One of Those Things." She stiffened in Blake's embrace, wondering if he'd recognized it, too. Of course he had. Vic had a very distinctive voice. No one who'd heard it before ever asked, "Who's that singing?"

"Go turn that off," she muttered.

"Gladly," he said tersely.

IN SPITE OF EVERYTHING, the evening turned out to be a pleasant, memorable one. The steaks were excellent, the mood almost dreamy, and because of Blake's light-hearted efforts, it remained that way. Shannon found it easy to respond, to forget her worries and uncertainties, to relish the very special tenderness she felt for him. He made love to her again after they went to bed, and she couldn't deny how wonderful that made her feel. Each episode left her spellbound. In such a state, one could forget problems.

But the sweet mystic aftermath could only last so long. Later, as Blake lay sleeping beside her, the worry came back and she spent a restless night. The sisters bothered her; she couldn't help it. She hoped she was wrong, but she suspected they wouldn't quietly forget the evening's encounter.

The following day she discovered how right she was.

CHAPTER THIRTEEN

REVEREND TOM ARCHER ARRIVED at the farmhouse at precisely two-fifteen the following afternoon. Shannon knew the exact time because the moment she heard the car in the driveway she glanced at her watch. Unconsciously, or perhaps not so unconsciously, she had been waiting for something unusual to happen all day.

She turned off her typewriter, folded her hands in her lap and waited. Several minutes later the back door opened; she heard two masculine voices, Blake's and another man's. An odd flutter of trepidation swept through her. Slowly she got to her feet and went downstairs. The voices came from the kitchen. She headed toward them.

"Ah, Shannon," Blake said when she entered the room, "I'd like you to meet a friend of mine. This is Reverend Archer. You've heard me speak of him. Tom, this is Shannon Parelli."

She pasted a smile on her face and stepped toward the short, sandy-haired man, hand outstretched. "Reverend Archer, how nice to meet you at last."

Tom took her hand. "It's a pleasure, Mrs. Parelli. So sorry I haven't been by to meet you before now. I've, ah, heard so much about you."

I'll bet, Shannon thought. She said, "And I've heard a great deal about you, too. Particularly your kindness toward Randy. I know how grateful Blake is."

"Yes, Randy. It's been gratifying to see the changes in the boy...all due to Blake, of course. His influence has done wonders."

"Yes, it has." The minister's discomfort was evident to Shannon. He wasn't here on a social call, she was sure. "May I get you some coffee?"

"No, no, thank you. I'm not much of a coffee drinker." Tom clasped his hands behind his back and stood in a classic clerical pose. "Are you enjoying our first touch of fall, Mrs. Parelli?"

"I'm sure I would, but I haven't been outside today."

An awkward moment of silence followed. Shannon waited with suspended breath, casting a nervous glance toward Blake, who was eyeing Tom quizzically. The minister rocked forward on the balls of his feet, unclasped his hands and rubbed one over his chin.

Finally Blake asked, "You wanted to talk to me about something, Tom?"

"Yes, I did."

"Would you gentlemen like me to leave?" Shannon asked hopefully.

"No, Mrs. Parelli. I suppose I should talk to both of you."

This brought a reaction from Blake. "Shannon, too?"

"Yes, I think so."

Shannon sighed inwardly. Here it comes, she thought, and she felt very sorry for Reverend Archer, who looked as though he wished he were anywhere else in the world. She pulled a chair out from the kitchen table and sat down. The two men did the same. All three of them folded their hands on the table.

Tom cleared his throat. "First of all, I want both of you to know that none of this is my idea. In fact, I'm appalled at the whole business and have said as much to certain people. Blake . . . I think it only fair to tell you that two of the board members plan to ask that your request for adoption be denied. They've even suggested that your suitability as a foster parent should be re-examined."

Shannon's heart constricted. She glanced across the table. Blake's face had set in a grim cast, and his breath escaped in a ragged hiss. "May I ask why?"

"For the record? It's because of your single status."

Blake's voice rose. "I've always been single. You said that wouldn't be a problem. It's not as though there are dozens of people lined up to adopt a fourteen-year-old. What do these 'certain people' think is going to happen to the boy if he's taken away from me? Tom, do you remember that I was your last-ditch stand? No one seemed overly concerned about my lack of a wife when there wasn't anyone else to take Randy. Is a detention home better than a single parent?"

"You know the answer to that one, Blake. Of course not. I'm not sure these people are thinking clearly. That business about the foster parent program, for instance. I suspect that was put in for its nuisance value."

Blake ran a hand through his hair. "Let's not tap-dance around the issue. The fact that I'm single doesn't really have a thing to do with it, does it, Tom?''

Tom sighed and shook his head. "No, not really. It actually has to do with . . ." A rush of color suffused his cheeks. "With the relationship between you and Mrs. Parelli.''

Blake uttered a sound of the utmost disgust. "What in thunder does that have to do with what kind of parent I'll make?''

"In my opinion, nothing. But I'm only one voice.''

"Those two women are behind this, right? Well, they're only two voices. How many people are on the board . . . a dozen? You told me that the rest of them favored the adoption. You were sure you could sway Mrs. Hatcher and Mrs. Prentiss to your side.''

"I honestly thought I could, Blake," Tom said earnestly. "They seemed to be leaning toward okaying the adoption. But . . . something's happened to change their minds. Mrs. Hatcher telephoned me this morning and said that she and her sister have decided the adoption is . . . unthinkable. That's the word she used—unthinkable.''

Blake's eyes narrowed. "Why? And don't tell me you don't know.''

The minister looked at Shannon apologetically. "Mrs. Parelli, I'm very sorry. This is difficult for me.''

"I know it is, Reverend," she said with as much poise as she could muster, although she was rapidly beginning to feel like a scarlet woman. "Please . . . tell us exactly why they want to deny the request." She was sure she already knew the answer.

Tom cleared his throat again. "It seems Mildred and Mary have decided that the two of you are living together without benefit of marriage."

"Oh, my God!" Blake exclaimed. "We aren't. I live with Randy in the mobile home, you know that. And what if we were? That's private and no one else's business."

"Blake," Tom said patiently, "people who want to adopt are often forced to reveal the most astonishing things about themselves and their private lives. Everything you do becomes the board's business. The sisters don't approve of...certain modern lifestyles that have become commonplace, and a man in my position can't very well rant and rave in favor of them."

"I don't believe this!" Blake muttered. "Not in this day and age."

"Mildred and Mary aren't of this day and age," Tom reminded him.

Again Shannon and Blake exchanged glances. She saw his heightened color, his chest heaving in agitation. She sent him a silent message: don't make things worse by getting angry.

"Tom, are you trying to tell me that the adoption is off, period?"

"Not exactly. But I am telling you that it might be difficult, unless..."

"Unless?"

"Unless Mrs. Parelli is out of the picture." The minister seemed vastly relieved that he had gotten it out.

"Reverend," Shannon interjected quickly, "I have to go back to New York soon. I hadn't planned to return until around Christmas."

"I'm afraid that won't be long enough. Mildred and Mary are . . . I'm not sure how to say it . . . ."

"Suspicious and cautious," Shannon finished for him. "Because of the young woman a few years back. I know. They told me the story."

"This is ridiculous!" Blake thundered. "Serving on an adoption board doesn't give those two the right to dictate people's lives!"

"They have a lot of influence," Tom said quietly, "and the board's decision has to be unanimous."

"What if I didn't even know Shannon? Then we'd be back to the single parent issue."

"I think we can overcome that obstacle with little trouble. Look, Blake, I merely wanted you to know what's going on, what's being said. You need to know what you're up against. I'm not here to tell you how to conduct your life."

"Good, because Shannon's part of it, and I want it to stay that way. And no one's going to take Randy away from me." His words were precise and deliberate. His jaw jutted defiantly.

Shannon watched him and wanted to cry. She didn't for a minute think that Blake was naive, but he was trusting. He was a gentle man in a very ungentle world, and he didn't seem to believe that those two women could actually prevent the adoption. She, however, recalled their pinched, accusing faces and found it all too easy to believe. Mildred and Mary wouldn't hesitate to heap misery upon anyone who violated their personal moral code.

She was sure she'd never felt more miserable. She had complicated Blake's life from the beginning— first Randy and now this. Under the circumstances, it amazed her that he even wanted her to stay. Yet he did, and if she ever needed proof that he loved her, she supposed that was it.

But she'd never forgive herself if the adoption was denied, for she would always know that she had been a factor in the denial. And in time Blake might not forgive her either, which was a sobering thought. But above all, a young boy's welfare was at stake. While Blake and Tom continued talking, Shannon forced herself to confront her own feelings. There was no doubt what she had to do.

Tom didn't stay long after that. His mission had been accomplished, and there was nothing else he could do except promise to stay on top of everything and report to Blake any new information that came his way. His regret was obvious and appreciated. One had to give him A-plus for courage; it couldn't have been easy for him.

Blake walked the minister to his car, and Shannon went back upstairs. When Blake returned to the kitchen and found her gone, he called her name. Getting no answer, he went up to the bedroom and found her seated on the edge of the bed. She was hanging up the telephone.

"Who were you calling?" he asked.

She didn't look at him. "The airline."

"What in hell for?"

"There's a flight out in the morning. It's a milk run—three stops between here and Kennedy—but I'm going to be on it."

Alarm, real and strong, cut through him like a knife. Until Tom's visit he'd thought the only real difficulties in their relationship would stem from her obligations back in New York. He hadn't anticipated this, not even with Shannon's warnings about the sisters. He'd thought she was over-reacting. He should have listened to her... not that it would have changed anything. "I was afraid of something like this. I saw the look on your face while Tom was talking." He walked to the bed, pulled her to her feet and into his arms. "Oh, sweetheart, call back and cancel your reservation. Leaving isn't necessary. All of this is going to work out just fine."

She slipped her arms around his waist. "I can't believe you really think that, Blake," she said miserably. "The good reverend wouldn't have taken the time and trouble to come here if he didn't think there was something to worry about. Things will work out fine only if I'm gone. I was leaving next week anyway. I'm just putting the trip up a few days."

"But Christmas is still on, isn't it?"

"I...I don't know."

"What do you mean, you don't know? Last night you were like a kid, making plans."

"That was last night. We'll wait and see how the adoption proceedings go. I don't think we should risk seeing each other until Randy is safely and forever yours."

"That could take months and months...a year!"

"I know," she sighed.

There was a moment of silence between them. Then Blake hugged her closer. "You know, there's a perfect solution to all this."

"Oh?"

"Uh-huh. Marry me."

She pulled away from him slightly and looked up. "You're not serious!"

He grinned down at her. For weeks he'd been thinking of a way to propose, but the words had popped out with the greatest of ease. "I've never been more serious in my life. What do you think I've been up to for, lo, these many weeks? I've been seducing you to my way of life. And aren't the sisters looking for a nuclear family?"

"Blake, I..." Swamped with dismay, she struggled for words. "People don't, or shouldn't get married in order to speed up adoption proceedings."

"That's not the reason I want to marry you, Shannon, and I think you know that."

Yes, she knew it. She knew he loved her, and she was beginning to think she loved him. But she'd hoped he wouldn't bring up the subject of marriage. She wasn't ready for it, she knew that with absolute certainty. For fifteen years she had lived in the shadow of a dominating personality, and Blake, in a less difficult way, was also a dominating personality. She didn't think he would ever be possessive and manipulative the way Vic had been, but he might unwittingly subjugate her. She had only the most precarious hold on an identity of her own. She couldn't risk losing it again so soon.

"It'd be great, sweetheart...the three of us," he said huskily.

"Oh, Blake, I...I can't. I'm just not ready for that, not yet."

She felt him tense. "This can't be much of a surprise," he said gruffly. "You must have known I wanted to marry you."

"I...I didn't think. I was too busy just enjoying each day. I...guess I hoped things could go on the way they were."

"You were wrong." His voice sounded harsh and brittle. "You might be satisfied with things the way they are, but I'm not. I want more."

She removed her arms from his waist, slipped out of his easy embrace and stepped back. "There's a lot you don't know about me, Blake."

He nodded. "I'm sure of it. I'd hoped you would tell me everything someday."

"You have no idea how confused I am, or what caused the confusion."

"Then tell me."

"It involves my marriage."

"I was sure of that, too."

Shannon took in a deep breath and sat back on the bed's edge. "Once I married Vic, I become Mrs. Parelli, no one else. Life was defined in relation to Vic. He married me for my youth and energy, then ended up resenting both. I don't think he ever saw me as anything but an extension of himself, and that in turn made me resentful. I find that I . . . like being Shannon, whoever she is."

"Surely you don't think I would ever see you as nothing but an extension of myself. I've been in love with you half my life!"

Tears filled Shannon's eyes. "Oh, Blake, you've been in love with some sort of ideal image. That girl you fell in love with years ago doesn't exist anymore."

"Maybe not . . . but I've discovered I also love the woman who does exist."

Why am I so full of uncertainties, she wondered. *Why can't I tell him I love him, too? It would make him happy to hear it, and I've often thought the words, felt them in my heart, even if I couldn't get them out of my mouth.*

"You can't really know me because I don't know myself."

"Oh, rot!"

"That sounds foolish to you, but not to me, not at all. You see me as I am now and think I've always been this way, but I haven't. I wish you had known me . . . oh, say a year ago. I was very blah, totally zip in the self-esteem department. I walked on eggshells and tried to please everyone in the world. Now I'm gradually changing. I've discovered that I won't be struck dead if I put myself first every once in a while. Who knows what I'll be like once the metamorphosis is complete? You might not like me at all!"

Blake stood over her, feeling impatient and frustrated. This sort of philosophic introspection wasn't his cup of tea. For most of his adult life he'd been too busy to wonder who he was or what he wanted. He'd stayed obsessed with the first love of his life for eighteen years, which was pretty unusual. And he'd never entirely forgiven himself for the Norma thing, though Shannon had helped him see that his guilt feelings might have been misplaced. Those were his hangups—pretty straightforward ones, after all. Shannon, it seemed to him, was engaged in a kind of emotional self-analysis that alarmed him.

"I don't understand this kind of talk, Shannon. I'm sorry, but I don't. You obviously don't think you know who you are. Well, I'll tell you—you're a kind, lovely, lovable woman. You've brought a lot of happiness to me and to Randy, who probably didn't deserve your efforts. I'd like to make that happiness permanent. I want you here with me. I need you. I love you. I . . . I don't know what else to say."

Her chin quivered. She studied a fingernail. "It makes me very happy to hear you say that."

"Yeah, I can see you're overjoyed."

"Sarcasm doesn't become you."

"Sorry." And he was.

"Whether you choose to believe it or not, I'm very happy to know you love me. But I have to be honest with myself, and in spite of the fact that you're the dearest man I've ever known and you mean so much to me, I know I don't want to get married, not now. I wish you would try to understand that I'm not rejecting you; I'm just rejecting the idea of another lifetime commitment at this stage of my life."

A heavy, weary feeling came over Blake. He sensed the end of something that, for him, had only begun. "You're being selfish," he said bitterly. "All this yammering away about a search for 'identity,' for God's sakes! You're only thinking of yourself."

She digested that. "Maybe you're right," she conceded, "but I think I've earned it. I think I'm entitled to a little 'selfish' time. Putting my own feelings first is something of a victory for me."

Silence lay over the room like a shroud. Blake desperately tried to think of something to say, something that would convey to her just how much she meant to him. Nothing came. He endured the silence for a moment or two, then said what he'd least meant to say. "I knew I should never have let you come back." With that he turned on his heel and left the room.

He was back in thirty minutes, looking harried, almost frantic. For half an hour he'd paced the mobile home, overwhelmed by a helpless feeling he hated. It had come to him with absolute certainty that losing Shannon, after waiting for her so long, wasn't something he could let happen. He needed a little more time, a day or two. Something would come to him. He'd think of a way to make her want to stay with him forever. He just needed time.

In the meantime Shannon had begun packing. Her typewriter had been put in its case and stood on the floor near the door. The manuscript was neatly stashed away in her briefcase. Her luggage lay open on the bed. She was cleaning out the dresser drawers when he burst into the room.

"If you leave tomorrow, you'll miss Randy," he said abruptly.

She darted from dresser to bed without looking at him. "I know, and I'm sorry. Tell him goodbye for me."

"He'll be...unhappy."

"He'll get over it. He has way too much on his mind now to waste his time thinking about me."

"You haven't even finished the book."

"There are only a few pages left. I'll do them when I get home."

"Dammit, Shannon, I don't understand the big hurry!"

She threw some lingerie into one of the suitcases and raised her face to him. He could see she had been crying, and for some reason that made him feel better. "Oh, Blake, I have to go back, so why postpone the inevitable? I'll stay in close touch. I'll call you often. I'll be anxious to know how everything goes once I'm 'out of the picture.'"

"The only phone call I want is the one telling me you're coming back for good. I don't want you flitting in and out of my life like a moth. I don't want to hear your voice long distance."

"That doesn't make much sense, Blake."

"Well, that's the way it is."

This was a stubborn side of him she hadn't seen before, and it surprised her. It also appalled her. She quickly recalled the first time she'd glimpsed Vic's inflexibility after their marriage, and what a shock it had been. Blake's attitude reinforced her decision to give marriage long, serious consideration. She faced him squarely. "You accuse me of being selfish. Did it ever occur to you that you're being very 'one way' about everything, completely unreasonable?"

"I tend to get that way when I'm frustrated . . . and right now I'm very frustrated."

The admission touched her. She closed the space between them and hugged him ferociously. "Oh, Blake, I know, and I hate that. I feel frustrated, too. I know how much I'm going to miss you."

"Me . . . or the way I make you feel?"

"You," she insisted, although she couldn't deny he had given her a whole new attitude about sex. "Marriage is only one of the relationships men and women enter into."

"Maybe so, but it happens to be the only one I'm interested in."

"I have obligations back home, but even if I didn't, I would have to leave. I'm removing myself as an obstacle. You should be grateful to me."

"Grateful? You can talk about gratitude when you stroll in here, turn my life topsy-turvy, then walk away...."

"If that's what you think I'm doing, then you haven't been paying much attention. I'll gladly come back when I'm sure Randy is safely yours."

Slowly he gathered her to him. He bent his head to kiss her gently. "And then what?" he asked as he lifted his head. "You'll stay how long? Until the book comes out and you go flying off to promote it? Then back until something else comes up?"

"I don't know. I can't predict what I'll have to do a year from now."

"Exactly. And I find that I want something a bit more permanent than that."

A lump formed in Shannon's throat. "Then we're at an impasse, aren't we? You want something permanent, and I want freedom from commitments. I wish I could make you understand that it has nothing to do with the way I feel about you."

"And I wish I could understand, but I can't."

"I was almost sure you couldn't."

Blake held her tightly to him, pressing one hand against the small of her back. Morosely he dwelled on the days ahead, days without Shannon. It made him feel sick inside. For years he'd been a loner who thought he needed no one. He'd discovered how wrong he was. Now there were two people on earth he needed as much as he needed air to breathe. It wasn't right that in order to have one he would have to give up the other.

She'd said she would come back, but would she really? He wondered if what he feared more than anything was letting her go back to that other life.

How did a man go about making a woman miss him, long for him intensely? It wasn't something he'd ever had to do. He called upon the only weapon in his arsenal—her desire for him. He didn't doubt his ability to arouse her, nor hers to arouse him. She didn't even have to do anything, just be there. With Shannon he seemed to exist in a perpetual state of insatiable lust. He crushed her closer still.

"Blake . . . this won't . . . solve anything."

"Won't it?"

"You know it won't."

"Well . . . we can give it a try."

Shannon felt the change in the way he held her. His hands slipped down to cup her buttocks and pulled her up to him. With a sigh she slumped against him. Despite all her misgivings and uncertainties, and they were many, she'd never questioned his love for her nor his ability to carry her off to a lofty plane where worries didn't exist and ecstasy reigned supreme. Her brain didn't function well when she was in Blake's arms. Emotions gained control.

And this time was no exception. She willingly and passionately responded to him. She sighed, closed her eyes and let her tension loosen. His lips wandered lovingly over her face and neck. He murmured her name, caressed her breasts and pressed her insistently against his swelling desire. She collapsed in his arms like a rag doll. When Blake was certain she was ready, he moved away from her, took the suitcases off the bed and set them on the floor. Then he undressed her. He was masterful. The ensuing lovemaking went beyond anything they had shared before, as though each sensed that this one encounter might have to serve for a lifetime of memories.

NOTHING HAD CHANGED, Shannon thought as she slid out of bed and began dressing. A few more minutes of ecstasy, and then they were right back where they started. She glanced over her shoulder at Blake, who was sound asleep...at five in the afternoon, yet. Did all men sleep after lovemaking, she wondered. Gazing down at his peaceful face, she felt her heart swell, then deflate. If things were different, if I were different ...

But she wasn't. Blake could make love to her every hour on the hour, and it still wouldn't change her reluctance to get married. And that's all he wanted. His inflexibility troubled her. Never again would she become an appendage to a man, adhering strictly to his notions of what she should be. She didn't think Blake would want that of her... but she hadn't thought Vic would either.

And face it, Shannon, you're not sure enough of yourself as a person to be positive it couldn't happen again.

As though it were any other night, she prepared supper and they ate in a compatible but quieted mood, carefully skirting the subject of her morning departure. It was only later, when they had retired for the night, that Blake finally said what was on his mind.

"I won't be here when you wake up in the morning, Shannon."

She turned in his embrace. "Where will you be?"

"I don't know, but I won't be here. And I'm not coming down to say goodbye to you, either."

"Blake . . . why?"

"I don't ever want to say goodbye to you again."

"I . . . I guess I understand that. I hate goodbyes, too."

"Never again am I going to watch you walk out of my life. It just takes too much out of me."

And that, too, she understood.

TRUE TO HIS WORD, he was gone when she awoke the following morning. Lethargically she went downstairs to fix some breakfast, but the kitchen was so spotlessly clean she hated messing it up. She settled for coffee, promising herself she would arrive at the airport early enough to get a quick snack there.

Somehow the next two hours passed. She finished packing and dressed in the coatdress she had arrived in almost three months ago. It would be totally improper for a New York autumn, but she had nothing else more appropriate. Back in August she hadn't meant to stay so long.

She made one last inspection of the house, wishing there had been time to give it a thorough cleaning before she left. From time to time she walked to the kitchen window to look up toward the mobile home, but there was no sign of activity, and she couldn't see his jeep anywhere. He obviously had left the farm altogether. Maybe he'd driven to Charlotte. She knew that the unsold townhouses worried him more than he let on. However, the roads had been completed, and today was a beautiful Sunday weather-wise, a good day for house-hunters. It would only take a few sales and he would be able to pay off the builder's loan. Then he wouldn't mind going into debt again. His power station could become a reality.

Her suitcases stood waiting at the front door. There wasn't much use in waiting any longer. She grabbed her handbag from the kitchen table and started for the front of the house when an idea caught hold of her. She didn't know how it would sit with Blake's pride, but she didn't care. Impulsively, she sat down at the kitchen table, took her billfold out of her bag and flipped it open to her checkbook. In her neat precise script she wrote a check for twenty-five thousand dollars and made it out to Blake. She then propped it against the toaster on the counter, and, ripping a sheet off a nearby notepad, she wrote, "Please use this. It will mean so much to me if you do. Love, Shannon."

Now there really was nothing left to do but go.

BLAKE RETURNED TO THE FARM late that afternoon. He had indeed been in Charlotte, and it had been a productive business day. The big ad in the Charlotte Sunday paper, coupled with the ideal weather, had brought sightseers out in droves. When he'd left, one of the townhouses had been sold, and he had hot prospects on two others. He had a feeling that the development was going to be a roaring success, and he'd been in the business long enough to know. A week ago he would have been on cloud nine. Now all he felt was an empty sort of despair.

Before going to the farm, he stopped at the school to meet the bus that brought the team back from Columbia. Randy was full of news about the trip. He announced that he could hardly wait to tell Shannon all about it.

"She's not there, Randy," Blake told him.

The boy's eyes widened. "Where is she?"

"She's gone back to New York."

"How come?"

"She . . . just decided she had to get back."

"Awful sudden, wasn't it? I mean, you'd think she'd stick around and say goodbye."

"Well, I guess that would have been too difficult for her."

Randy slumped in his seat and stared ahead thoughtfully. He didn't say another word until the jeep turned onto the lane leading to the farmhouse. "Are we gonna stay in the house tonight?"

Blake knew with absolute certainty that he couldn't go into that empty house right now. "I don't think so. All our stuff is in the trailer, and you need a good night's sleep. I'll start moving in the house after you go to school in the morning."

Entering the farmhouse the following day sent his emotions spinning wildly. He could feel her presence even if she wasn't there. Like a man bent on self-destruction, he made his way upstairs and found the bed they had slept in the night before now neatly made up. Roughly he jerked back the bedspread and stripped off the sheets. There was no way he could sleep in that bed with the smell of her still in it. In the bathroom, on the ledge beside the tub, he discovered a box of dusting powder she had forgotten. That went in the wastebasket. He gathered up the pile of linens and carried them downstairs to the laundry room off the kitchen. That was when he spied the check.

For the longest time he stared at it, disbelieving. *Shannon, the last thing I want from you is money!*

Unbidden and unwanted, memories of another time sprang to mind. He wondered if the way he felt in any way mirrored Norma's thoughts on that long-ago day. It was so easy to buy yourself out of a difficult situation. The sheets he was holding fell in a heap at his feet. He reached for the check and tore it into as many tiny pieces as he could manage.

CHAPTER FOURTEEN

A VERY PLEASED ANTHONY THOMPSON regarded Shannon over the rim of his coffee cup. "Shannon, it's a pretty damned good book," he began enthusiastically. "Better, much better than I expected."

"You've already read it?" she asked in surprise, for she'd delivered it to him by messenger only two days earlier. Since then, like legions of writers before her, she had thought of dozens of ways she could have improved it. When Anthony had called that morning and asked if he could stop by to discuss the book, her heart had palpitated like mad. What if he didn't like it? What if he wanted to scrap the project altogether? She had thought of so many different things he might want to discuss with her, none of them good. Only now was her nervous stomach calming.

"Yes, and I enjoyed every page of it," Anthony said. "And if I liked it that much, the public is going to go wild over it. When I read, I nit-pick, but the average reader doesn't do that."

"Thanks." Shannon smiled back. It would have been impossible for her to describe the elation she felt over the publisher's praise. She had burned the midnight oil the night she returned to Long Island in order to finish the book. Emotionally, it had been just what she'd needed. When the last page had rolled out of the typewriter at two o'clock in the morning, she had been exhausted and had fallen asleep immediately. Very unlike subsequent nights when she had lain awake until the wee hours, thinking about Blake, missing him, wondering what the future held for them... if anything.

"It just moves right along," Anthony went on, "but..."

Shannon looked at him questioningly. "But?"

"Are you sure this is the book you want published?"

"Why wouldn't it be?"

Anthony tugged on his chin. "You see, I rather envisioned a gossipy little book full of anecdotes about famous personalities. This is... much more than that."

"I know," she said solemnly. Even though she was a novice, she knew she hadn't written a piece of fluff. "Yes, it's the book I want published. I think it's... honest."

"And entertaining. He was an interesting man," Anthony said.

"Yes, he was."

"Not much like the happy-go-lucky crooner the public knew."

"No, I suppose not. But I've come to realize that his laid-back image was the real Vic Parelli while he was performing. I think that's when he was most at ease, most confident. He wasn't fooling the public. I'm not sure the public can be fooled for long, and Vic was a star for over thirty years. And his generosity was genuine."

Anthony nodded. "The list, for instance. Incredible. Are there really that many names on it?"

"Oh, yes." She had decided to tell about the list. No names were mentioned and very little details given, but she thought the list attested to Vic's generosity and gave a gentle dimension to his very intricate personality. "Anthony, arc you trying to tell me something? You said you liked the book."

"I do, I do! I'm just surprised by it, that's all. I think it probably has bestseller written all over it." He leaned forward and set his cup on the coffee table. "In fact, I'm re-thinking the publicity campaign we'd planned. The book calls for something more provocative."

Shannon tried to envision herself as a bestselling author and found she couldn't. After all, the book was no lifetime dream come true. It had been a challenge dumped in her lap. It was enough that someone knowledgeable thought highly of her efforts.

"You'll be getting a call from your editor in a few days," Anthony told her. "Her name is Kay Matthews. I think you'll like working with her. She's experienced and tough, but I don't think you'll regret trusting her instincts."

"This is all so new to me. I'm flattered that you took the time to come all the way out here to see me personally."

"Oh, it's a beautiful day, and it gave me an excuse to get out of the city. Besides..." He smiled charmingly. "I have a golf date not far from here."

Shannon laughed. "It's nice anyway. I'm sorry you have to leave so soon. Jerry's due in a little while."

"Too bad I have to miss him. I don't see as much of Jerry as I'd like. Nice man."

"Yes, very. A good friend."

"His devotion to you and your husband came across nicely in the book."

"I'm glad. I've discovered it's easy to write about people you know well and like a lot. Not so easy to..." She set down her coffee cup and folded her hands. "Anthony, I didn't do a...hatchet job on anyone, did I?"

"No, and I watched for that, believe me. Didn't you read the clause in your contract that deals with lawsuits?"

"Good," she sighed. "There were some I could have butchered. Vic was a...gregarious man. He loved having people around, and he...wasn't always wise in his choice of associates. Jerry was one of the few who never used him. I'm not worried about being sued, because there's not a word in that book that isn't the unvarnished truth."

AFTER ANTHONY LEFT to keep his golf date, Shannon gathered up the coffee service and carried it down the hall to the kitchen. Nicole and Ginger were sitting on stools at the enormous stainless steel work-island that occupied the center of the room. Both jumped to their feet when she entered, embarrassed at being caught idle by the mistress of the house.

Shannon smiled brightly. "Keep your seats, ladies. I'll just put this here."

"Mrs. Parelli, you should have rung for me," Nicole said. "I didn't realize the gentleman had left."

"No problem, Nicole. Ginger, thanks for making the coffee, even though we didn't drink much of it. Those crispy little wafers are wonderful. You put cheese in the dough, right?"

"Yes, ma'am. Parmesan."

"And you used real butter, right?"

Ginger was surprised; to her knowledge, Mrs. Parelli didn't know how to boil water. "Yes, ma'am."

"I thought so. Delicious. Nicole, I'll be upstairs going through some of Mr. Parelli's closets. I'm expecting Mr. Thorpe this afternoon, so have him come upstairs when he arrives."

"Very good, ma'am."

The two servants watched as she left the room, then turned to each other.

"She's changed a lot," Nicole commented.

"A lot," Ginger agreed. "A lot. Can't quite put my finger on what it is, though. For sure she's more interested in what's going on around here. She asked to see last month's grocery receipts. When I showed them to her, she studied them for the longest time, then asked me to start making up a week's menus and to only buy what was absolutely needed. Mr. Parelli always wanted the larder full at all times and didn't care what it cost."

"She seems...nicer somehow," Nicole mused. "I hate to say this, but the mister wasn't an easy man to live with. I always thought the missus was sort of...oh, I can't think of the word."

"Intimidated?" Ginger offered.

"That's it! Mr. Parelli seemed to intimidate her. Maybe she's more relaxed now that he's not around, though it's awful to say so."

"Well, one thing's for sure...she's not any happier than she ever was, and I never did think Mrs. Parelli was really a happy woman."

SHANNON HURRIED UPSTAIRS and shrugged out of the shirtwaist dress she had hurriedly put on before

Anthony arrived. Now she put on jeans, a crimson sweatshirt and some disreputable sneakers. Running a comb through her hair, she scrutinized her new hair cut and recalled with amusement her longtime stylist's reaction when she'd shown up for her appointment the day before. "My God, Mrs. Parelli, your hair looks dreadful! What have you been doing with it?"

"Nothing, Connie, not a thing."

"It shows. Well, go get shampooed and we'll see what we can do with you."

The day had been one that Shannon had set aside just for herself. She'd had her hair done, a manicure and a facial, and after leaving the salon she'd stopped at an exclusive boutique she often patronized and bought three dresses she didn't need and might never wear. In the past, that kind of day could be counted on to lift her spirits. Yesterday, however, had done almost nothing for her. During the drive back home she had chastised herself for her extravagance, unwillingly thinking of what Blake would have to say about it. When she'd returned to the house, it had been just as empty as before, and she had felt just as lonely as before. The loneliness seemed to be eating her alive. That was when she had finally forced herself to start going through Vic's things. It had proven to be an emotional and formidable undertaking, but it was something that had needed doing for a long time. She returned to the task now and kept at it until she heard Jerry's voice calling her name.

She met her friend in the upstairs hall. "Hi, Jerry. Couldn't Peg come?"

"No, she had a meeting of some sort. God, that woman's got her fingers in so many pies I wonder that she can keep up with them. She said she wouldn't be home until late this evening."

"Then stay for dinner." Why was it "supper" on the farm and "dinner" here? "I get tired of eating alone. Besides, I need to talk to you about so many things."

"Problems?" Jerry asked with a frown.

"Not really. Just unfinished business. Come in here, and I'll show you what I'm concerned about."

She led Jerry to the second floor room that had been Vic's private retreat. It was a large room, filled with things Vic had considered important. Two huge walk-in closets occupied one end of it, and it was to one of those closets that Shannon moved now, flinging open the door. "I've finally started going through Vic's things," she said, "and I want you to look at all this stuff. I had no idea what was in here. Maybe you can tell me what on earth to do with it."

Jerry went into the closet and studied the myriad assortment of things Shannon had unearthed. Box after box of photographs, his earliest recordings on 78 rpm, tapes of all his television shows and specials, letters, awards...the memorabilia went on and on. "Good Lord!" Jerry exclaimed. "This stuff must be priceless!"

Shannon nodded. "That was my first thought, too. The other closet is just as full, and I haven't even been in the attic yet. I wish I'd known all this was here when I was writing the book." Idly she fingered a dusty photograph album. "No doubt John and Rosemary will want a few things, but we're talking about rooms full of stuff. Surely there's someone, or several someones who would want it. I simply can't stand the thought of just throwing them away.''

"I know.'' Jerry frowned. "Maybe I can get in touch with someone who'll have an idea.''

They stepped out of the closet and Shannon closed the door.

"That's why I wanted you to see what's here. Over the years you must have met plenty of people in the industry.''

"True. I'll call around tomorrow.''

They left the room and went into the hall. "All those things coupled with all this...'' Shannon's arm swept around to indicate the house as a whole. "has me overwhelmed. So many of the things Vic owned are quite valuable. That vase over there, for instance. He bought it in England. I almost fell down when he told me what he paid for it. Some of these things probably belong in a museum.''

"Have you considered an auction?''

"It crossed my mind.'' She frowned. "But isn't that just selling everything, after all? Vic clung to his possessions so tenaciously.''

"But that was Vic, not you, Shannon. You don't need to be tied to these things. If you ask me, the entire place looks like a museum. Why don't you just hang out a sign and charge admission?''

Together they descended the stairs. "Funny... if Vic were still alive and, for whatever reason, didn't want to live in this house, he'd probably love the idea of turning it into a museum. He liked nothing better than to show his friends around this place. He even threw open the closet doors!''

Jerry smiled. "As hard as he tried, Vic never entirely got rid of his poor-kid-from-Philadelphia outlook."

"I know. Maybe none of us ever shakes his roots. Vic used to tell me he'd never been able to take all the country out of me."

They reached the bottom of the stairs and moved in the direction of the den. "Speaking of that, tell me all about being out among the cows and hay." This was said with a note of cheerful derision. Jerry was a dyed-in-the-wool New Yorker who loved the vitality and energy of the city. Even Long Island was too rural for him.

With forced casualness, Shannon said, "There weren't any cows and there wasn't any hay. The farm isn't really a working one, not yet."

"The place must have been bursting with old memories."

"Yes, it was." But the new memories were the ones that haunted her. She wished Jerry hadn't mentioned the farm. She had managed to go almost all day without consciously thinking about Blake, although he lingered just on the periphery of her thoughts all the time. She missed him twice as much as she'd thought she would.

When she had landed at Kennedy last Sunday, she had psyched herself into a state of utter confidence. Things would work out. Blake wouldn't remain stubbornly set on marriage or nothing. She'd half expected him to call that very evening.

He hadn't, and her confidence had waned with each passing day. The silent telephone was like a slap in the face. She wouldn't have dreamed he could hold out so long.

Of course, she could call him, but she wouldn't, not just to chat. Damn, she wished she knew what was going on down there, and if Blake had any sense at all he ought to know she would be burning with curiosity. Maybe he didn't care.

"Something wrong, Shannon?" Jerry asked solicitously.

She turned to him with a jerky motion. "No, no, nothing. Why?"

"You looked like you were a million miles away."

"No, not quite a million. Now, Jerry, did you bring the household accounts with you?"

"Uh hmm." Jerry was more than just a little curious over Shannon's sudden interest in how her money was being spent. She'd never been extravagant—far from it—but like most women of her financial status, she had spent money without giving it a thought. Now she wanted to know where the dollars were going, and that was smart. But what had motivated the interest?

They went into the den. Shannon sat behind the desk, and Jerry took a seat nearby, after first spreading a computer printout before her. She studied it carefully while Jerry waited. Finally, she sat back and looked at him. "This is ridiculous!" she exclaimed.

"Didn't I tell you?"

"There's no reason for this house to cost so much to run every month. The waste must be tremendous."

"Shannon, thrift has never been a by-word in this house."

"I had no idea."

"I know you didn't. And every time I mentioned it to Vic, he said he never wanted to give money a thought again as long as he lived."

"There's a difference between not worrying about money and spending it like there's no tomorrow." Shannon frowned. "Leave this with me, Jerry," she said, tapping the paper before her. "I want to study it some more. I know these costs can be reduced."

"Sure. May I ask what brought on this sudden concern over finances?"

"No one has the right to over-consume," she said tightly, leaving Jerry even more puzzled. "I don't need this place."

"Haven't I been trying to tell you just that?"

Folding the printout, she slipped it into the center drawer. "Well, what say, Jerry...are you staying for dinner?"

"I have a better idea. How about letting me take you out to eat? Peg's having dinner at that meeting. Guillermo's for paella? How does that sound?"

She smiled. It would be good to get out of the house for a few hours. The walls were closing in on her. Jerry was right; the place was like a museum. A very expensive museum. "It sounds great. I'll fix you a drink and you can sip it while I'm getting ready."

WHILE SHANNON AND JERRY were having dinner at the charming out-of-the-way restaurant, Blake and Randy were seated at the kitchen table in the farmhouse, their meal long past. The boy was intent on the latest issue of Sporting News, and Blake was talking on the phone to Tom Archer. The news the minister had for him wasn't good.

"Blake, Mary Hatcher is convinced that Shannon has gone away only long enough to allow the adoption to go through."

"That's not true, Tom. She had a lot of loose ends to tie up in New York. She'd always planned to leave."

"Is she coming back?"

Ah, there's a question, Blake thought. "I honestly don't know."

"Well, Mary and her sister are intent on dragging this thing out, but I have an idea. How about a private attorney? South Carolina allows private adoptions, so you might be better off by-passing the adoption board altogether. I haven't mentioned it before because, frankly, it's expensive."

"I don't care what it costs!"

"I've been told that any attorney who specializes in these things will want a retainer of a thousand dollars or more."

"No problem."

"Then let me give you a name. Jim Bernstein. He's supposed to be the best. I don't have the number, but it's in the book."

"Just a minute. Let me get something to write with." Blake motioned to Randy, who jumped up and got a notepad and pencil off the kitchen counter. "Okay... Bernstein. Right, I got it. Thanks, Tom. I appreciate it."

When Blake hung up the phone, Randy looked at him across the table. "Shannon's not coming back, is she?"

"I don't know, son."

"Why doesn't she call us?"

"I guess... because I asked her not to."

Randy frowned. "Why'd you do a goofy thing like that?"

Blake stared at the phone. "I don't know that either," he admitted.

"Well, if you told her not to call you, she won't. So seems like you should call her."

"Think so?" The temptation was strong. He had endured a week of the loneliest nights he'd ever experienced, and he was beginning to realize how absurd his ultimatums to Shannon had been. Wasn't part of her better than nothing at all? Randy was right; she'd never call first. And he probably should tell her he'd torn up that check. He wouldn't want her account to get screwed up. Lame excuse, but at least it was an excuse.

"Come on and call her, Blake," Randy insisted. "I want to tell her what the coach said yesterday after practice."

Blake grinned. "Well, as long as there's a really good reason for the call..."

The deposit slip she had given him in the motel parking lot last April was still folded and tucked inside his wallet. Reaching for the phone, he dialed the number she had scribbled on the back. It rang three times before a woman's voice answered.

"Parelli residence, Nicole speaking."

"May I speak to Mrs. Parelli, please?"

"Mrs. Parelli isn't in now. May I give her a message?"

"I, ah, what time do you expect her?"

"I really couldn't say, sir. She's gone out to dinner. would you like to leave your name and number?"

"No, I . . . I'll call her another time." Blake replaced the receiver and struggled to hide his very real disappointment from Randy. "Sorry, son, she's not home."

"Call her again later."

"Maybe. Right now I want to talk to you. Reverend Archer has a new idea about the adoption."

Out to dinner, he fumed. Why had he ever imagined her moping and pining over him? Wasn't this what he'd feared—that once she got back to that fancy life in New York she'd be too busy to miss him or even to think about him? What a fool he was! What a fool he had always been about Shannon.

ONE MISERABLE WEEK LATER Blake, his courage and confidence bolstered by three cans of beer, again tried to call her, only to be told that Mrs. Parelli was spending the day and night in the city tending to business matters. If he'd like, the woman named Nicole said, she would be glad to give him the number where Mrs. Parelli was spending the night.

Why the hell didn't Shannon ever stay at home? Again he declined to leave a message, and he damned sure didn't want a phone number. He didn't even know what he'd intended saying to Shannon if he'd been able to reach her. In the mood he was in, it probably would have come across as gibberish.

When Shannon returned home the following day, Nicole thought to tell her about Blake's phone calls. "A gentleman has called twice, ma'am, a week or so ago and again last night, but both times he declined to leave his name and number."

A spark of hope rose up in Shannon. Blake? Was it even reasonable to think he might have been the one who'd called? The hope died quickly, however. If Blake had finally relented enough to telephone, he surely would have left his name. He would want her to return the call, wouldn't he?

"Thank you, Nicole," she said, and dismissed the calls from her mind.

CHAPTER FIFTEEN

SHANNON SAT AT THE TABLE in the gracious dining room and ate her superb but solitary Thanksgiving dinner. At her elbow was a copy of the New York Times, lying open to the article headlined PARELLI HOME TO BE AUCTIONED. It had been a hard decision, one she had agonized over night after sleepless night. After first making sure that neither John nor Rosemary was interested in the house—"Good Lord," Rosemary had said, "I can't imagine being tied to all those things."—she had considered the idea of turning the house into a museum in order to keep Vic's possessions intact. Upon investigation, however, she'd discovered that such a project would have taken years to see through to completion, provided several local government agencies approved it, and there was no guarantee they would. She simply wasn't prepared to give it that much time. The house was a burden, and she was bent on ridding herself of burdens.

In the end, she felt an auction was the only course open to her, and making such a decision was another milestone for her. She had kept a few things for herself and had asked John and Rosemary to take anything they wanted. Then she had donated some of the more priceless mementos of Vic's recording career to the Academy of Recording Arts and Sciences. That done, she had contacted one of New

York's most reputable auction houses and made arrangements for an on-site sale in January. People from the firm had filed in and out all week, asking her advice on the best way to prepare the rooms for viewing and on which room would best serve as the auction hall itself. She had experienced a few stabs of guilt while all this was going on, but she was somewhat consoled when both John and Rosemary agreed she was doing what they would have done themselves.

Then and only then had she told Jerry of her decision. That made it hers and hers alone. He had been pleased, as she'd known he would be.

One by one, matters had been taken care of. Each decision became easier than the one before. Shannon had consolidated all of Vic's enormous estate and placed it in a trust fund, which would simplify her taxes and care for her handsomely throughout her life. The trust would also handle Vic's list every month, another burden done with. Only once during all those negotiations did she falter; that was over the matter of beneficiaries. She had no heirs. As things now stood, when she died, her large estate would go to several worthy charities.

The book was finished. She'd had no idea what working with an editor entailed. In her case, it had meant two pleasant luncheon meetings with the delightful woman named Kay Matthews, and a few days spent on revisions. Now the book was on its way to production, whatever that meant.

So there was little for her to do; just pack the things she wanted to keep for herself. And, of course, find a new place to live. She would leave Omar boarded at the Post-and-Paddock for the time being. She didn't have to worry about Nicole and Ginger.

Nicole was using the changed circumstances as an excuse to go live with her sister, who lived upstate and was newly widowed. And once word had gotten around the Parelli's social circle that Ginger would be available, the cook had been beseiged with offers of employment. Ginger was going to work in the household of the recording executive who had signed Vic to his first contract thirty years ago.

Shannon forked in a mouthful of Ginger's delicious stuffing and stared across the great expanse of the dining table. Holidays alone were awful. Of course Jerry and Peg had invited her to have Thanksgiving dinner with them, but their house would be packed with their kids, some aunts and uncles, nieces and nephews. Today, after all, was the most family-oriented holiday of the year. She would have felt like an intruder, although all the Thorpes would have turned themselves inside out trying to make her feel anything but that.

Pushing away her plate, she raised a goblet of white wine to her lips just as Nicole hurried into the room. "Are you ready for some pumpkin pie, ma'am?" she inquired pleasantly.

Shannon patted her stomach and smiled. "I think I'll wait a while, Nicole. I'm afraid I couldn't hold another bite. Please tell Ginger she outdid herself this year. The food was marvelous."

"Yes, ma'am, I'll tell her. She'll be so pleased."

Instead of immediately clearing the table, Nicole stood nearby, shifting her stance uncertainly.

"Nicole, is something wrong?" Shannon asked.

"No, ma'am, but...you see, Ginger and I were just talking about how this is the last Thanksgiving any of us will spend in this house. It's been a long time...twenty years for me and almost as long for

Ginger." The little woman's voice wavered slightly. "And...ma'am, what Ginger and I would like to say is...it's been a pleasure serving you."

Shannon's eyes grew hot. She blinked several times. "Thank you, Nicole," she said with some difficulty. "And thank Ginger for me. I...shall miss both of you, very much."

Nicole nodded and began clearing the table. Shannon quickly got to her feet and carried her wine into the den, where a fire blazed cheerfully in the fireplace. She sat down behind Vic's desk with the idea of concentrating all her thoughts on where she wanted to live. She'd had time for only sporadic house-hunting, but she had to find a place before Christmas if possible. Nicole and Ginger would be leaving, the pre-auction preparations were beginning to get on her nerves, and since she had to move, she wanted to get it over with.

Her mind, however, was a blank. In spite of her good intentions, she found her gaze riveted on the desk telephone. Why didn't Blake call? Why was he so relentlessly stubborn? If he had called, even once, she might have made a quick trip to South Carolina to spend the holiday with them.

Exactly what he didn't want, she was reminded. What would he and Randy be doing on this Thanksgiving Day?

The urge to call him was strong, as it had been ever since returning home. How many times had she picked up the phone and gotten as far as dialing the area code? Dozens. But she'd always hung up before completing the call, for Blake's voice would come to her loud and clear: "the only phone call I want is the one telling me you're coming back for good." Even now she wasn't sure she could do that.

She took another drink of wine; the golden liquid slid smoothly down her throat and created a mellow glow within. Suddenly her hand reached for the instrument. It's only a phone call, for heaven's sakes! No one could order her not to make a phone call. Part of what had been wrong with her life was her easy acquiescence to ultimatums. She didn't care if he fumed and snorted. He could even hang up on her. All she wanted was to find out how they were.

She would use the check as an excuse for the call. It hadn't cleared the bank, so knowing Blake, he'd probably torn it up. Knowing Blake, she probably shouldn't have left the dumb thing in the first place.

Quickly, before she could change her mind, she dialed the number, only to sit and listen to its endless ringing. Acutely disappointed, because she knew how long it would probably take her to get up the nerve to call again, she frowned. Where would a man and boy who had no other family go on Thanksgiving?

THE POPULAR GREENVILLE CAFETERIA was even more crowded than usual on the holiday. Most of the patrons, Blake noticed, were elderly, although in one corner of the establishment several tables had been fitted together to accommodate a large group composed of all ages, from seventy-plus down to infants in arms. It took ten minutes for him and Randy to reach the serving line. "Load 'er up, son. Turkey and all the trimmings," Blake said.

"Do I have to take the broccoli?" Randy asked, wrinkling his nose.

Blake grinned. "I don't guess so. How about the squash or peas?"

"Aw, Blake, it's a holiday. Do I have to eat vegetables today?"

"Tell you what... if you'll take a salad, I won't insist on vegetables."

They found a table by a window. Dinner in a crowded cafeteria might not spell Thanksgiving to most people, but for Blake it beat all the solitary holiday meals he had endured in his life. And Randy was getting a huge kick out of it, which was the important thing. The boy ate with gusto, as he always did, and he seemed to be growing taller by the minute, yet he remained reed-thin. Not even Shannon's good cooking had put any weight on him.

Blake put down his fork and took a drink of water. She'd been gone a month, and still he couldn't stop thinking about her. He felt her presence in every corner of the house. He hadn't dreamed a person could actually ache from loneliness, but he did. Lingering memories, which he had sought to avoid at all costs, existed in abundance.

In one of his more irrational moments he had wished he hadn't been so careful during their lovemaking. A baby on the way might have kept Shannon by his side. But he'd immediately been ashamed of himself and knew he didn't mean that. Of all the reasons for a woman to stay with a man, pregnancy was probably the worst.

Maybe Norma had realized that all those years ago. Maybe she really had been the realist she claimed to be.

What in hell had made him think that? Damned if he hadn't turned into someone about as pleasant as an irritated mongoose!

"This is really neat!" Randy exclaimed enthusiastically, his eyes roaming the cafeteria.

"What? The place or the food?"

"Both. But I'll bet Shannon could have really fixed a meal!"

"Yeah, I'll bet she could have, too," Blake agreed. Randy talked about her all the time, which didn't help matters. The boy seemed to have conveniently forgotten that he'd ever considered her a threat. To hear him talk, one would think they'd never been anything but friends.

"I think its weird that she hasn't called us," Randy mused. "I don't care if you did tell her not to. I thought she would anyway."

"I guess she's busy, son. There was a lot she had to do back in New York," Blake said, wishing he could think of a way to change the subject.

"Too busy to make a phone call?"

"Randy, eat your food before it gets cold."

"She doesn't know you're building the power station?"

"No, she doesn't." By now she'd know he hadn't cashed the damned check. He'd thought she'd be a little curious about that. He could tell her he'd sold six of the townhouses. Would she be pleased?

"She doesn't even know about the lawyer, does she?"

Blake shook his head. He was encouraged. Jim Bernstein, the young lawyer he'd retained, seemed to think he could obtain the adoption without any trouble. There were certain channels he had to go through, but he knew the system and foresaw no problems. Now the sisters no longer posed a threat. Everything in his life was slipping neatly into place, everything but Shannon.

If she knew about all this she might keep that Christmas date with them. But Blake had reached the point where he no longer knew if he wanted that. She'd only leave again, and he'd had enough of Shannon's leaving to last several lifetimes.

"Are you gonna tell her?" Randy asked.

"I don't know, son."

"Wish you would. She might come back to see us when she's not so busy."

"For someone who couldn't stand the sight of her for a while there . . ."

"Yeah." Randy smiled sheepishly. "Dumb, huh? She really was nice. You know what I bet?"

"What?"

"I'll bet Shannon's the only woman in the whole wide world who knows Larry Bird's from French Lick, Indiana."

Blake cleared his throat and wiped his mouth with a napkin. "Say, Randy, how about us having some pie and then taking in a movie while we're in town?"

"Hey, neat!" the boy agreed, and the subject of Shannon was dropped for the time being.

THANKSGIVING DAY FINALLY DWINDLED into evening. The day had dragged on leaden feet. Shannon had waited an hour and called the farm again, but still there was no answer. She didn't attempt another call; what was the point? She'd forgotten what she'd been going to say in the first place. She tried pushing Blake and Randy out of her mind, but it didn't work. She tried to be glad they were busy and not missing her. That didn't work either.

Well, this is what you wanted, her inner voice reminded her. *Independence, freedom from commitments, a chance to find yourself. Are you any closer to knowing who you are than you were a month ago?*

Yes, was the answer. A very definite yes. She had discovered she was more decisive than she'd imagined possible. That, in turn, had inspired a new self-confidence, a liberation of her spirit.

Yet, she'd also discovered that freedom and independence didn't cure loneliness and emptiness. Her life still had no clear-cut goals, nothing central to focus hopes and ambitions on.

It could have. Again her inner voice nagged her. *There's Blake. You could be with Blake tonight.*

The thought sent a tingling current up her spine.

She went upstairs early, bathed, then propped up in bed to try to lose herself in the new paperback novel everyone was raving about. She had been reading half an hour when she suddenly put down the book.

This was ridiculous! Sitting there missing Blake when he was only a phone call away was absurd. What difference did it make who called who first? That was high school stuff. And as long as she allowed some foolish qualms to prevent her calling him, she was admitting she wasn't in control where he was concerned.

Her hand reached for the telephone at the precise moment it rang. She jumped at the sound. Blake? Hope bubbled inside her. She didn't answer the phone; she never did. She waited until Nicole tapped on her door and peeked in.

"It's Mrs. Thorpe, ma'am."

Shannon shook off any disappointment and smiled, reaching for the phone. Now she would be treated to a full and detailed account of the Thorpes' Thanksgiving. She would call Blake afterwards. "Hi, Peg?"

"Oh, Sh-Shannon, it's Jerry! He's had a heart at-tack."

Shannon's heart lurched up into her throat. "No!"

"It's critical. Come, please. We're at Metropoli-tan. I need you here with me. Everyone else is fall-ing apart all around me. Please come."

"I'm on my way!" She hung up, flung away the bedcovers and made for her closet. "Nicole!" she cried.

The maid, having sensed the agitation in Mrs. Thorpe's voice, hadn't strayed far. She appeared in the bedroom immediately. "Yes, ma'am."

Panic tinged Shannon's voice. "It's Mr. Thorpe. He's had a heart attack. I've got to go..."

Nicole's hand went to her throat. "I'll bring the car around."

SOME TIME LATER Shannon stood in the front of the emergency room, her arm around an anguished Peg Thorpe. Seeing her friend in such a state of despair was a shock almost as great as the news of Jerry's heart attack. She had known Peg over fifteen years and had seen her display only two moods: happy as a lark or angry as a fire ant. Now she was stunned and frightened, and the expression on her face shook Shannon down to her toes. She ruefully wished all the "friends" who declared that Peg was empty-headed and lacked depth could see her now.

There were few vacant seats in the waiting room. Shannon recognized the faces of Jerry's son and daughter, though she hadn't seen them in ages. They had grown up. The girl was crying uncontrollably, and the young man looked as though he had been kicked in the stomach. She also recognized Jerry's

sister, whom she had met once before, but she'd forgotten the woman's name. Other members of the
family were present, most of them out-of-towners
she had never met. All of them were trying to comfort one another. Their faces registered stunned
disbelief. What had begun as a family holiday had
turned into horrible tragedy.

"What happened, Peg?" Shannon asked.

"H-he was so quiet all day, preoccupied. I . . . just
supposed he was worried over an account. But then,
after dinner, we were all watching TV, and I saw the
strangest look come over his face, as though he was
in pain. I asked him what was wrong, and he said
heartburn." Peg's voice broke. "A . . . few minutes
later he grabbed his chest and slumped out of his
chair onto the floor. I . . . oh, Shannon, he . . . can't
die!"

"Shhh. He's not going to die, Peg. Keep that
thought."

Time passed with agonizing slowness. It was well
past midnight when the emergency room chief put in
an appearance. Cautiously he announced that the
patient was stabilized but still in very serious condition. Jerry was being taken to the coronary-care unit
where the fight to save his life would go on. He suggested they all go home, for there was nothing they
could do there. He would notify them immediately
if there was any change.

"I can't go home, Shannon, I just can't," Peg
whispered.

"Please go, Peg. You can't do Jerry any good if
you become exhausted and get sick yourself."

At that moment the Thorpes' daughter approached and took her mother by the arm. "Come
on, Mom, let's go home. The doctor said he'll call."

"Please, Peg," Shannon insisted. "I'll be back in the morning to sit with you. And every day until we know he's all right."

Peg nodded and brushed at her tear-stained cheeks. "Thanks so much for coming, Shannon. Jerry loves you, and so do I."

"And I love both of you."

Shannon glanced at the rest of the family. They were gathering near the entrance to the emergency room. Their faces were portraits of fear and despair. She felt so very sorry for all of them, but thought how fortunate they were to have one another at a time like this.

If I were in that coronary-care unit, hovering between life and death, who would rally around and keep the vigil?

FOR TEN DAYS Jerry remained in the coronary-care unit, fighting for his life. Shannon didn't miss a day at the hospital, although she, as non-family, wasn't allowed in to see him. She stayed with Peg, consoled her, ran errands for her and other family members, handled phone calls and sometimes spent the night in the Thorpe home when she was too tired to make the drive to her own. Outside the hospital's grim walls, New York was being decked out in her Christmas finery, but none of them noticed. Their days were consumed with waiting and praying.

Jerry lived and slowly responded. Finally he was moved to a private room, where his long convalescence began. Shannon marveled at Peg's quiet, sure strength and steady resolve. She stayed as close to Jerry's side as was allowed and seemed to be willing her husband to live. The fluttery little social butterfly was gone, replaced by a stoic, determined woman with a take-charge attitude.

Eventually the day came when Jerry's recovery was sufficiently assured to enable Peg to talk about the future. "I'm taking him away from the city, Shannon. He's never going to work hard again. He always did, you know, only I was too busy to notice. We both just rushed, rushed, rushed from one place to another. I don't know what we were trying to prove. Sitting beside him in the ambulance that night, watching the medics working on him, I thought—my God, we've wasted so much of the last twenty years!"

"Away, Peg?" Shannon asked with a painful twinge. "Where will you go?"

"To my mother's place in Maine," Peg replied without hesitation. "It overlooks the ocean and has the most beautiful natural garden. I...always thought it too provincial and primitive for the likes of sophisticated city people like Jerry and myself, but now it seems like a haven. Mom isn't well, and she would adore having us there. Jerry needs peace and quiet—the doctor says so—and it's the perfect place."

A picture of the farm suddenly flashed through Shannon's mind. "How do you think Jerry will take to the country?"

"He probably will balk at first, but I don't care. We'll have to lower our standard of living considerably, but I don't care about that either. I can do without Gucci and Galanos and servants, but I can't do without Jerry. He'll...never really be well again, Shannon. You know that, don't you?"

Shannon gulped and nodded. "I know."

"Never again will he compete for a big account or entertain important clients. He wouldn't be able to stand enforced idleness here in the city, but it won't be so bad at mom's. In time, if he wants, he can dabble in tax returns or something like that, but I'll never again allow him to become a workaholic."

"I'm going to miss you."

"Lord, don't you think I'm going to miss you, too!" Peg exclaimed. "We'll have to stay in touch, forever and ever."

"Of course."

"I can picture us still having yearly reunions when we're in our eighties."

"Sure."

The two women were seated in the hospital cafeteria having lunch. Once the meal was over, Shannon was going home and, for once, staying there. Peg and the hospital had been virtually her whole world for weeks, but now she had things to tend to. Both Nicole and Ginger were leaving right away, and she was closing up the house. The auction firm was taking charge of it now and had appointed caretakers to look after the place until after the January auction. The proceeds of the sale would go to the trust. Shannon couldn't get away from the place fast enough.

Peg reached across the table and covered Shannon's hand with her own. "For weeks now we've talked about nothing but Jerry. You've been a rock, Shannon. I don't know what I would have done without you. But now let's talk about you. What are you going to do?"

"I don't know, Peg. Not surprisingly, I've not thought about it for a while. I do have to find a place to live, though, even if it's only a temporary apartment."

Peg sighed wistfully. "Ever since Vic died I've sorta hoped you would decide to move into the city, get a place near me. But now..."

Shannon smiled. "But now 'near you' will be the coast of Maine. You're the dearest friend I've ever had, Peg, but I'm not sure I want to move to Maine."

"I'm worried about you, Shannon."

"Please don't. You have enough to worry about."

"Isn't there any place in this whole big wide world that really appeals to you?"

Shannon stared out the cafeteria window for a moment, then turned to her friend and said, "Yes, there's a place." She paused, then added, "And a person."

Peg's eyes widened. "A man?" she asked breathlessly.

Shannon grinned. "Why did you automatically assume that?"

"Come off it, Shannon! Are you telling me there's a man in your life and you haven't told me about him?"

"Is Blake in my life? I wonder."

"Blake? I don't know a Blake. Oh, my God!" Peg breathed. She glanced at her watch. "I have thirty minutes before they'll let me in to see Jerry again. Now, I want to hear all about this!"

Hesitantly, Shannon told Peg about Blake. All about him and the farm and Randy. She concluded with, "And that's the way we parted. Either I come back for good, or I stay away altogether. And, frankly, that rankles."

Peg placed a hand on her forehead. "Oh, Shannon, that's the most romantic thing I ever heard! He was in love with you for eighteen years, and you never knew it!"

"So he claims."

"I'm not too sure I'd want someone like that to get away."

"A time or two I've been sorely tempted to go back, to commit myself to Blake in every way, but then...then I think of how good it feels to be free, and..." Shannon paused, for she was venturing into an area of her life she'd never discussed with Peg. "You see, Vic had become unbearably possessive. He almost...smothered me."

"Do you think I don't know that? I could see it."

"You could?"

"Oh, of course, and I often wished you would talk to me about it. I liked Vic, really I did, and goodness knows he was good to Jerry over the years, but I would have had to be blind not to see the way he held onto you as though you were a life vest or something. He resented everyone you liked, even me. I think he was scared to death of losing you."

"Peg, you amaze me, honestly you do. That you paid so much attention..."

"Hey, you've been my best friend, and I care about you. I always thought it was a shame you couldn't enjoy life without having to fight Vic's disapproval all the way."

"Living with him had become...difficult," Shannon confessed. "Things had changed so much in the last...oh, four or five years."

"Vic was fighting the calendar. Once he passed the fifty mark and felt all that youthful energy slipping away, he resented yours."

"I think you're right. Maybe if I had understood that, had understood him better, I might not have been so resentful."

A moment of contemplative silence followed before Peg said, "Now you feel free, and you don't want to give up the freedom. Oh, Shannon, I can understand that, truly I can. But this man in South Carolina sounds divine...." Peg paused to roll her eyes. "Like someone who wouldn't cling to you but would let you lean on him when you needed to. And that is nice, believe me. I've leaned on Jerry plenty during the last twenty years, and now he's going to learn to lean on me. Not all commitments are suffocating. I guess I'm looking at life a little differently now. I think about the kids and how I often accused them of being ungrateful, selfish monsters, but look how they rallied around like little Minutemen. In fact, everyone on both sides of the family has been wonderful."

"I know." For weeks Shannon had been watching all of them banding together like an impregnable force, shoring up each other's spirits when they began to sag. While misfortune was never easy to deal with, the difficulty was mitigated somewhat when there were others to share it with.

"Alone isn't a good place to be, Shannon," Peg continued. "I've discovered that family is everything, everything! Everyone needs someone who cares, and this man sounds as though he really cares."

Shannon smiled wanly. "I know he cares, but he's stubborn as all get out, and I wonder if he wouldn't easily become just as possessive as Vic did."

"Do you honestly think you would allow that to happen now? Think of how much you've changed

since you married Vic. In the early days you used to
remind me of a frightened puppy who'd strayed far
from home. But think of all you've accomplished on
your own. Do you think for a minute you would let
a man dominate you now?''

"I guess not. No, I wouldn't! So that might cause
problems. And, too...I wonder if I'm willing to
commit myself to Blake's way of life. I mean, we are
talking about a man who keeps a snake in his garden and wants to make his own soap!''

Peg chuckled. "A far cry from a mansion on Long
Island, huh? Ah, but what's life but a series of
changes and choices?''

"Why, Peg...how philosophical!''

"One of my mom's famous sayings. She has one
for every situation under the sun, and in my ripe
middle-age I'm beginning to see the truth in most of
them. She used to tell me that a commitment to another human being is always a calculated risk. How
right she was! There were so many times when Jerry
and I might have failed, but we always chose to stay
together because together just seemed better than
apart. I'm so thankful we did. He needs me now as
he's never needed me before, and I need him to really
need me. I think we'll be even closer than ever, and I
can't imagine growing old without him.''

Who will I grow old with, Shannon wondered.

"I've always wanted you to be happy, Shannon,
and you've never been, not really. You've lived just
on the edge of happiness. If you think the man in
South Carolina can make you happy, then I'd sug-
gest you run to him. Follow your heart. Do what
seems right and natural to you.'' Peg stopped and
smiled sheepishly. "Aren't I a treasurehouse of advice? You know...speaking of my mom's famous

sayings... she says there's one thing every woman should save for her old age.''

"What's that?" Shannon asked.

"Her marriage."

SHANNON WALKED OUTSIDE and stood for a moment in the dismal, sunless December afternoon. A man and woman hurried by, entering the hospital with their arms laden with gaily-wrapped packages. Tomorrow is the day before Christmas Eve, she suddenly thought in surprise. The time got away from me. I haven't done any shopping. Her next thought was, *Who pray would I shop for?*

Another couple walked by, also going into the hospital. "Merry Christmas!" they chorused.

"Merry Christmas," Shannon answered and burst into tears.

CHAPTER SIXTEEN

THE HOUSE WAS ON A SIDE STREET in one of Greenville's oldest neighborhoods. A blue sedan pulled to a stop in front of the small frame structure. Blake and Jim Bernstein got out of the lawyer's car. They walked up the sagging front steps and knocked on the door. Several minutes passed before the knock was answered. The woman who stood in the doorway was fortyish, short, thin and pale. She eyed them suspiciously.

"Mrs. Sloan?" Jim Bernstein asked in his lawyer's voice. "Thelma Sloan?"

The woman's eyes narrowed further. "I'm Thelma, but I haven't been Mrs. Sloan in a long time," she said gruffly.

"Oh, of course, but that's the only name we have."

"It's Meadows now."

"Mrs. Meadows, my name is Jim Bernstein. I'm an attorney, and this is my client, Mr. Carmichael." The woman glanced at both of them but made no acknowledgement. "We're here to speak to you about Randy."

At this the woman stiffened. "If the kid's in trouble again, you've come to the wrong place. I washed my hands of him long ago."

Anger boiled inside Blake. He had agreed to let Jim do the talking, so he kept his mouth shut with some effort.

"The boy's in no trouble, Mrs. Meadows—far from it," Jim assured her. "Mr. Carmichael wants to adopt him, and we need your signature on a couple of papers. That's all."

"Yeah?" The woman opened the screen door and stepped out onto the porch. Her eyes swept over Blake in a total assessment. This was one of the rare occasions when he had elected to wear a business suit. He looked every inch the prosperous executive. "What's in it for me?"

"Mrs. Meadows, there is no monetary exchange in these matters, if that's what you mean," Jim explained patiently. His tone implied he was sure that's what she had in mind.

"Then I'm not too sure about signing anything."

Blake flinched. Jim had warned him that Randy's mother might want money; still her attitude appalled him. For the first time in his life he experienced the very real desire to hit a woman. He glanced at Jim, whose cool professional manner hadn't slipped one iota.

"Mrs. Meadows, your signature isn't abolutely necessary since, as you pointed out, you 'washed your hands of him long ago,' and the court is aware of your negligence. Mr. Carmichael has been Randy's foster father for almost a year. Your release, however, will make the adoption completely uncontested and would speed things along considerably."

"Well, it seems to me that if this fine-looking gentleman wants my boy, he should give me something. Randy wouldn't be around if it wasn't for me."

Jim shifted his gaze to Blake, who nodded curtly. The lawyer then looked at Randy's mother. "In return for your signature, Mr. Carmichael is willing to give you a cash settlement of a thousand dollars."

On cue, Blake withdrew his wallet from his hip pocket and slowly began counting the fifty dollar bills he had gotten at the bank for just this purpose.

The woman's mouth dropped. Flustered, she said with affected casualness, "Well...I guess...that's all right. Seems fair. Listen..." She glanced around furtively. "No one's gonna know about this, right? I mean, my old man doesn't have to get wind of this, does he?"

"Rest assured, no one will know about the money. I will require you to sign a document, however. It states that you waive all rights to Randy forevermore."

The transaction took place with dispatch. "Would you like copies of these papers, Mrs. Meadows?" Jim inquired wryly.

"Hell, no!" she sputtered, took the money from Blake and went inside the house. Blake and Jim walked back to the car.

"Charming woman," the lawyer commented caustically.

"Yeah, a real sweetheart," Blake said.

"Well, Blake, I'd hoped to make you a daddy by Christmas. We won't miss it by much, though. Right after the first of the year, I reckon."

"I don't know how to thank you, Jim."

"Don't mention it. By the way, where's Randy this afternoon? School's out for the holidays, right?"

"Right. He's at the gym with some of the team. I'm going there right now to tell him the news. Then we've got to go buy a tree. A house with a kid in it has to have a tree. I'm afraid Christmas sneaked up on me this year."

"Yeah." Jim grinned. "Well, you've had a lot on your mind."

An understatement, Blake thought as they drove back to the lawyer's office where his jeep was parked. It seemed his mind was never at peace anymore. He had been worried about the adoption, of course, but now that was taken care of, he could place the blame for his restiveness where it belonged—on Shannon. And on the days that had slipped by, one after the other, without word from her.

He'd swallowed his pride once more only a week earlier and telephoned her yet again. This time the servant named Nicole had informed him that Mrs. Parelli was at the hospital.

"Hospital!" Fear had sliced through him, searing his insides.

"Yes, sir. A friend has been very ill, very ill. Are you sure you wouldn't like to leave your name and number?"

Quietly he'd replaced the receiver. Well, he wasn't going to call her again. And he had to be realistic about this. With each passing day, the chances that she would call became slimmer and slimmer. He'd tried to put himself in her shoes. From the little bit she'd told him he had guessed that her husband had been domineering and possessive. She must feel like a sparrow who'd been kicked out of the nest and was trying her wings for the first time. She wouldn't want to get tied down again. He hoped he could accept that and get on with his life.

"BLAKE," RANDY SAID with youthful frankness, "I gotta tell you—that's the worst looking Christmas tree I ever saw!"

Blake stepped back and studied the fir he had set up in the corner of the living room. "Does have a couple of bare spots, doesn't it? And the trunk's crooked. Guess you shouldn't wait until two days before Christmas to buy one."

"Turn it the other way... toward the fireplace," the boy suggested.

"Like this?"

"Uh huh. That looks a little better. Still got some holes, though."

"Well, all that tinsel and garland we bought will fill them up, don't you think?"

The boy shrugged. "Guess so. Do you know how to put all that stuff on a tree?"

Blake shrugged. "What's to know? How hard can it be?"

"Lights have to go on first."

"I know that much."

For over an hour they ineptly labored with the tree decorating. Finally they moved to the center of the room to study their efforts. Neither spoke for a minute. Then Randy said, "Doesn't look too bad, I guess."

"I think when we get the tinsel on it, it'll look better."

"My homeroom teacher says you gotta put it on one at a time."

Blake glanced down at the box containing what appeared to be about a million silver strands. "That's ridiculous!"

"That's the way she did it with the tree at school."

"That'd take forever."

Randy went to the window, lifted the drapes and peered outside. "It's pitch dark. Can we finish this later? I'm starved!"

"Okay. I'll heat up soup and make sandwiches."

"Soup? Sandwiches? I'm tired of that. We haven't had anything good to eat since Shannon left."

"Do me a favor, son. Let's go all the way through Christmas without mentioning her name. I think it's best to accept the fact that she's probably not going to come back." He had given up. If she hadn't called by now she never would. It was done and he was going to forget. At least he wasn't going to think about her until some distant time when he could relive intimate moments without falling apart inside.

"Yeah," Randy said sadly. "All right."

"Okay, Randy, you're starving and you want something good to eat." Blake forced some cheer into his voice. "Let's go out in the kitchen, and I'll see if I can't rustle us up some real food."

A few minutes later he backed out of the refrigerator. "How about ham and eggs? There are some frozen hash browns in the freezer, and here are some canned biscuits. How does that sound?"

"Sounds pretty good. I'm star-ving!"

"You're always star-ving."

SHANNON DREW IN A DEEP LABORED BREATH as she turned the rented sedan onto the lane leading to the farmhouse. Days were short now, and night had descended swiftly. She stopped the car and stared ahead at the house. Lights were on, and Blake's jeep was parked in the drive. The courage that had propelled her this far crumbled like clay. Rash and impetuous she'd never been. She couldn't believe she was there. She couldn't believe she had come without telling

Blake to expect her. She guessed she hadn't called because she hadn't wanted to give him a chance to tell her not to come.

Five hours ago she had locked the doors of the Tudor mansion behind her forever, after spending twenty-four of the most hectic hours of her life. Yesterday she had driven home from the hospital with Peg's sage words ringing in her ears. Alone isn't a good place to be—that had stuck with her more than anything. And if ever anyone had been alone, it was she. It had come to her in a blinding flash of insight that she didn't want to spend her next forty years alone. And on the heels of that decision came another—she knew where and with whom she wanted to spend them. Her life was in order, she had proved what she'd needed to prove, and now she knew what she wanted.

She had arrived in time to say goodbye to Ginger, who had promised her new employers she would be available to them in time for Christmas Eve festivities. The goodbye had been difficult. Nicole had fussed over her, brought her coffee and, later, reheated the dinner Ginger had left for them. On an impulse, Shannon had telephoned the airline and discovered there'd been a cancellation; otherwise she'd never have gotten a reservation on the day before Christmas Eve. It had seemed something of an omen.

Naturally she had called Peg to tell her of her decision, and they had spent twenty minutes blubbering like a couple of saps. The remainder of the evening had been given over to packing. That morning she had arranged for a neighbor to keep her car until she could make plans to ship it, sell it, whatever. She had also said goodbye to Nicole, a task that

had been twice as difficult as saying goodbye to
Ginger. Then she had taken a cab to the airport...and here she was. She stepped on the accel-
erator, and drove ahead until she pulled to a stop in
front of the house. She waited a moment before getting out. Every cell in her body seemed a knot of
acute tension.

IN THE KITCHEN neither Blake nor Randy had seen
approaching headlights or heard footsteps across the
front porch. The doorbell's peal startled both of
them.

"Who the devil could that be?" Blake muttered.

"I'll get it!" Randy called as he bolted out of the
room. Jerking open the front door, he blinked, then
gasped. "Shannon!"

In the kitchen Blake almost dropped the carton of
eggs he was holding. He hadn't heard what he
thought he'd heard, he was sure. Carefully setting
down the eggs, he moved toward the front door, his
heart thudding in his chest.

She was standing in the foyer, wearing a deep blue
wool coat that was cinched tightly around her waist.
Her hands were thrust into its pockets. Her face was
flushed from the cold night air. She looked younger
than her years and far lovelier than he remembered.
A space ship landing on his front porch couldn't have
stunned him more. For a moment their gazes locked,
and Blake thought he had stopped breathing completely.

"I..." Shannon began, then faltered. She could
read nothing in his expression. He didn't look glad,
mad, sad, anything. She had fretted over the greet-
ing she would get more than anything. "I don't sup-

pose either of you would believe that I just happened to be in the neighborhood and thought I'd drop by."

Blake crossed the foyer in a flash and had her in his arms. She withdrew her hands from her pockets and clutched him ferociously. The only sound she could hear was Randy's delighted boyish laughter.

"I'M AFRAID I didn't come bearing any gifts," Shannon apologized as she scrambled eggs and kept a watchful eye on the biscuits.

Blake and Randy, seated at the table, exchanged glances. "Good Lord!" Blake exclaimed. "I forgot all about Christmas shopping."

"Me, too," Randy said.

"Well, maybe we can all go into town tomorrow," Shannon suggested. "Won't the stores stay open until late afternoon on Christmas Eve?"

"Probably. Let's plan on it."

Shannon filled their plates and carried them to the table, then returned to the stove for her own. When she joined them at the table, she looked at Randy, then at Blake, smiled radiantly and said, "Well, it's good to be . . . home."

Blake felt the weight of several worlds leave his shoulders.

RANDY PICKED THAT NIGHT of all nights to stay wound up like a five dollar watch. Bursting with excitement, he didn't want to go to bed. He wanted to tell Shannon everything that had happened with the team since she'd left. "Coach says we're gonna win district. Not just maybe we'll win but we will win. And did you know Blake got a lawyer and I'm gonna be adopted right after New Year's? And Blake's started the power station."

"That's great!" Shannon responded enthusiastically. "All of it."

"'Spose you can help us with the Christmas tree? It looks kinda . . . scraggly."

He wanted to watch something on TV; he wanted a bedtime snack. And because these weren't unusual requests for a non-school night, Blake tried to mask his impatience. He held back his questions and stifled his urgency. Once in bed, Randy would sleep like the dead and not awaken until nine or so tomorrow morning. There would be time for questions, for . . . everything else later. Shannon was here! He wouldn't let his thoughts go further than that.

"Are we gonna sleep in the mobile home tonight, Blake?" Randy asked.

Blake didn't look at Shannon. "Oh, I don't think so. That's a lot of trouble. I'll just take the sofa."

Shannon got to her feet. "I think I'll go upstairs and unpack," she said in a small, nervous voice. "Goodnight, you two. Sweet dreams."

Blake couldn't tear his eyes off her as she left the room. He studied her erect carriage, the movement of her hips beneath her skirt. Her casual elegance always fascinated him. In some ways she seemed as out of place on the farm as a hybrid rose in a patch of field corn. In other ways she seemed to belong.

Just having her in the house made everything so different, so much nicer. Incredible that just by walking through the door she could change everything. A whirlpool of emotions assaulted him. He patiently endured Randy's bedtime stalling tactics as long as he could, then ordered him upstairs with, "We've got a busy day ahead of us, son. Get on to bed."

Randy issued a few token protests, but he didn't dawdle long. Blake waited downstairs and listened to the boy's sounds overhead. He methodically walked through the rooms to switch off lights and check door locks. He pulled out the sleeper sofa in the living room, though he had no intention of sleeping in it. At last, when he decided Randy had had more than enough time to fall asleep, he went into the kitchen, poured wine into two long-stemmed glasses and carried them upstairs.

Light welled from beneath the door to his bedroom. He walked past it and peeped into Randy's room from the half-closed door. As usual, the boy was out like a light. Smiling, Blake returned to the door to his own room, his heart pounding. He pushed it open with his elbow, then closed it behind him with his foot.

The bed had been turned down. Shannon was propped against the pillows, shoes off, ankles crossed, but still dressed. A soft smile curved her mouth as she watched him approach the bed. Silently he handed her a glass of wine; she sipped gingerly, then set it on the bedside table. Blake took a hefty swallow of his and placed his glass beside hers. Slowly he sank to sit beside her. Taking her hands in his, he leaned forward and kissed her gently on the mouth. She closed her eyes to receive the welcome touch of his mouth on hers, then opened them when he lifted his head. They settled on him, wide and luminous, full of excitement and love.

"I assume I was expected," he said huskily.

"I would have been terribly disappointed if you hadn't come," she admitted. "I'm so thrilled over the adoption. How did the sisters take it?"

"They were miffed as hell over having their authority usurped."

"I can imagine. Everything...seems to be going your way. The power station...I'd like to see it tomorrow."

"All right. Drink your wine."

"I don't need wine. My head's already spinning. I suppose you want to ask me some questions."

He nodded. "What the devil keeps you so busy in New York?"

That caught her by surprise. "I don't understand."

"Every time I called you were out to dinner or at a friend's or..."

Shannon sat up straight and squeezed his hands tightly. "Blake...you called?"

"Half a dozen times. You were never at home."

She uttered a little laugh. Dropping his hands, she placed hers on either side of his face, and held it tightly while she planted two light kisses on his lips. She laughed again. "Oh, Blake, I called you, too! Twice on Thanksgiving...you weren't at home either. I was going to call again that night, but Jerry got so sick...."

"Who the hell is Jerry?"

"My friend. My best friend's husband and Vic's business manager. A dear, dear friend...but only that."

A smile crossed his face. "Now that that's settled, I can ask you why...why are you here, Shannon?"

"Isn't that obvious?"

"Christmas, you mean?"

"No," she said softly. "I missed you so terribly. I wanted to be with you. I've realized things...."

"What things?"

"That I love you to distraction, for one. That I don't want to try living without you, for another."

"If there are other reasons, I guess I don't need to know what they are. Not now anyway." His spirits soared off on an uncharted course. He kissed her again. "Do you remember what I said? The conditions..."

"I have a few conditions of my own," she said slyly, "but I don't want to talk about them right now. In fact, I don't particularly want to talk at all." One hand crawled up his chest, and its fingers deftly flicked the first button out of its hole. "Please...we can talk later."

There was a catch in his throat as he spoke. "Okay, lovely lady. I'm all yours."

Shannon felt sublimely content as he drew her into the comforting circle of his arms. He held her tightly; she held him as though she couldn't bear to let him go. For a long moment they sat locked together before Blake broke the embrace, got to his feet and pulled her with him. A weakness invaded her legs, and she leaned against him, drawing on his strength. It flowed through her. There was such an air of vigor about this man, and she had been drawn to it from the beginning.

Blake's hands shook as they moved to her shirt-front. The touch of his hands on her breasts sent the fire of desire roaring through her. "Help me," he said thickly. "I don't seem to be able to do a damned thing...."

Shannon's hands were none too steady as they worked to divest herself of her clothing. Her silk shirt and wool skirt were removed and carelessly thrown aside. She wriggled out of her slip and pantyhose and let them fall in a heap at her feet, but when her hands went behind her he covered them with his own. "Allow me."

Her arms fell to her sides as Blake unhooked her bra, removed it, then brought his hands around to fill them with her smooth creamy breasts. The look on his face was one of pure pleasure. His dark passionate eyes gripped and held hers. Since he seemed incapable of moving, she unbuttoned his shirt, jerked it free of his pants and pushed it off his arms. Then she unbuckled his belt, unsnapped his jeans and slid the zipper slowly down. Her hand rediscovered the part of him that throbbed with life. She could hear her pulses pounding in her head.

Blake felt as if he were strangling. Heat and vitality coursed through his veins. He had risen and hardened moments before, and now he couldn't stand waiting another second. With a groan of exquisite torment, he dispensed with the remainder of his clothing, which joined Shannon's on the floor. Lifting her slightly, he placed her on the bed, covered her body with his and locked his hips between her parted thighs. She accepted him eagerly.

They made love hungrily; abstinence had made both of them avaricious. Together they quickly found the rhythm. Though both of them would have liked to make the union go on and on, it wasn't to be, not this time. The climax was quick, sure, powerful and good.

"ARE YOU READY to talk now?" Blake asked sometime later.

Nestled against him with her head on his chest, feeling warm and thoroughly satisfied, Shannon didn't particularly want to talk at all. "I never knew you were such a one for conversation."

"Did you ever find out who you are?"

"I'm going to ignore the facetiousness, because I'm so easy to get along with. That probably sounded ridiculous to a man like you, but I was completely serious about it. As much as I missed you, and it was a lot, the past two months were good for me, Blake, really good. The answer to your question is yes."

"Then tell me all about this person named Shannon."

She thought a moment before speaking. "I'm stronger than I thought I was. I can make decisions and stick with them. I like kids and animals and the whole idea of family... and I like me."

"Is that a fact? Well, I like you, too." A little laugh rumbled up from deep within his chest, but then he turned serious. "Are you back for good, Shannon?"

"Would I have come back otherwise? I remember all too well that rather pompous ultimatum of yours—all or nothing at all. Isn't that the way it went?"

"Being 'one way' about everything. I remember that accusation. And what was the other? Unreasonable?"

"You left out stubborn. I guess I'll learn to live with it."

"The loose ends are all tied up back there?"

She sighed. "Almost. There are things I'll be required to do once the book comes out."

"Now, goddammit, sweetheart..."

"Hush and listen to me, Blake." She sat up and looked down at him. "No more ultimatums, please! I'll do what I have to do. It might take a couple of weeks, tops, and that will be a year from now. You have to understand that I'll never be completely dependent on you. I have too much money, for one thing."

"Good. You think that disturbs my ego or something? Forget it. I'm relieved I don't have to be the one to keep you in the style to which you've become accustomed."

Shannon smiled an easy smile. "And another thing—I'm too old to be a clinging vine."

"Also good. Farm women have to be self-reliant, strong and sturdy and able to cope. Also able to pitch hay and milk cows." He apparently thought this the height of humor, for he laughed huskily. "You'll love it!"

She groaned. "Very funny. It so happens that I am self-reliant, strong and all the rest. If I have to pitch hay and milk cows, I'll do it."

"I'll just bet you will." Under the covers, one of his hands leisurely traced the outline of her curves. "I really want you soft and feminine, like now."

"I'm that, too. At least I am when I'm with you."

"You mentioned conditions earlier. What conditions?"

"I have my car, a Mercedes, parked in a neighbor's garage. I'd like it shipped down here."

He shrugged. "It's your car. I guess you can do with it whatever you please. A Mercedes, huh? I'll bet there are damned few farms in South Carolina with a Mercedes parked out front. The novelty of it appeals to me."

"And I have a horse boarded at the Post-and-Paddock back home. I'd like to truck him down here."

"Suits me."

"Omar is no ordinary horse. He'll require a rather fancy fence...."

"One fancy fence coming up. What else?"

"I want to write a book about you."

"About me?"

She nodded, grinning. "About turning a run-down farm into...well, into what you'rc going to turn it into. Homesteading." The idea had caught and held her during the flight down. Why not? She had proved she could start and finish a book. She'd often thought she could write a book about Blake.

Blake thought about it and discovered he was pleased. "Okay. Just don't make me famous."

"And I'd like to turn the spare bedroom into a study. In fact, there's a lot I want to do upstairs. It's rather blah."

"Fine. See how agreeable I am? Anything else I can do for you ma'am?"

"That's just about it...except for making an honest woman out of me."

Blake rolled over and covered her body with his. "You can be very sure I plan to do that, since marriage was always my only condition. Shannon, I was only kidding a minute ago. I don't want to turn you into a *hausfrau*."

"You couldn't. No one can turn me into anyone but who I am."

"No one wants you to be anyone but who you are, least of all me."

Shannon locked her hands behind his neck and smiled up at him contentedly. "These past two months, when I didn't hear from you, when you didn't cash the check...." She stopped. "What did you do wtih the check, by the way?"

"I tore it up."

"I imagined as much. Why?"

"The last thing I wanted from you was your money."

"You're not going to be stubborn about that, are you? I have a lot of the stuff, and now it's ours. Someday Randy will inherit a bundle."

"Let's not let him know that for about a dozen years, okay? Now, you were saying about the past two months...."

"Oh...yes, when I didn't hear from you, I really got nervous. I thought...you might have decided you didn't want me after all."

Lovingly he kissed her mouth, then, with utmost seriousness, he said, "Shannon, my romantic fate was sealed an awfully long time ago. I couldn't stop wanting you if I tried. And now that I have you here in a marryin' mood, I'm not taking any chances. We're going to get the license the day after Christmas. Then we'll both adopt Randy. We're going to be a real family!"

"Oh, Blake, what a merry Christmas this one is going to be! It's one we'll never forget. I do want to thank you for...well, for a lot of things, but especially for waiting all those years."

Blake was overcome with emotion. There was so much he wanted to say and didn't know how. "What else could I have done? I was a hopeless case where you were concerned, sweetheart."

Shannon closed her eyes and basked in pure contentment. "Love me," she said softly.

"Now and always. I guess..." he said in a choked voice. "I guess I would have waited for you forever."

He made love to her again in the room they would share for the rest of their lives. As it turned out, "forever" had lasted exactly eighteen and one-half years.

EPILOGUE

THE GYMASIUM WAS PACKED to the rafters, standing room only. Tickets had been at a premium, although Blake and Shannon, as parents of a player, hadn't had to worry about that. Their seats were on the third row behind the press table. Interest in the local team was running high, since they had given the school its first winning season in a dozen years. Shannon took advantage of a time-out to go to the concession stand, leaving Blake, who had suddenly become the world's biggest basketball fan, to view the game interrupted.

She was returning to the stands when she almost collided with a woman hurrying from the restrooms. She murmured an apology, then was startled to be looking into a very familiar face. "Well, hello, Mrs. Hatcher. Are you a basketball fan?"

Mary Hatcher's smile was stiff and forced. "My niece's son plays on the Greenville team. How nice to see you again, Mrs. Parelli."

"It's Mrs. Carmichael now," Shannon said, juggling soft drinks and popcorn.

"Oh, yes, so it is. Reverend Archer mentioned it at the last meeting of the adoption board. I believe he performed the ceremony."

"Yes, right after Christmas."

"How nice." The woman's voice was like ice. Her eyes dropped of curiosity, then widened. "Why, Mrs. Par... er, Carmichael. Enceinte?"

Shannon smiled radiantly. She was wearing a rose-colored dress with an empire waistline to emphasize her condition. She was roughly three months along, which made her suspect the baby had been conceived the night she'd returned to the farm. She could easily have gotten by without maternity clothes for another month or so, but she hadn't been able to wait.

She was still reeling from the knowledge that she was going to be a mother. At last she knew unadulterated joy. Her age had worried her for a while, but her gynecologist had soothed her fears. "While I'd be the last to advocate waiting until thirty-seven to have a first baby, Mrs. Carmichael," he'd said, "I find nothing to worry about in your case. Come September, I'm looking forward to delivering a normal, healthy baby."

Blake was beside himself; one would think he was the first man in the world who was going to become a father. And Shannon had immediately called Peg, catching the Thorpes only days before they left for Maine. After learning that Jerry was recovering as rapidly as could be expected, she had blurted out her incredible news to an astonished Peg.

"Oh, my God!" her friend had screeched. "I'm trying to decide whether to laugh or cry. Listen, Shannon, I'm going to give you my mother's phone number. Now you've got to keep me posted, and when the blessed event arrives, I'll be there to hold your hand."

And Shannon was sure she would be.

Anthony Thompson hadn't been overjoyed with the news. He wasn't particularly happy that a Mrs. Blake Carmichael would be plugging Shannon Parelli's book. He would have preferred a grieving widow, and on top of that, when the book came out, Shannon would have a five-month old baby to worry about. "But I'm not one to rail against fate," he'd said during their phone conversation. "I'll keep these new...ah, circumstances in mind when I'm making plans. We'll work it out. And...er, congratulations."

Now Shannon faced Mary Hatcher. "Yes," she said demurely, "We're expecting in September."

Mary folded her hands in front of her and appeared to be trying to think what to say next. "Well...how nice. A real family."

"Nuclear enough for you?" Shannon couldn't resist asking that.

Mary coughed. "Still and all...it's a shame that there'll be such a difference in the children's ages. I mean, there won't be any real sense of being siblings between Randy and the baby."

Shannon's chin lifted defiantly. "Mrs. Hatcher, would you like to know what one of the wisest men I've ever met told me?"

"What's that, dear?"

"You can't sweat the small stuff."

Smiling a goodbye, Shannon hurried back to Blake and took her seat in time to see Randy make a free throw.

Harlequin Superromance

COMING NEXT MONTH